Daybreak Massacre

Order this book online at www.trafford.com
or email orders@trafford.com

Most Trafford titles are also available at major online book retailers.

This is a real work of fiction, the characters, incidents, and dialogues are products of the author's imagination and are not to be construed real. Any resemblance to actual events or persons, dead or living, is entirely coincidental.

Printed in Victoria, BC, Canada.

ISBN: 978-1-4269-3380-6 (sc)

ISBN: 978-1-4269-3381-3 (hc)

ISBN: 978-1-4269-3698-2 (ebook)

Library of Congress Control Number: 2010907073

Our mission is to efficiently provide the world's finest, most comprehensive book publishing service, enabling every author to experience success. To find out how to publish your book, your way, and have it available worldwide, visit us online at www.trafford.com

Trafford rev. 6/15/2010

www.trafford.com

North America & international
toll-free: 1 888 232 4444 (USA & Canada)
phone: 250 383 6864 • fax: 812 355 4082

ACKNOWLEDGEMENT

Most Supreme Lord, all glory and Honor be unto Your Holy Name, for instilling in me the zest to accomplish this great work within a short while.

Great Kudos goes to Mr. Aike Emeni and Mrs. Ifekam Emeni. They are both united in marriage for their non-relenting support and editing of the work piece. Mr. Scott Almona and Mr. Russell Anamali both of Agip oil Company; Double Chief Reece Almona for his final torch in the editing work.

Also thanks to "Field Marshal" Richie Emeni Chairman Remens Investment Ltd. Hon Mercy Almona Isei member Federal House of Representative for her financial support, Hon S.A.E. Emeni for his fatherly and historical orientation and guide, Idise Emeni for his financial support, Mr. Gordon Emeni a mastery of politics, Mr. Benaebi Aigbe my favorite cousin, Barrister Chukwuma Dafe on the logics of law, Chuckwuwinke Dafe Barrister to be, Nicole Collahan, my admirable friend Uche Ogude, Onoharigho Festus Dafe, a man of repute for his constant advice on life itself, Raymond Njekwe My political associate, Dan Opuma a nice guy, Ewere, Edith, Geraldine and Tega. Last of all my able "Gen." Enexto Uti who contributed his computer as his token of assistance for free to enable the effective work output progress.

CHAPTER ONE

"I can't remember when last I visited that town of mine despite the fact that the streets and outlet are well known to me." Jim said as he gazed at the wall. Well, 'I promised myself that I would not go back a upstart. "As such, I must be an accomplished man before I can go right there to settle."

He spoke loud enough to be heard. "Jim what are you insinuating?' You mean the target cannot be reached, simply because of your myopic reasoning? "Not really" "I guess you must have misunderstood me.' It is just a side way Reflection."

"Then talk to me." Nicky said. "The operation is going to take this tune." Phase! He corrected.

'First we are to recruit 5 active men to have a standard unique force of a 7-man team, comprising of two look out operators that will serve as backup" "You have an ideal plan Jim said. Who can handle the wheel perfectly? he asked. Ken of course is an angel, a real masterpiece Nicky added. All right, one down: get in touch with Jude and one-man kill; they are always in the same boat. "Do that as quickly as possible." Commanded Jim.

No stress! Nicky said. You know time is our greatest enemy; every thing has to be as snappy as the fox. 'Arrange a meeting so that we can meet with these guys' Jim called after him. 'It has to be urgent, 'do you mind?' " I repeat no time loss." It's an order." Right! "Go ahead call them on my handset." As he walked past, Nicky snatched the handset and started dialing. "Hi, who is on the line Can I be linked to Jude Let him know its Nick? Just a minute; Jude, Nicky is on the line," she called. "Hi Nick what is new?" as if remembering he said. "Tomboy, 'what has gone wrong with you? You've not been associating lately." "Man you have to come off your shell." "Speak up" Nicky said. "I have a never failing offer for you, real man! "Get across to one-man kill and come over to my apartment right away, as usual." "Man! Can't you give me a breakdown? Tomboy asked.

No it's of no use." Get started! Nicky commanded. "All right, you're the boss. Don't keep long,"

Nicky said and he hung up.

"Hello! Who is this?" Nick, "listen to me" drive master, I have a master-piece, get along right now. "You know what? I don't want any question okay?" You need not remind me, I'm at your Service, he hung up, I've done it. Nick clapped his hands in excitement; I know they will be here in a jiffy. Good work, Greg said.

"Let's have the details of ammunition and plan B for this operation." Greg Suggested, we need three AK 47 riffle, one kalashnikof and two to three .25 Silencer guns, four hand grenades, some flip knives, two bullet proofs, a Jackboot Uniform and a government car with tinted glasses to match." "Someone's official car" Nicky added. "Once it is zero hour, we will snatch a government car drive straight to the bank; disarm the security operatives, our men get in and move out with the cash. In less than an hour we are out of the bank premises." "Remembering that every move has to be done with the speed of light." That sounds real good a masterpiece." Greg applauded.

"We also have a program for the unexpected." Nicky said. "If by any way we encounter opposition from the onset; we will be forced to use the hand grenade to daunt the people from advancing." "In that case, we should increase the number of grenade to 7, Jim Suggested. That is settled. Greg said.

CHAPTER TWO

It was a dark cloudy day. The sky looked as though it was about to rain, but thanks to the dry Season as the rains were not expected at this time of the year, being the 1st quarter. The people both old and young gathered at the traditional shrine awaiting the pronouncement and declaration of the yearly festival. Normally, every year Ukuraibo in conjunction with Ubeumu and environs embark on festive activities, which are marked to remember the Ancestors. This tradition goes way back into the time of their fore fathers and is celebrated on a Yearly basis till date. Way back in the 18th centuries, a group of warriors from Ubeumu along with their leaders, Egbe and Osamu comes to Ukuraibo to celebrate an accord to start the festival. Since Uku Uzuko clan and Ogwezi of Ukuraibo migrated from Ubeumu with three other clans namely: Ogbe Iso, Onya and Ogbe "Ubeumu called Uzuko Nta."

When preparing for the yearly festival, the warriors come twice to Ukuraibo to enquire about the date that the festival is to hold while on the third visit, a date is fixed for the festival to commence, which holds differently. The warriors will then trek back to Ubeumu dancing on their way back in anticipation of the commencement of the festival.

As the people waited patiently for the festival to commence a skinny looking old man appeared with his all gray hair depicting the only visible part of his body, he was supported by his walking stick and a helping hand; he looked frail "Okpala Uku" the people greeted. He sat on a soft chair designed with Tiger skin. Being the oldest man in the village the people called "Okpala Uku," he was about to declare the festival open in the town's shrine. "Where is the ebubu?" he enquired from his Ogbuemi "his assistance." The ebubu was presented to him by the ogo "server." First thing first he said. "We must observe tradition, he prayed over the ebubu. Declaring the festival open he rose from his sitting position displaying his staff of office he shouted… The people celebrates the commencement of the festival by eating of Crumbled yam, mixed with palm oil and roasted fish called, "Ebubu"

Once the people were through in escorting the general Onutu-Uku and the Okpala- Uku to their houses, a song was raised. "Okpala Oli Ebubu Olite Oshioline Kpowe." The oldest man eater of crumbled yam after eating he says he didn't eat. They kept singing until they were through with the Onotu-Uku.

On accomplishing the assignment of seeing the Onotu-Uku to his house they separated into various dance group and continue in this manner of singing. Mostly mimicking various classes of people who by their life style have done wrong or dented their image. 'For example, anyone who has slept with a married woman will be mocked because both the Christian and the African Traditional Religion frowns at it.'

CHAPTER THREE

"Darling you promised to stay with me tonight why are you rushing off? " Remember, a promise is a bond." A man's honor lies in his words. "Come here!" he stretched forward to reach her. "You and I are meant for good tidings remember?" off to get the goodies. He held her in his arm gently caressing her; she submerged her lips in his. She started kissing him voraciously like a loosed object from a snake squeeze. He melted into her grip, the urge to stay built up. "I've got to go." He pulled out of her grip and moved to the door, opened and slammed it immediately without saying good-bye. He did not want to fall into the trap of seduction which can easily distract him.

Knowing that Jim does not call if there is no big stake for keeps, he got into his Bora and drove off towards Nnebisi road; as he got to the T- Junction, he became tense on seeing the traffic. The whole place was filled with traffic, everyone wanted to be the first to leave the hold-up. 'One could easily lose one's hearing potential with the alarmist that kept sounding their horns.' He thought. On a second thought, Jude moved towards the right turn, he was able to cut off the bloody hold up and was at the other end of the road through an outlet created due to bad road, he linked Asubi road through Umuonaji 12s and found himself at the Robga express road linking Ahstino. He turned left facing Ahstino, he had to drive as though he was going to Ahstino; before turning off the express road into Ezeinei Avenue.

Jude made it at exactly 14:00 hrs. He pulled up at house no 15 and waited inside the car with the intention that if there was any body in the building, the person must have seen him from the open window. One-man kill was entering the bath when he noticed the car packed outside, he quickly went to the window to take a look; he was marveled on noticing the man on the wheel. Dam! What on earth has brought Jude over. He unlocked the door and moved over to the house entrance to receive him. "Man! What has brought you to this neighborhood?" "Don't tell me she stays around" Buddy cut it off Greg wants to have a word with you, let's go. "Come on, you can't bump on me like this and expect me to leave my work and hop into your car?" "I've got to tidy up before stepping out." On a second thought, one-man kill decided to give in. "Could it be an emergency? He thought, guess what? Give me 15 minutes 1 will be right there ." One-man kill said. "See you then" Jude said.

Drive master wondered for a few second what the deal would be like, this time around he knows for sure Jim does not call you just for the fun of it. Jim kind of person is strictly for cash business as usual. He quickly entered the bath allowed himself to be soaked with water; it drained down his body. He reflected on his last assignment, which has turned his life. He switched off the shower wiped his body with his customized handkerchief. He was able to maneuver through the hold up and was in Kings Street. He packed his car a block before Jims building, an habit developed to guard against uncertainty,

Guess what? Drive master is here. Jim announced, he quickly went over to the door and opened to allow him in. Old boy! You've changed within these few months of rest; "what is the secret?" he asked as he moved inside Where is the boss? He is inside. Good to see you fresh and sound. Drive master I guess you've not finished your goodies. I wouldn't rush this fast if there is any left. They both laughed. Sit down the rest crew members have not arrived.

And he was about accelerating when he noticed the car in front was a stationary one, he slammed on his brake while the car behind almost hit him on the right side: cracking the side mirror. What a funk! The man did not stop; he moved on, Jude did not bother to go after him knowing he was wrong, an unusual behavior though. He drove fast to meet up his appointment with Jim.

One-man kill was almost knocking off the brandy he was in a deep thought which degenerated into a trance he remembered his last assignment that almost got him killed. This time around he has to be more careful. The operation was well planned but was flooded with amateurs who, could not differentiate between a set up and walking into a trap. "Well for once I must be very grateful to God Almighty for sparing my life, thereby giving me a second chance of retiring." "How can one retire when the system is so expensive and investment is not paying off? He thought.

You succeed in a deal after a short while you're out of fund making life utterly miserable. I hope this past experience will not repeat itself;' he thought aloud. He switched off the shower wiped his body with his face towel. He moved over to the wardrobe picked his pair of trousers knowing the distant from his apartment to the meeting spot can't be more than 10 minutes. He decided to take his time. His mind was on a constant race, on the kind of Job this time. He slipped into his Honda 'Legend' and drove off.

At exactly 30minues after Jims called Jude was making Ahstino Kings Street, he felt elated for he knew the team was time conscious. The Ahstino bridge holdup was alarming he sweated profusely as he checked his timepiece! Not what is given to the gods did he get, it demanded to eat more than enough.' It took him 25 minutes to leave the holdup scene.

'Greg I guess that's Jude? Yah! Oh! one-man kill is right behind' Your presumption has paid off he said as he was able to confirm it as he was at the window expectantly waiting for the whole crew to arrive. Get the door open fast, they were already at the door by the time it was swung open.

Old chaps I miss you guys! Nicky said. What's this whole thing of 30 minutes business deal about? Can't you get in first before asking question? Nicky said. Jude and one-man kill got in and sat next to Greg; whom they both have great respect as the team leader. As they sat Greg was looked upon to speak.

"Business hour" he said and pulsed: "we just have to slog out this thing for once." Jim offered them the remaining bottle of brandy and high weed. "That is all I've got." He explained. "As you all know our holiday is over, Greg said. When you stay too low you get yourself out of business, by so doing you run yourself down completely, without knowing it." Maybe you will now attribute it to witchcraft or home trouble. They all laughed. "We have a real job at hand;" "I implore you all to listen carefully so that we can actualize our individual dreams." Men! The need has arisen for us to go for the big stake." Jim said. Jim and I have a masterpiece 'plan' on how to get across to the Fedson bank Ukuraibo. Greg continued. You are all aware it has been our entire life dream to get involved with a bank so that we can all retire from active service to our homes and start a new life. Any comment from the team? He asked. Go on Jude said, you are on course.

Our target is to get all the cash available in the bank's vault on a Monday morning. Before they think of carrying any cash away, we shall be there with them to resume banking proceedings. That will be as early as 08:00hrs, the official opening hour of every bank. Knowing full well that there is Saturday banking of deposits only, the team will walk in and make do with our share. We go on a raid as early as possible, hijack a government vehicle with tinted glass. Jim chipped in. Jim will wear a Jackboot uniform, as an oddly while Jude will be our look out man; Drive master knows his work I need not tell Him: one man kill and I'll go for the kill any obstruction on entering the bank will be resisted. The security guards will be disarmed hook or crook. Okay? We swiftly enter the bank, saunter into the manager's office, solicit his cooperation, move over with the bag of cash and we're out on our way to Nadabi.

I presume there won't be any complication. If we encounter any when leaving, the need for the hand grenade arises, if not it will be safe in its stead. He said. You guys must ensure there is no exchange of fire or any form of shooting unless the need arises. I don't want innocent people to get hurt. I've communicated. One-man kill, Rap it off. But you want innocent people's cash? All laughed. Better get serious Greg cautioned.

How many security men do they have in the bank? One-man kill enquired. Three I suppose. Drive master answered. Then you had better check it out so that we don't have complications. Remember no guesswork. Greg? I suggest that we all take a cruise to Ukuraibo on a Saturday to check things out ourselves. Jim suggested. 'Jude and I will get the necessary materials needed for the operation.' Greg said. "The weed was depreciating faster than usual" man where did you get this grass? One-man kill asked.

It taste real good he countered, it is of a high quality. "I don't know why these grass dealers always give us staled weed for Christ sake." Drive master said. Then get along with the supply business so that we can get better stuff for upkeep, Jude said. Hearing this, the whole team burst into laughter.

Drive master did not find the joke funny because, he is from the main hub where high weed is commercially produced for distribution. As widely speculated, the farms are devoid of all other produce apart from grass. Even the Jackboot and the drug enforcement agency "NDLEA" find it difficult to raid the area because the farmers are combat ready at any given point in time.

"Well I have to run along, you guys made me break a promise this evening and I need to go back and redeem it. Jude said. One man kill shall we. Run along you, I'm not through with this stuff yet. One-man kill checked around for the razzler he could not find it; he picked an alternative paper called kanako to wrap the weed "please help me to fold this weed," he said.

It took Jude approximately two hours to maneuver his way out of the hold-up to get to his apartment. He had to meditate, a habit he had picked up since he joined the team. He rang the bell but to his dismal, there was no response at the same time he felt better since he would have pleaded for time alone if Kel was at home. He brought out his keys to open the door, but the door gave way without him turning the keys. What are fuck! He entered the house hoping to see Kel sleeping on the cutch but she was nowhere to be found. He moved over to the bar and poured himself a shot of "501" brandy. He was so disturbed that no matter the calmness of the hour, he badly needed a seat. As he strolled to the sofa, his mind drifted to the proposed Saturdays Visitation/ rehearsal.

Jude waited at home for the rain to subside. He knew his limits; time was not on his side. It is a rule of the game not to be late no matter the circumstance. His mind also drifted to one man kill. As ever one man kill in his usual self despise is the main bane of being late for appointments, he thought, to be on the safe side, he picked up his hand set and dialed one man kill to remind him. The phone rang as he picked the handset. "Hello!" "Who is this?" "You had better get your ass to this place if you know what is good for you." He retorted. One mans enough of this. The team is waiting. You know you can't keep us waiting. Jude said. He quickly poured himself a cognac took his car keys and left for the garage. He slides beside the wheel. Just as he had anticipated, Jude got to one mans-kill's apartment when he was about leaving to find an alternative arrangement since the ignition was on he put the car on drive and in no time he was driving towards Nnebisi holdup. The hold up was so terrible that he had to force his way through the coming traffic. By doing so, he earned insults from all corners, which made him laugh. All he wanted was to get out of the jam. They drove off through Ezenie Avenue to the express. It did not take long to reach Ahstino Bridge but because of the heavy down pour, the bridge was not accessible.

"Let's call off this meeting" one-man kill dialed Jim's number; it was answered on first ring as if Jim was expecting the call. "Hi what's the matter with you?" You should have called earlier to keep us informed. Jim said. "I'm sorry"." Replied one-man kill. We had ourselves trapped in dam bottleneck he continues. "Just ensure you leave early next time;" Jim snapped. Say me well to Jude and he hung up. He says our target's security update has to be checked, but you had the blue print of the security update. Jude reminded him. Yes you never can tell; Just in case we have to prepare for the unforeseen.

It was exactly 12 noon when the whole crew arrived at their meeting point. "Gentlemen, when we get to Ukuraibo, Nicky will rent a bike as we check into a hotel and go on area surveillance." Jude you will have to go straight to the supermarket opposite the bank buy something and ask to wait for someone there; your duty is to know the structural pattern of the premises. Look out for the security operatives. While I drive straight to Akarba and back through the old road to detect the bad spots on the road:" "When you are all through with the assignment you fall back and wait. Instructed Greg.

"Roughly in the next 1 hr 30 minutes we should be at our contact point, lest I forget, Nelson will take a bike round Ukuraibo, pass through the link roads to know those areas that are completely inaccessible. Get your pen ready for this." He continued. "We are going to continue this rehearsal for the next one week. Hope I 'm clear?" Greg said.

"After the days assignment the crew will meet at Uzuko guest house before proceeding to Irraw to spend the night." The security man opened the gate while the Jackboot officers walked towards the back entrance. Jude waited at the shoemakers his eyes blinked as he saw the Jackboot officers emerging from a close circuit room.

"How did it go?" Asked Jim. Jude was the first to respond. "Well I feel the operation is going to be a smooth one because the town is so peaceful and there is no jackboot patrol team. The bank watch is not effective from the look of things." "More so the Jackboot station is far off from the bank; it will take men with fiber guts to come to the scene of the operation." He concluded."Well, I guess we are progressing." Nicky said. " Then we had better leave this place." Jim added. Who in turn took over the steering. He reversed the car, got down and beckoned on Drive master. "You can start your assignment now." The station wagon

Primera car crawled into Iama road, drive master took his time to maneuver the wheel on getting to the express he slowed and turned right accelerated and seconding it one two three he was on the 4th gear as he passed Amoyam clinic. They were at Akarba heading for Irraw via Uke town.

At Abonima port in River State Teddy sat with a group of pals expectantly waiting for his pals to come back from the field. "Hey lady come sit here with me" Alex said, "meet my friend Tom, he is a mariner: "owns a barge, a big man to reckon with. That is Nicky he is usually shy when it comes to the opposite sex, he is a nice man." He continued. This guy here is Gab has no job but owns a car. How he makes his money I don't know. Here is, 'don't hide your face, come on I know " all laughed" you? His enormous head reorganizes him. 'They all laughed'

"Mister don't look else were, I know you very well' He enters any mariners car. Alex said. He is Charles brother to the governor who refused to tar our roads but employed laborers to sweep the road. As the introduction was on someone moved the table and the drink splashed on the girl. Talk of the devil ' they all laughed' hahaha! Anywhere he goes there must be problem. Facing the girl he said sorry my dear, get a rag to wipe this mess, he told the attendant. Haven introduced you to these guys does not mean they are good enough for you. Alex said.

The real man I will recommend for you is Tom, because he will take proper care of you. He's not married' ha,' don't mind him I 'm a married man. Every body laughed. He put on an embarrassed expression. But that's what he asked me to tell you. Sorry it's a plan between us that he has just uncovered. That tells the kind of man he is. "Service he called, get more beer on the house!" "Who is going to pay? Charles asked. No problem I will settle for this round. Alex said, I just remembered today is my mums birthday; we have to celebrate Nicky said.Cheers every body. Alex raised his glass up; the guys on sipping raised their glass up as well, cheers! Brothers Alex said. The table was full with different bottles of beer. Nicky walk out of the bar feeling drowsy as he was so drunk that he almost fell off the pavement; he hailed a cab ' take me home.' He said. "Hey where is Nicky gone to? Gab said 'I can't find him' come on, you worry too much let him have fun; he deserves it. One-man kill said. I'm out of here one-man kill announced.

On Monday morning Jude was asked to go alone to Ukuraibo to enquire on the process of opening an account in Fedson bank. 'This will enable you study the bank critically. Jim said. 'Getting the numbers of staff at the counter is very necessary. Possibly demand to see the manager so that you can know exactly where the guy's office is situated, then move on.

Jude left the hotel room very early as directed, he hailed a taxi but the man refused to go his direction, then he decided to pick a bike straight to P.T.I junction. How much would it cost to and fro to Ukuraibo?" He asked a Red Cross member of the road transport union. #2000 flat the man said. Without pricing he said, "let's go" when he got to Ukuraibo he instructed the taxi driver "take me to Mezu guest house!" he paid the taxi driver part payment. "You've got to wait for me, feel free take a drink on me" he said, he quickly walked through the old road to the bank. He stopped at a chemist shop 'do you have super multivitamin tablet' he took a side vie at the bank and smiled on seeing the security lapses.

Inside the bank, he moved over to a woman sitting alone. "Good morning," "yes can I help you?" 'Definite' he said, "I want to know what it entails to open an account in this bank." "Is it a savings or current account? she asked. "Both" He replied. "Well you need 3 passport photographs, a minimum of N10.000. Your business registration papers and tax clearance, that's all about the current account but on the other hand, you don't need a business registration and tax clearance for a savings account and the rate is N5. 000." She concluded. "Thanks," "If I may ask, what if I want to deposit in a fixed account?" Then you will have to see the manager to know the various terms. "It is imperative I see him then?"

"Walk straight down, that door facing you is the secretary's ask her if you can see him." Thanks once more." Jude said. You're welcome," she said smiling. He moved over towards the secretaries office knowing full well that he did not need to see the manager cause, he had gotten to see all what he needed to observe. He cautiously walked out of the bank and moved on to Mezu guesthouse. "This man mere seeing you one would not know you can imbibe 4 bottles of star." He paid for the star beer, "let's go or you want to have some more? The driver kept accelerating until he reached PTI junction. He took his handset and dialed Jim's number. "I will be with you in the next 15 minutes cheers!" and he hung up. He did not want to converse on the phone for fear that the taxi driver was all ears to his conversation.

"Buddies, Jude is back from Ukuraibo." Nicky announced. "The way he sounds I figure he has gotten the necessary information in place." Jude finally got to the hotel at about 15:05hrs, paid the taxi driver and proceeded to the hotel room to meet his colleagues. He gently knocked three times on the door, three times to let them know he was the one and the door was opened without much formality.

"What do you have? Jim enquired. "I guess it went as planned?" Greg asked. Smiles all over him," the team is going to have a swell break through. He said.

As you all know, the bank is situated along the major road, the security men are stationed outside displaying their riffles. "The bank manager's office is on your right, as you enter the banking hall facing you directly is the cashiers stand while there is another door on your left hand side." "When we get to the bank Jim and one man takes care of the two security men outside, we move into the bank get hold of the manager to open the vault, as soon as that is accomplished, we collect as much cash as possible and we leave the bank."

"I must warn that our time in and out must not exceed 20 minute. I hope I 'm well understood. Any question so far?" "No" they said in unison. "That means this phase is done with." "That reminds me," there was a sudden air of authority. Greg said "this operation is going to be a clear picture of self-employed graduates of crime.' We are to get in touch with Steve and Andrew at Nadabi, whom will serve as our back up team to enable us get maximum security as possible." "Steve will station a car at the outskirt of Ukuraibo while Andrew will be at the other end of the section going to Akarba."

"Their position will be organized in such a way that it will look like a break down, their duty will be to watch out for Jackboot alert team coming to the bank." "If we have problem we know from the onset, in that case the operation will be aborted immediately." Man you got it well arranged" Drive master said. The crewmembers were so sure of their plot that they all moved over to celebrate the day's success.

At the bar the music by "Robert Nester Malley" 'no women no cry' was being played in an under tone. They all echo, "Could it be love let be love, let be love. Don't let them fool you." One man kills left without being noticed. He called one of the waitresses to himself. "Hi, would you mind being my guest tonight?" "I have many goodies to offer.

"Handsome to know anything good is not easy to come by." She said. "Come on here he held her close to himself, his mind racing with the intension of laying her but for the brightness of the day he would be seen by anyone coming from the entrance, he released her reluctantly. "Les's go to my room" He said,"But I 'm on duty." she resisted. "He handed her a clean bill of two N500 note, use this as means to my room. Okay?"

"Hey man! Where have you been?" Jim called. "Having fun of course I 'm off to the room I, have got company." "Nelson you can't do without getting these old lay." Man my time is up, he walked to the room surprisingly she was right there waiting for him.

They all assembled in Jim's hotel room at 8:00 hour to plan their next line of action. Jude was first to speak, "we are running against time you all know we have not notified Steve and Andrew." "I have tried contacting them over the phone, not bad still we would have gone to Nadabi later on." Then we had better go park our luggage and be out of this place." One-man kill suggested. "Sure" was all Jim could say. They all left their individual rooms and within the next few minutes, they were in the hotel lobby checking out. The bags were neatly arranged in the car booth. Drive master wheeled the car and the tyre rotated, as if it wants to turn round. The car screeched while reversing, they all stepped in, and he zoomed off. With little traffic at the airport road junction, the car in no time was speeding through Elepas road. The road was almost free of traffic as it was a little two early, most transporters had not started the days business. Before Agosom, a small Community in Elepas Local Government, well known for the mass production of Garri, coupled with the high rate of crime, every body in the car had slept off leaving drive master and Jude.

Master drive did not reduce his speed one bit; he wanted to beat Nineb's hold up to make his targeted time of getting to Nadabi. He was able to make it to Nineb tollgate in calculated 1hr 30 minutes. At the tollgate the federal high way patrol team stopped him. In demanding for the vehicle particulars master drive confidently handed it over. As the federal Jackboot officer wanted to pass it back his eyes picked on the date, "wait a minute" he said "mister this particulars has expired?" Master drive looked him in the eye "oh yes but it's just a week" The Jackboot tactically extorted N500 five hundred from them and they were able to continue their journey, drive master had to reduce his speed because of the bad bumpy nature of the road. He needed no fortuneteller "Soothsayer" to remind him, remembering how the road had dealt with two of his tyres the last time he plied the road. He preferred passing the Ile Ife road, linking Nadabi express way. It was at Nadabi ring road that he was forced to wake Jim up, knowing he was in charge.

"Just drive straight to the crown royal hotel for a change, from there we shall secure an apartment in town, for old time sake. Crown royal hotel was built with the same fanciful bricks of the Sheraton hotel, Sogal. The difference is just the size; the entire interior bore similar characteristics. The owner wanted a unique size for a change.

Jude did not hesitate to call her as she passed. She wore a cream Jeans, and top to match her leather shoes, with a very flat heel, her height was not affected by the flatness of the shoe. She was not wearing any make up. Everything about her was natural; her hair treated to size. She was an epitome of black beauty with ebony eyes. All Jude needed was composure; he knew this was who he needed to take care of his home.

"Hi love," he said she walked past as if she did not notice the caller. Jude walked up to her and held her shoulder, she flipped and stopped. "You're the finest creature I've ever set my eyes on, down here in the South West and there in the South East." He said. "I want you to consider marrying me not just going out with me; as most guys propose" She smiled, which of course revealed her dimples.

"Come off it, you are not kidding?" " I'm not." He said "But you know I can not just love a man I'm seeing for the first time," "I don't even know your upbringing, your back ground and that. "That will come later," he said smiling. "Let's have a drink. I' m Jude from South East. It is a pleasure meeting you. Well she hesitated, "I'm Bukky from Osun State but my parents reside here in Nadabi. "I will want to meet them today" Jude said, she laughed as they both walked into the hotel lobby. "Where're you putting up in town?" she asked "In a hotel but that will not be for too long, as I intend contacting a friend of mine." "Once I'm through, I'll move in with him. "You're okay by that I suppose?" "If you say so, "She laughed. they both laughed.

Jude had difficulty in locating Steve and Andrew cause they had moved from the known apartment. He went to a pub they've visited in the past, but the joint also no longer existed. He packed by the road junction with his mind racing seriously.

"Hey! Jude is that you?" he was surprised to see Jude in such a mode, more-so the blond seating in front of his car captivating his reasoning made him to be more confuse. Jude hissed wiped off sweat from his agony- ridden face and was alert once more. "Jude what's the problem all about?" "Frank man! It's been hectic for me; can you imagine that I can't trace Steve or Andrew? Not a big deal replied Frank. "I'm on my way to their home." He got inside with Jude while he engages the gear and zoomed off. It wasn't a difficult drive this time around for Jude, cause Frank knew his way around. All the access roads in town were in his fingertip. They had to take the Major Ademoyo way to cut off the built-up traffic caused by military checkpoints. It took a century's drive to find a way to Johnny Street, which terminated at Nadabi ring road, connecting the crown royal road. "Turn right." "Okay you've got it Jude." "Do you think he will be at home?" Jude asked. "Sure; "I just called him a couple of minutes ago before leaving my office." replied Frank.

'For God sake where has Jude gone to?' Jim was the first to break the silence. "Man don't you think he's having problem locating these people?" "You should have gone with him." Nick said. Look at me, I have forgotten my handset." said Jim. Good gracious we can call him. The phone was given a hurried dial, Jude's line was busy but Nicky kept redialing the number.

At the other end Jude was busy getting use to the girls around him that he for once forgot that he was on assignment. The phone ranged tentatively before he realized it was his. He quickly went to the lobby clicked the phone and it went off. It rang again. "Hello!" He answered, but there was no response from the caller. He put off the phone and went back to his position with a strong conviction it would ring again. But on a second thought he dialed Jim's number.

"Hi what's happened to you?" "I've been calling your number" "The last time you picked up the phone, your voice sounded faint." Sorry I've not mastered this cell phone "I had problem in locating our men." Jude replied. Give me time I shall be back soonest. He assured him.

"Bola the holiday is over" "I shall take my leave but will be back." " Are you sure you will come back?" A slim looking dark eyed girl asked, if not for her protruded boobs she would have passed for men. " Of course." Answered Jude. "Let me get back to the crew." "They are eager to see me."

"I won't have done it if my position was not to play back up" 'you know buddy we are retired." I 'm well off with my joint. "I don't want to see nor hear no evil." "Well we'll just be fine by His grace," countered Andrew. They all sat around a conference table awaiting the coming of Steve's girl. "Your blonde promised coming over with her ally, has she called? Yah she will be here shortly. "Tell me Steve what's been happening to you guys?" I can see you're settled and contented." Said Jude.

"Jude, I almost got killed in the last operation some young but not talented kids got me into." "I spent four months out of circulation." "There and then I decided my fate." He unrolled his sleeve "you can see the scar"

"You know we've come a long way," said Steve. "Never mind, this whole thing is well arranged," assured Jude. "Your part is as simple as selling beer at a joint," unless of course, a nut rakes a bottle of beer on your old head. Thanks for your concern. Said Steve. "Who is going to run your joint since you'll be proceeding on leave? "was it a make shift arrangement for Steve to be with the team on this operation?" Asked Jim. "I have a very capable manager who takes the joint as his own business." Said Steve. He is a nice lad, just got out of high school. He lost his parents in a ghastly car crash.

Any way, he finds the job amazing. He goes to the movie only after closing hours. Maybe he can be trusted with our family business when we are retired." Jim said. "Oh no not this kid, he has an elephant task ahead of him. He wants to study medicine and he is saving money from his salary to register for JAMB Exam." "The guy is quite smart." "The whole ladies want to go to bed with him but he has never succumbed to them. Jim counted N5, 000 and handed it over to Steve. "Give this to him for his Jamb enrolment forms."

"Man this is solicitous of you!" "I should have taught of this ever since, but business has been at a snail pace." "Jim you're God sent, you must learn to be a good fellow" Jim said

Steve walked to the manager and they both strolled into the office. "Sit down mike.' " It's time we both discussed your education." As you well know the business has not been any boost since you joined us but you've been able to keep it going. I just realized I've not been a good friend to you all this while. It occurred to me when I was discussing you with a friend and he without more ado gave me this," " He handed the money over" to give you for your JAMB Examination. Mike was dumbfounded; he embraced Steve like he would his father. "Oh! My God, he exclaimed. "I love Jesus.' He said. "Well the person is Jim go thank him."

Jim assembled the whole crew to inform them of the need to leave Nadabi on Saturday. "If we wait until Saturday, we might not have enough time to prepare our unit." "We have to catch up on that commissioner guy cause if we miss him we cannot proceed." " I've been able to monitor his movement for the past weeks." "Our best bet is to track him on his way back to Abasa on a Monday Morning." "We shall intercept him along Elawk Abasa express immediately we return through Nsukwa via Utumu to Ukuraibo agreed. They all echoed. Go on Jude said.

The whole team was fagged out as they arrived Irraw, they checked into a hotel on a Saturday night. "You can't believe it we slept all night" Jim was discussing on the phone. Okay! Did you say he is in town? "Please call me and give me feedback and you get your pay at once."

The man at the other end knew what his mentor wanted as such he guided the prey to his hotel. Thanks to the usefulness of the Econet GSM, he calls his associate. "Oga Ralph!" "That's me, once it is 18:00 hr the operation is called off. Okay! Fidel did not need any other information to function. As the driver approach the lonely road he alerted his men who mounted an emergency roadblock.

CHAPTER FOUR

Teddy woke up startled. Normally he has a fixed timer by his bed side that conditions him each day to an early wake as he made to the bath but on a second thought put on his pair of Jeans, not minding his casual dress code he stepped out he was surprise to see restive youths all over the place. He instinctively recollected his dream, which alerted his reasoning "there is bound to be trouble"; he wondered whether the community was witnessing another dawn. It was as if an alarm was used to channel the people to one direction. They engulfed the whole place. A slim tall boy wearing a black baseball cap, which covered his face from all view, passed an order.

"Organize yourselves and block the whole road leading to the bank," he said, the addressee did not complete his last world before the boys swung to action. They fleetingly took it as their sole responsibility to defend a just course, hurry! Tell Peter to block the road sideways with his lorry. Peter was no where to be found a lorry was commandeered to block the road with it's face positioned in such a way, that it crossed the road in an angle adjacent to the building;

assignment achieved. " Where is Nat? He is inside Stanley answered. Please called him Nat do us a favor; use your bus to block the road. they moved over to the old road leading to the market. The group close to the bank was being shot at aimlessly as they could not do a proper job cause they were scared. One of the robbers shouted as he aimed firing at the sky. "I don' t want to shot you guys'. The shot missed someone's head, "Oh boy we can't die here ooh! They all flee their position leaving the job incomplete.

I've come to abase any one who thinks he's man enough to defy me here in the open. Davidson barked. This is for real he waved his gun to and fro aiming at the masses while he took a stride backward to the bank. "Where is the manager? He enquired as he walked into the banking hall. The man was speechless. "Look you guys must be warned, I'm here for business, and not to trade peanut." "I want your absolute cooperation while we are here because we don't intend to take much of your time." I repeat, "Business is business." "I suppose I have made myself clear for this is a settled issue." "Except my being here is misconstrued, I don't want to repeat myself." He wore a horrifying look, smiling as he spoke knowing the man he addressed was scared, there was tension allover; the bank manager in a confused state ran out of his office leaving a client behind. As the group strolled in, the bank manager was addressed, 'you must cooperate cause time is money' Greg said.

"Sorry I am not the manager," "you're not what?" He was not given time to express himself as he shook in disbelief at what was happening to him. He was instantly hit on his head with the magnum .45-silencer pistol, which exposed part of his inner skull.

"Get the manager down here or we start a shoot out." Greg barked. The fear of not succeeding got hold of him. "Listen no body gets hurt unless it's necessary." Greg said.

"Please we will cooperate with you people don't hurt anybody in here." The manager said, as he rushed back into his office "Who holds the key to the vault?" Jude asked. "Bring him here immediately!" The man trembled to the manager's office with the whole keys raised above his head.

"I know you will do just as you're instructed" and you II be okay right. Greg said. Yes Sir." The man said panting.

"Marsha, get down with him to the vault." He ordered. "You have the spread of ten minutes to return with the bags understood?" "Yes Boss.

"Paul, hand over your car keys to Simon so that he can alert the Jackboot at once." "After all, we have done part of their job, it will be much easier if they turn up to assist." Eddy said. Not withstanding the human traffic along the road he took a swift drive to the station the whole surrounding was a cluster of living beings.

"Good morning Sir." "What can I do for you?" The Jackboot man on duty asked. "I want to have an audience with the DJO." "He is very busy now." Then you can be of assistance? Simon asked. There is a bank robbery; we need a break. The whole road leading to the bank is blocked. The Jackboot man did not show any sign of concern he kept on writing." Sir! Well we're indisposed," he said nonchalantly. "Why?" "There is neither vehicle nor ammunition for such operation." "What?" "You have to do something, tell the DJO, we can't just let these hoodlums get away this time."

At the bank arena an instruction was passed but Nkem, an Okada rider did not wait for confirmation, he took his bike keys out of his pocket and got on the way in a gas pedal. As he got off the bike, he rushed in.

If there is anything you people can do to help yourself go on with it, he said without looking up. As Simon stepped out Nkem entered the station. "A bank robbery!" he said panting as he spoke, "Can we go at once?" No we can't.

said the Jackboot man. "Man calm down, we can't just rush out." "We have a procedure." The Jackboot Officer said." "I've explained before there is no operational vehicle and the reinforcement's team for this kind of Job is not readily available." "We have to be patient till the patrol team comes back from Utumu."

"Sir, you mean you don't have a radio system to alert the team on patrol?" "Young man I hope you have not come here to give me orders." "Sir can't you see, it is a matter of life and death." "People are all trapped in the bank and as you know, they will be under pressure by now." "My friend get out of this station now! I've had enough of your complain."

The young man left the station grumbling, "Nkem did you get the Jackboot cooperation? He hissed, "can you imagine we are accommodating enemies in form of Jackboot officers. "You should have known that the Jackboot in this country do not work where there is nothing to eat." The man replied. "Dam the Jackboot." we can do without them. The information circulated in a swift moment amongst various groups: individuals decided to go and see for themselves at the station. As they got to the station to their astonishment, the Jackboot officer was busy reading a novel.

"No body moves!" "If we don't do it, no one will do it for us, we have to save our people from this humiliation and unholy menace of armed robbers." Papa said. "Everybody! All ways lead to the bank." Everyone answered yah! There was a mad rush towards the bank. "Ensure the express road is completely blocked all roads leading to the town need maximized security alert." Nkem added.

Precisely, the whole communities were out watching with Keen interest. Along the old road masked men patrolled as if the town was a war zone. "Operation clean Ukuraibo town is our watch word," "keep singing, if we are not in this we can't be." they sang. A group matched towards the bank premises while a look out guard mounted roadblocks leading to the bank from all road junctions.

"I hope our men are at alert, Mr. Mike?" "Cause it wouldn't sound well if we don't apprehend this society nuisance." Papa said. Lets rest in hope our team is all prepared for action?" Mike reassured him. "We succeeded in deploying the hunters for this purpose. I have full confidence we're on guard." It is not right for these numb men to take over the bank premises without us stopping them.

"Guess what Andrew?" There is nothing to guess at, at this crucial hour." He was in no mode for jokes. "We are all on course." Dad stepped out with his newly acquired plasma rifle to check the outlaws. Everyone quickly followed him.

"We can aim at those rats from this angle." Papa Andrew addressed the boys. "This is for real, anybody, I repeat, anybody who feels offended should come over so that we can sort it out over here without formality." One of the robbers shouted.

From a distance Andrews's dad, a tall lanky fellow in his fifties pulled out his rifle and aimed directly at the robber standing outside the bank premises. The man slumped. "What is that?" Jim barked. His fellow robbers dragged him inside. Let's get the hell out of here before we get snags." One-man kill opened fire indiscriminately to disperse the crowed building outside. "You! Carry these bags to the car" Jude said. Soon as the whole bags were dragged to the entrance they used the bank customers as shield till they successfully loaded the vehicles with the bags of money. They dragged the injured robber along as they entered the car. Once put inside, move! Greg barked; as they drove out of the bank premises one-man kill kept sliding his trigger back and front firing at the dispersed crowd.

The people mounting guard took to their heels as the driver maneuvered through a loosed blockage and rode off through the old Akarba road. Immediately the whole town cursed and chased the robbers. Some people went on their motto bikes. There was a general out burst towards the new road. An alert Jackboot van was off towards Akarba maneuvering the various roadblocks along the express.

"Alu- eme!" meaning Bad thing has happened. "For Christ sake is the Jackboot out to aid the robbers in ruining our banking system in Ukuraibo?" Everyone questioned. Subsequently various groups started walking towards the Jackboot station as if they were summoned.

At the station the crowd present created serious tension, the DJO in fright began to address some community leaders, while there was a section of the youths conversing on the need for Jackboot overhauling in the country.

"Fellow kings men," he stated I must thank you all for your efforts this morning in helping to track the hoodlums. You and I all know our effort were in vain simply because we had in our mist traitors as Jackboot officers. Who we must not fail to understand aided and abated the robbers to snatch away huge sum of money from Fedson Bank Plc." The speaker waited for the people to digest all he has said. "This you know is hard earned money that strangers and people of this community suffered for." "Do we blame them?" "No off course" Gab said. My people remember " When a hunter is possessed he can no longer hunt, that is our position with the Jackboot force in Ukuraibo. If not, why would the native hen then say "urinating is easy when the chicken cannot do it. My peoples hard earned money on a drift. The government has caused us much pain by deploying this ill-fated deputy superintendent of Jackboot to ruin us but, I tell you, courage brothers we shall resist the agent of the devil, cause it is worse than the devil itself.

"Men, please you must bear with me, the situation as you can see is not beyond my control. We shall do all things humanly to bring these robbers to book." The DJO said.

"Just go back to your various houses so that the Jackboot can do its job." "Look at him medicine after death, can you give a patient drug when the patient is dead." Johnny said.

"We can do without the Jackboot," an onlooker shouted. "Please this cannot degenerate into community crises," the DJO said. "Oh! You want us to have community problem?" "DJO you are the sole cause of this problem." Papa said, "We have asked you to leave our town time without number but you've been adamant. Well it is your cross so carry it vulnerably."

"Let's not argue over insignificant issues." The DJO said. "You can call it insignificance?" questioned papa. "Wait until robbers rubbish your earning completely in one night then you will realize the pains we have been through these past months." Cried Nat.

"Have we not time without number requested your assistance concerning the escalated robbery cases?" asked Stanley. "We have to be calm, two wrong can't make a right." The DJO lamented. "Oh you know you've been at fault?" Ikemna said and hissed.

"The Jackboot are all the same all over the country," said Cyike. "I cannot listen to any explanation unless." "I see the robbers' hand cuffed in front of me." "Let's think of other important issues." Ben said. " You remember the page one incident? "Wait a minute, innocent citizens of this great country were arrested and carried to an unknown destination? Even one of the boys constantly pleaded with the special anti robbery squad to let him go, considering the fact that he was in town for the renovation of Obiagele grammar school classrooms. To further humiliate the government the "SARS team," went with one of the boys to the bank under gunpoint to withdraw #70.000 as a bail bond. How cruel they have become over the years in disguise. They are the horror in uniform." He walked to regroup with the boys

At Akoru town the vehicle took a turn and stopped as the 230 green Mercedes Benzes with Sogal registration number approached. "stop there! Your life or your car, which do you, want? One-man kill said as he flew out of the car. "Oh my life, you can have the keys." The driver got out hands above his head. "Bring down your hands," No wise attracting any on lookers, you will pay dearly if you do." One man kill said as he collected the keys, be firm," one-man kill snapped. "Common open your booth," the driver was ordered to carry the bags from their car. The Benz driver in absolute obedience didn't hesitate but helped the robbers in transferring the two bags of money into his own car. "I will cooperate," he persistently said. Can you see the strength in a pointed object Jude was amuse as the instruction was let out. "Look at that." "He is even fidgeting." "Look why not go help so that we can leave this place?" "I'm not comfortable, one-man kill snapped.

"Oh, no the Devil incarnate is scared too." Jude said. He quickly got out to help. The whole bag of cash was neatly starched inside the booth of the newly acquired car. Mister, Jude said. "Listen carefully, don't go to the Jackboot and you will see your car along the road." "Okay if you like take a tip go to the Jackboot and we shall burn the car." We are on air; will be on our way, good luck." The government vehicle was abandoned while they drove off in their newly acquired car. This was tactically done without attracting on-lockers who were standing at a distance. The man stood and watched his car being driven away; he was speechless. His mind was racing whether or not to comply with the directive given by the robbers, or to go to the Jackboot. He knew the Jackboot's corrupt nature, but on the contrary, considered drinking a bottle of beer. "Madam give me one star please." The chillness of the star beer relaxed his nerves as he drank the bikes from Ukuraibo arrived. "Did you see?" They were on their way out when an Okada rider on passing them spotted their gun pointed outwards. He turned to alert his people behind. On seeing the Okada's quick response one-man kill fired continuously to distract their pursuers. A woman who was in her private sawing institute heard the sound of gunshot; the various shattering of gunshot fired, quickly called her little kids together and entered into the inner room. The door was half closed when she heard a vibrating sound that shattered the machine inches away from her. She half struggled to pull her two kids together with all her strength. She was almost dazed but the spirit in her was a courageous one, not wanting to fail her little kids. In fear, her daughter asked "mummy what was that?" "Never mind I will explain later as she closed the door."

In the open, angry youths stood by with great expectation. "What have these Jackboot men got to offer?" Papa said. "Nothing I suppose." Ben answered. "Then we have to excommunicate them." "You re right Adams." What are we waiting for bring down this building cause we don't have need for the Jackboot anymore." "Absolutely you're right Chris," a man was busy beckoning to the crowd. "Fellow Kinsmen, enough is enough of Jackboot collaboration, the time has come for us to do our job in this town without the Jackboot force, it is of no use having this bunch of thieves. Exploiter, charlatans uniformed robbers in our community and we are constantly intimidated harassed day and night by robbers." "The lingering agony is still new in most houses where not just robbery cases but killings, we must send this people to where they belong."

The response that followed triggered the crowd; the spokesperson was not allowed to complete his speech. The youths rushed to the station, as the DJO was about going out. In self-defense he started shooting to disperse the crowd. This singular act infuriated the youths, they rained stones at the DSP who nevertheless saw it coming. He quickly entered his car and drove off. The cell was bust open while the in- mates were release; after carefully removing people's belongings every other accessory in the station was set ablaze.

The Jackboot officer noticed the rioters were quick to swing into action, he quickly opened the armory made away with the ammunition available unaware that a passerby was watching him from a distance.

"Ensure that no body removes anything from the station." Adams the rioter ordered. The groups ensuring that nothing was removed from the station were unaware that the Jackboot officer was busy removing the weapons from the armory. As he came out of his hideout he was accosted. "Stop that Jackboot officer!" Where are you coming from? What is your name? . Charge him for hiding when he was supposed to do his job as a Jackboot man." Someone identified him as the desk Jackboot man who refused to grant audience to the people. He was knocked down before he could say a word.

The crowd was so much that Teddy's advancement depended on their dispersing as they were seen from two sides of the road. While others came from the street he was about to turn into; the remaining groups took a narrow path that led to the main road. Teddy could not proceed in that direction so he had to drive along with the crowd to their destination.

"Burn everywhere!" the crowd screamed. 'Lets complete this process' I believe this will create an impact in the mind of all that has conspired with the Jackboot. "Lets go to the DJO's house, at least he should be the specimen goat for now who is to serve as deterrent to others." Someone shouted. They all welcomed the suggestion and the various groups trekked out of the station yard that remains of ash and tick black smoke. An expert in burning who made it look more or less of a dilapidated building mechanically effected the final damage to the building and left the walls in such a way that will give way once given a slight push. Other valuable items were seized.

CHAPTER FIVE

The rioters moved along Ubeumu road to the express, a distance of about 300 meters from the express. On reaching the express they met with some other groups who barricaded the road awaiting the robbers.

The regrouped partakers were briefed of the next line of action without questioning the authority joined to reunite with the first set. Approaching was one of the least distributors of soft drinks. On seeing the truck, the rioters swung into action. "Stop there!" They commanded, the driver an elderly man of average height with a funny set of teeth blackened as a result of excess intake of tobacco in panic stopped before the command was let out. Come down! Someone backed. He quickly disembarked and raised his hand in solidarity. Instantly the youths moved to the truck and reached for crates of drinks. They descended on the bottles of soft drinks as though they were drinking water, for they were very thirsty after the day's hectic job. "No! No! No! We cannot finish this stuff, we've had enough, let him go." The group leader said. The driver in a confused state; in want of what to say said, "thank you leader invariably thanked the leader for an ample opportunity to defraud his company. His motor boy was not a company staff, so the boy knew little or nothing about company ethics.

They matched along the busy express road linking Akarba and the bypass to Nineb. Due to the incident, the road was less busy instead human traffic occupied the road. In no time, the rioters turned off to the link road that terminates at the DJO's house.

Teddy pulled out of his compound with the intension of fetching water. He has a habit of fetching enough water to last for the week. The simple truth being that he is not always in the town; his business compels him to travel almost every day and to return late in the evening or at night. The street he drove on had a lot of ditches as the Local Council refused to grade it. He moved his car up and down on the road. As he approached the main express road, he noticed the crowd, which was multiplying by the second. On the notion he was well known in town, he moved on, he drove across the main express, this time he did not bother to delay in watching out for vehicles since the whole vehicles coming from both direction were stopped momentarily. In the mist of the rioters he recognized an old associate who by his age margin should have been discourage from the act of rioting. He was still wondering what was amidst when they passed him. Someone called from the crowd Teddy! On a second glance he reorganized the whole crew. A man who had his face covered with a white hair tie walked up to him in the old rickety Brown, Datsun 200L as if he wanted to exchange pleasantries. "Oh! it's you?" He said. "Lets move on," said another member of the group who stepped forward to rescue him from greeting.

The whole youths in solidarity all carried branches of "leaf" some tied their head with scarves making it impossible to identify them. The scenario was free of happiness; the youths had sadness written all over their face. In pursuance of their demand, they began to sing a war song "Ojukwu wanted to divide Nigeria, Gowon say Nigeria must be one we're are fighting to defend Nigeria, Nigeria must be one." Whorea! Neither do we want Jackboot, in this town of Ukuraibo. Echo

On till that day Ukuraibo clan will not know peace we Ukuraibans will fight we find it necessary we know we shall win, as we are confidence in the victory ami war. Echo wars in the east, war in west war up north, war down south ami say war in our land ami say war. Teddy incredulity of the on going film show was totally excited. He was no longer in a hurry to move on. He waited until the last man was out of sight before moving. On reaching the DJO's residence the crowd rushed towards the building. "Oh! No!' "Not like the station." "We can not function here the way we did at the station, do you know why?" The leader asked. Yes someone said. "This building belongs to someone else" "A good citizen I suppose, unlike his tenant. For posterity sake we cannot set it ablaze." "So what do we do now?"

Ada, one of the girls who had been with the groups from the on set responded; "you are right." "We can only bring out his belongings out in the open, here set it on fire." "Do we agree?" They all responded. Sure. Inside the house a Jackboot man on hearing the persistent murmuring outside called on the girl with him. "Sister' I don't think we are safe with this kind of noise." "Watch out." He called. He quickly pulled his uniform, ran to the back door and dragged the girl along. He remembered that as a Jackboot officer he had to treat his superior's girl friend as he would his own, when ever his superior is not around.

The door was hit with an axe, which gave way easily without further hitting. Before the crowd could step into the house, the Jackboot officer and the girl were in a safe distance. "Oh! My God! Exclaimed Ada, "just don't stand watching pack out everything to the open." "The people must see for themselves that this man is an accomplice." He succeeded before, but not anymore with all this to show. What if we take a picture of these items to serve as evidence? Benson suggested. Oh! No we don't have time for that. We must finish this assignment on time.

The properties were carried out side one after another. These included chairs fridge fan electronic rugs bed est. Surprisingly under the bed were found cartridges of Ammunition and bags of various sizes. The bags were eventually open to the astonishment of all-present different currencies of many domination were found. Also found was, pot of charms neatly arranged in one corner and a sack containing compressed Indian herm. These items were carefully arranged in a Datsun bus packed outside. A fireman was invited into the scene. "Stop, there! Where are you taking the video to?" "Bring it back and put it right here." He was fluff up at the house corner, Pablo administered him with fresh slaps neatly he received whipping but the group did not want an in house fight. "You people are warned for the last time." "This one can be pardoned." Ensuring no camera was in sight they burnt every item that came out of the house

Teddy stood amazed he thought of great contras in that the leaders of the group of rioters would have been wise enough to leave some of the items recovered to serve as exhibit in the course of investigation. His reasoning was based on a human right seeker of justice, because when a Jackboot officer has in his possession different domination of naira and foreign currency one starts to question his neutrality in crime. He reasoned. For the items could be items recovered from criminals or gift from same set of people. If the items recovered is from criminals, why will it be stored at the divisional Jackboot officer's house. More so different ammunition discovered would have raised eye brows coupled with the allegation by the same Jackboot that its armory was raided whereas it was his Jackboot men that looted the armory which goes to show the caliber of Jackboot they are.

"Whatsoever, I repeat nothing must be removed from this place."Every property goes just as the cash that left Fedson Bank Ukuraibo this morning." Papa said. "Fellow Kinsmen" he continued, lets not spoil the good work done by indulging in petty stealing or what ever name you may find fit." " We are on sanitation exercise; as such any bandit will not remain in our mist." "Thank you all for listening." The firemen poured Petrol inside the bus and opened the fuel tank of the motor. He was handed a long stick with its tip ties with cloth, he soaked it in fuel, he ignited the matchstick, which attracted the fuel, and the bus was engulfed in flame. The people cheered. "We are done with this what next?" Dandy said.

"Do we have losers in our mist?" "No!" they echoed. "We go now to the bank manager's house and carry out the same duties." The group after burning the DJO's house decided to extend it to the bank manager's house; who happened to leave in the heart of the town called Agnabgal street, adjacent to the bank building before Iama road from Akarba end of the town. The distance is similar when coming from the area of attraction. "The bank, they passed Nwaiko Rd, which took them to an off cut through an open compound having its front entrance along a bypass terminating in Agnabga street, proper. On entering the fenced compound some minds were softened, coupled with the sticker seen on the managers door. he was instantly identified as a member of a renowned religious body in the town, notably believed to house all prominent men and past leaders of the community.

"Brothers," Felix said. "It will be on us if we at the end of the day burn an innocent man's property, please lets see reason now that we can think. This man is not the only

Bank Staff, if there is a bad egg within the system, for sure as a manager he would not be able to detect the public enemy, more so he is not the person who attends to customers."

"I feel his position is that sensitive that he would not want to compromise his job by motivating crime in an area within his immediate jurisdiction." "Please lets have a rethink." "I can foresee we are taking this too far another speaker added," "we might have other plans but not this house." Unknowingly the speaker made a mark because the number of people in support of burning the house after the speech diminished. "Should we suspend this one?" the leader asked. Yes! They echoed. As they were about going, someone voiced out. "What of that, 'good for nothing' light skinned guy that works in the bank?" "An accusing finger cannot just be pointed at him." Another shouted. "He must be bad for his bad countenance he has to be administered with severe punishment. Someone else concluded.

Their spirit was awakened; they moved in one swift in search of the accused person as predicted an evildoer couldn't hide. Lock ran out on him as he was about entering the bank " that is him," pointed the team leader instantly the crowd averted him from entering the bank premises. "Tell us now or you die where your friends are from." someone hit him with a sledgehammer, all this while he had held it with his shirt serving as cover. Different hands slapped him as he tried to defend himself, various raking hands to his face he was dragged to the open road pulled back and front. Most people were kicking at him not for the offence as proposed but his nature as a poser. Naturally the beating would have continued if one prominent chief did not come to his rescue.

"Stop that, do you want to kill him." If he is guilty of an offence send him to the appropriate quarters. Not the Jackboot sir, "Okay send him to Okpala Uku's Palace for interrogation" yes sir. this put a stop to the beating of the bank victim. "If not for Chief Derrick I would have suggested a second round of beating." Papa said. 'Is like you were reading my mind' Felix voiced out. "This guy feels he is the Managing Director of the bank." At all weird time he goes with girls as if he is filled with demons.

As the crises persisted, some prominent citizens called in their lads perceiving the situation was getting out of control. The scenery took a different dimension young men who did not partake in the offensive gradually joined in the display of arrogance to the detriment of a few, whom were single handedly figured out as sacrificial goats.

The streets of Ukuraibo were invaded by angry youths who used this as an opportunity to avenge any offender. They mounted roadblocks along the express, to boost the effectiveness of the roadblocks; bottles were broken all over the place. This served as checks to most motorists that would not wait to comply with the simple rule of roadblock. Since they knew the outcome, the unlucky drivers were forced out of their cars and in turn receive the beating of their lives. The rioters mounted the vehicle and by so doing displayed their new role of leadership in the territory. Everybody within reach was exited. They drove round town under the influence of Alcohol enjoying the supply of the various brands of dry gin, gulped directly from the bottle; making the scene to be in conformity with carelessness and youthful exuberances.

"Obey before complaint!" snapped the Youth leader. He addressed a driver. So you are an indigene. "And you do not know the happenings so far." "I tell you, you had better join in the celebration now or face the wrath of any mob attack." The youth leader said. "This is an advice from a brother not just a friend." "What is he saying?" Papa asked. "Oh! No" "Forget him we are just discussing." The leader answered. The stranger who happens to be an indigene packed his car and joined in the celebration of victory over the robbers and Jackboot. "The driver who solely masterminded the notorious group, known as DBS "destroys before settlement" when he was resident in town. Now as a tanker driver his behavior has not altered one bit. As an insider in Irraw refinery it takes mainly guts to handle the tanker drivers when they are provoked. That is why it is mostly advised not to allow an issue to persist at times of demand and claim. The man sees himself as a complete youth as his perpetual adolescence frame gives him confidence that he is a youth. He is dark in complexion about four ft two inches tall with sets of legs mere seeing him you would think he is one of the zuru fighters, with his bushy hair. He positioned himself as the bail master Order, Russell shouted, what! No car is allowed to go without confirmation Pat said.

"Look I cannot continue with all this." Edmond said pointing at a youth who instead of collecting money from a driver passed him on self-recognition. "You know at this crucial time no one is exempted," better go back and join the group. Papa slammed his fist on the guys back. "Behave yourself! Okay." "You don't have to complain Jeff is right." Mike said. The guy suppressed his anger and moved to his new duty post.

"It is high time we discontinued this act of intimidation." Solo said. We started this in good faith; we therefore just have to end it in like manner." A murmuring Nat said.

"We cannot take laws into our hand for so long unless we are calling for reproach from the authority." My advice any way is to discontinue." Solo retorted. "Look who is talking – why start what you can't accomplish?" Andrew said, "We are in this and it has to continue." "We don't want the Jackboot any more." "Get that straight into your fucking brain." Nat barked.

"You think I 'm happy doing this, Edmond said. If you don't know it we are sending signals to the appropriate quarters." "They should feel free to stop us if it is their job to encourage mugger and harass innocent citizens." Edmond screamed. "We will know sooner or later if they are in support of our being intimidated by the muggers." "Let me give you a tip lad, they can't stop us. Nat added.

The molestation continued non-stop as such motorist avoided the new road to take the old road but similar act of oppression and intimidation was the order of the day along the old road. This brought to an end, the unnecessary traffic along the old Elepas Robga Road.

CHAPTER SIX

Naturally anything that has a beginning must have an end. It is a saying that decency must be recognized as a rule for being clean. After witnessing the dramatic encounters of the people, Teddy drove to his destination. Since it has been a hectic task for him all morning, he walked up to the borehole attendant to pay him his due who incidentally was his schoolmate at the secondary level. "Hi Josh" he said what is new? Teddy asked. Nothing much, replied Josh. "Please since you are mobile could you help me buy diesel to run my generator?" "My boy did not tell me he had used up the liters left as at yesterday." Josh an ardent opportunist did not want to miss this golden opportunity. "No problem" Teddy said, "what are friends for if not for inconveniencies?" Teddy collected the money from him without counting, knowing he must have counted time, without number. Once in such trade, you have to be meticulous with cash since it's not easy to come by. He thanked him in anticipation for he knew in no time; his cash will be exchanged for diesel.

Not as anticipated Teddy drove through wire road to Ubeumu road then turned right towards the express. Along Ubeumu road a heap of refuse was dumped at intervals along the road. He was about going to the corner to allow fellow road users to pass when his tyres suddenly rotated and climbed the sandy heap. "Oh my God," he screamed. As his hand hit the steering, he received a sharp pain on his finger. He got down from the vehicle. "Who must have deposited this waste?" He was furious. Unknowing, he spoke aloud to be heard, a woman standing in awe of the days activity came to his rescue as she heard him. "This is the handwork of our local government chairman." She said. "Then where did he get these hazards?" "His hotel of course, these dumped materials now served as hazards for the space to drive through the road were so narrow that most cars unconsciously climbed the heap of refuse. It took him less than three minutes to reach the elf filling station, Ukuraibo from Ubeumu Junction.

As he was waiting to buy fuel, because of make shift scarcity based on the shortage of staff. Suddenly the staff started drifting towards the back of the station abandoning their duty post. Teddy turned to face the road. "Oh!" "At last we have been expecting you guys." Teddy said. The mobile Jackboot officers disembarked their vehicle and walked towards the town with the vehicle as lead behind. Their posture like the American solders who invaded Iraq in operation desert storm, they were combat ready with their guns held upright pointing in one direction.

"Wait a moment" Teddy said. "Why are you guys running?" He addressed the attendants. "I suppose you've not committed an offence." "It's only criminals that react this way." "You had better come and attend to me." "Can't you see? If these Jackboot men capture you there will be nowhere to run oh!" the attendant said, as he hid behind a fuel thank. The set of mobile Jackboot force walked past without looking in Teddy's direction. In all, they were about thirty men, with a big truck and jeep as escort backup.

The fuel attendants ensured that the team had passed before they resumed selling. "You people are frightened over nothing." "These people are meant to protect you and be your friends as well." Teddy said. "I rather have a bandit as a friend sir." The fuel clerk said. "It's not like that with present Nigeria." The Jackboot would rather dine with criminals to earn their living." "I hate their guts, a mugger will spare his buddy but as for the Jackboot men." The attendant said. "Unless there is a general over hauling of the Jackboot unit, Nigeria cannot know peace." "You have forgotten so soon that without bribe 'egunje' they don't work, neglecting their main call to duty." "A Jackboot officer would prefer a criminal to be an innocent citizen when money has exchanged hands. Thanks for your time and the lecture too." The attendant said.

"I begin to wonder if we would ever have a change," Teddy thought as he drove off. As the mobile Jackboot men passed the filling station approaching a road junction, they boycotted the expressway through Ubeumu road, the road that was a clear picture of an abandoned community, no sign of government presence. The team entered the ditches created by heavy downpour; the villagers avoided the Jackboot team as such, the road being free of human beings. They were astonished at the level of havoc done to the station. But it did not infuriate them as one of the team member rightly said. "This is government property not our own." Suddenly the whole place was charged up as in a chemical reaction. The siren awaked the whole neighborhood from a distance, the Jackboot men started reorganizing themselves, as the car got to their position it slowed to a stopped, while the car door was swung open by the oddly and the commissioner of Jackboot came down, all stood at attention. Those that did not know him were jittering. He inspected the parade alone, as the commissioner walked toward his car the DJO quickened his step to meet him. "Look all I want is result the deputy governor is on my neck." Yes sir. The people hovered around hoping to hear him. "Call me once your men goes to the field." was his last word, he closed the door of the car that was steaming and the driver drove off.

The DJO called the Jackboot men together and started briefing them on the nature of the assignment as briefed by the commissioner himself. He was about leaving when one of them called. "Sir we leant your property was destroyed?" "We would want to see for ourselves." "It's of no use inspector just do your job as directed." The DJO said. "Sir the men are insisting on seeing your house." "Alright, we move from there. The inspector shouted, by the left forward match. They started on their sight seeing mission along the express road; they intercepted an onlooker who refused to run as other people were doing. He was brought down by a single kick, pulled on the floor along as they proceeded, intermittently he was flogged with the whisk "koboko" they held. The Jackboot men took advantage of the man because he had a bad leg such he could not run. The man took his fate in his hands even when others at a distance were signaling on him to plead with the Jackboot to let him go. He refused. He was later set free. There was a general out burst of people taking cover as if the robbers were back to unleash another round of agony on the people.

"Oh! No. it is the mobile Jackboot force." "They had come on time a by stander said. "Our people we quite know if given 100 miles take 1000 miles for sure." Henry said. "I feel this will calm the situation." "Henry, you're just ignorant about these peoples ordeal." "These men are destroyers, number one: public enemy number two." The Jackboot men boycotted Ubeumue road entered the express road, which was free of human traffic. They trekked straight through the express and turned through the bend that led to the DJO's house. As they reached the Danfo burnt bus, the DJO stopped. He started by showing them the havoc done to him. As he spoke, his eye was brick red but was able to control himself before his subordinates. "Commander, you can see for yourself, my whole life, I came to this town thinking I was in a safe neighborhood, but with Jackboot protection I was proved wrong." "My property, belongings name it, all gone in a single drift." "Look at this, I bought this bus some couple of month's back." "I intended putting it on transport once I leave the town" "In here, they packed my belonging, whole lot they burnt to ashes. The remains of my belonging; "I believe you can bear with me that this was born out of hatred from a fellow human being."

"Sir, if I may ask; who is that person?" "Never mind, I want you to do your job rightly." "You must understand that the people of Ukuraibo are number one enemy of the Jackboot." "At the station, if I did not run for my dear life, I may not have been opportune to give this account." "I was chased out of the Station; I narrowly missed the mob attack." "Over 500 angry youths stormed the station in protest." "But trust our skill I left without being hurt." With this analysis he was able to influence the Jackboots reasoning

"I can't bear this any more." "We have to teach these people the lesson of their lives maybe when they hear a Jackboot officer's name they will give absolute respect." "If we don't, this town can never respect the Jackboot." ""You can see for real the cruelty of man's inhumanity to man" "How could this thought be conceived by human beings? "We had better treat them like animals if we must succeed in this crucial mission." "Please you see the neighborhood, I've lived here ever since I came to the town and I've not had problems with any body." "Sir but Ukuraibo is Ukuraibo." I know, just do me a favor deal decisively and aggressively with people across the road especially Uzuko and Akabgu. Ensure to arrest chief Edeja, hold some few as bond for the government.

The Jackboot assembled in front of the old burnt vehicle. The commander shouted "Jackboot regroup" The entire Jackboot officer stood at attention in a single file. He shouted. Doubles, The first man moved to the right while the second to the left, they continued in that form till they had a double line. You have seen for your selves at least you have your own views so treat as you deem fit the people of Ukuraibo.

The first victim was apprehended at Mandela junction. Maybe this revenge of the Jackboot is on the armed robbers who have caused havoc in the past a un- looker chipped in.

The people did not know that the Jackboot force had received induction. He was rushed at before he could take a stride backwards towards his store. "Leave me oh! Nat wailed, I 'm not a rioter." "Shot up or I 'II kill you." The Jackboot said. And Nat responded, though he spoke to himself. "You fit, on seeing the barrel pointing at him he kept quite. He was flogged; Kicked his short was pulled from his waist. As the Jackboot tried to draw him close to the truck he saw a free exit and ran for it. "Let him go." the commander said. He has suffered enough. "Move on now!" The Jackboot was so aggressive that they not only waited for someone to run into them, but also left their normal single file course and started chasing people back and forth. A man was stopped; before he could say a word a Jackboot man slapped him. What for? You don't have the right to slap me?" Have you finished slapping your friendly criminals?" on hearing this, he was routed from the ground by a single kick that came from about four jackboot officers at the same time, he struggled with the Jackboot men and was raining all sorts of abuse on the team of mobile Jackboots. He was carried into the Jackboot van but without proper check, he jumped down and ran away

"I agree with you Justine, but I think we need the Jackboot at this junction." "Any way, I will travel out of this, town first thing tomorrow morning." Festus said. 'Me too' Henry said.

At Iama road junctions, they seized two girls who were returning from the market. Both were forced out of their bicycles, "please we did not join the protesters" one of the girls said. "You have a succulent breast," the Jackboot officers said as he touched her nipples. The girl fidgeted and held her breast. They lashed them with "Koboko" and massaged their breasts. "Help" the girls cried. But in the circumstance, help could not come. Every body ran helter scatter in total confusion. On lookers were seen standing at a distance not minding the consequence of being caught. They wondered why the Jackboot would be treating girls in such a manner knowing they didn't partake in the crime of the day. Never did it occur to them that the girls were single handedly picked to pay for the crime perpetuated by angry youths who burnt the DJO's property. "Can you imagine that these Jackboot officers are not bothered about the station?" This gives you an insight of the kind of Jackboot unit we have in this country. Jonathan said. "Can you imagine?

Shops along Iama road were temporally closed as the owners abandoned for safety. A man was taken away with his facemasks in blood, despite his constant plea and protest. He was led into the awaiting Jackboot van.

Iama road, which is a very busy link road in the town, was temporarily out of business. The whole road, with the exception of a few portion was crowded by on lookers who acted like arm chair analysts." "If we regroup to "attack" run, this Jackboot men don't you think they will give in." Hector said. "By so during this will stop this act of intimidation" a by stander moved as if to commence action but, reconsidered the act and withdrew. He was not man enough, slowly slowly he phased out of the scene. As the crowed built up, the Jackboot acted spontaneously by spraying tear gas to disperse the crowd. This was accomplished with the aid of the tear gas gun: which has a provision that accommodates, "smoke" being fumed from the gas chambers, the air was polluted, without warning individually the crowd dispersed in various groups. The teargas was sprayed randomly; this reduced the tension faced by the Jackboot. They carried on as if they were not scared but deep within them; they were almost overtaken by fear.

"Our people needed a little resistance to check the activity of the Jackboot but who will bear the cat? Festus asked. Since we failed to stall this act of intimidation we are bond to regret. How can our youths be scared of the Jackboot officers? You that is talking can't you act if you're not a coward. Pablo shouted at him. It is obvious that the Jackboot would have withdrawn if the youths mounted pressure on them, but no body was ready to take the lead thereby placing his life on hood for the emancipation of his fatherland. The Jackboot who noticed the people's unwillingness to challenge their action capitalized on the people's weakness and this generated into acute molestation. The people watching from afar sent a wrong signal as the Jackboot officers tried to ward them off by firing tear gas into the air. Surprisingly the people remained calm someone from the crowd walked up to the smoking tear gas. It's fuming, the people shouted. While picking the object he sniffed it and chucked it back to the sender.

As they approached the house, adjacent to the old Jackboot station Dickson pointed. "That one on the edge" you are sure he is in there? The commander asked. Yes, Ama the conspirator said. "Open the door or we break it." The man inside knew he would be looked for. He did not listen to their threat, which was as good as real. He stood on top of the stool gently he opened the window noiselessly not minding his size he squeezed through the window in the process he sustained slight brose. The door was slammed open as one of the Jackboot officers heaved his weight on it. "We have missed him." "Look he must have left through that open window." a Jackboot officer said. "What next" the 2nd in command said. The commander looked at his Wright watch. Yes! The market, the Jackboot officers drove to the market area, the market was in full section as it was on a market day. The traders far and away come every 4th night: directly in front of the market, the Jackboot officers parked their truck. The team leader collected a canister of teargas from his colic, facing the market he fired the shot right into the market. As the Jackboot officers saw the teargas gun fired they screamed "yah ho!" the Jackboot officer smiled" "at least this will hunt the old and young" the teargas sent a frightening signal amidst the people, in disarray the traders and buyers old and young ran in an attempt to run away from the teargas. Some people began to loot and scattered goods especially tomato, pepper and bottles of oil. The whole market was in a mess couple with the untidy nature of the Ukuraibo market, most people fell when pushed and others stumbled and fell on others, all in the name of teargas fired"

The whole market was in hysteria; uncertainty was the order of the day in the market. Goods worth thousands of naira were littered allover the place. "This strange behavior of the Jackboot in Ukuraibo must have its roots" Johnny said though it's not a strange behavior with the Jackboot force. "They are ruthless, and heartless even in most cases, robbers are more humane than the Jackboot." The Jackboot saw it as pay back to the youths, whom most of their relatives would be affected. The same act of inhumanity preached against.

"Where is that area called Uzuko?" A low rank asked. "Wait, I'II go and find out from commander." He quickly boarded the car and drove off. The Jackboot officers waited calmly for their man, the traders ran midway out of the market they collided with the Jackboot officers and ran back into the market.

"Yowa! Uzuko" He said pointing at the other side of the market. "It is over here. Opposite the market, that means this whole area must be Uzuko." Directly opposite the market they started their invasion, the crowd that greeted them at first sight reduced without being noticed, the compound was as empty as a graveyard. The action singly informed every body within the neighborhood of the need to be most alert as far as Ukuraibo is concern. It is generally known in Ukuraibo that one is prone to hazards if one resides at Uzuko. As such, one's approach to life is simple, when a person watches his footstep, one can't fall into a unexpected pit. Also there is a saying that "you scratch my back and I scratch your back" with this information, the news of the day's mishap traveled faster than ray of light, since no one knows when he needs such information.

Austin was in no mood to visit Ukuraibo but for his rent he had no choice, he was on the way to his office when Chike slowed to a stop. Austin he called, as he turned he almost walked on but for decency sake he went to meet him. "Chike you mean all these months you have been in this town? I can't believe it even with the entire story that filtered round town, that I've been relieved of my job. Man you wronged me badly, after all what are friends for if not for inconveniencies. You did not bother to look me up-why? Friends cannot be for pleasure ride alone." He enquired.

"A guy is not your friend if he can't be there for you, when you need him most." Austin said sympathetically. "I don't what to go into that analysis" Chike said, "it has past and I belt you we all had our dose of problem." You can't tell me to allow it rest when you are still insisting to be a saint. "All right I accept my wrong and I am sorry." That's my friend. Austin laughed. So where are you going? "I've just had a call from our head office to come over" that means you're passing through Ukuraibo Chike asked. You're right, he thought for a while "I've to forgo the office and go with you."

"Our best bet is to go round through Unugo to be free of this impending hold-up." That's right Chike reverse and followed a link road by shell estate he was on the Unugo expressway with ABS on the right, Atled broadcasting service.'

The pleasure ride to his town was rewarding for he was able to obtain a cash gift of #5000.00 from his friend. He bid his friend goodbye, moved as he remembered his mission, normally when he visit like this he collets his rent first before seeing friends. A tradition he would be expected to spoil the table, this set rule he did not forget. As he stepped past his caretaker's home he saw market women running towards his direction. "The frantic mode they bear prompted him to ask. What's the matter? He was surprised that the traders did not stop to answer him, all he heard from the crowd is 'Jackboot and teargas" as they hurriedly past him. He was able to put too and too together to understand what was going on. Not far from his position he saw Jackboot truck in front of him, he knew his town just like Irraw is crises infested so he need no body to advice him. He tactically averted the bank since a truck was stationed there, meaning he has to follow another root to his house. 'Uncle,' a kid in his compound called. "You are wanted." Who wants me? He asked as he moved to see the person, he was met by an old pal. "You just have to leave this neighborhood at once; this is no time for question and answer. He quickly went inside instead of moving out he was more relaxed, he reasoned.

"So there is nowhere to run" 'how can? even his own house is not safe.' Sure belt he needs to chastise his parents for residing in Uzuko.

Basically in Uzuko clan, all forms of crime namely 419, Rape and petty stealing are perpetuated in high degree. An Alhaji positioned in a small Cabin some where in the community this enables him to extort money from peasant traders living in neighboring villages that usually come to trade in the market. Luck ran out on him as the Jackboot officer storm the area; he was the first to be apprehended. "Well done the traitor said. "This is the head of the 419 in Uzuko" the 419 thrive because of greed as such the victims are easily dispossessed of their wealth. "Why would someone want to reap where they did not sow? The adage of the game states that: a "mogul" can only be wise when he has been duped. As such he would be initiated. When a "mogul" as the victim is called is deceived, he would be made to take an expletive, so that he would not tell the secret that is passed on him to a second party. One is made to perform such acts so that the game plan will be taken seriously. All these happen to further portray themselves as real. What most people don't understand is why one has to be taken to a shrine. The "Mogul" as they term the victim is mostly from one of the villages that solely believe in Juju. This could be why the tricks work with ease. Even girls in Uzuko help in the act of 419 by luring their male toasters to their well-arranged group that eventually pretends not knowing their partners in crime. The traitor explained.

A few Jackboots mounted a road bock by the bank while the remaining moved into town. A teenage boy wearing a school uniform was held. "Let me go." he groaned but was hit on his mouth. "Keep quit," the Jackboot shouted.

"It is saddening that age is not on my side," Responded an old man who was carried in a black Mercedes Benzes as he passed the scene. "If not I would have taught those pigs the lesson of their lives." "The army with their military might was unable to hold this town to ransom during the civil war not to talk of these untamed pigs."

The man, in his eighties was still very strong. His looks portrays a different view concerning his age, one would have thought he was approaching seventy. He could not restrain his anger for the sight was awful.

At the old Jackboot station, someone was being taken away from one of the shops. Oh! He is one of the conspirators whom initiated the early morning burn fire. The people's concern was, who was behind the information? Ukuraibo knew no peace from the moment the Jackboot force set their foot in the town; the Jackboots were busy with arrest. Fear rose to a peak when the Jackboot officer in rang started breaking all the doors at Uzuko but to their dismay they met empty "bunks." They were highly disappointed since there was a tip off from good people of the area. The Jackboot continued in their manhunt with the hope of taking at least, some people from Uzuko as prisoners.

In an attempt to arrest a lad and his brother the eldest of them smashed the Jackboot officer's arm and push his brother to run while he took to his heels. He exhibited a show of brevity. "In physic' starting energy," once started cannot stop unless a force is acted upon it to stop. Most people got arrested because of their ego. They did not want to run and the Jackboot officers capitalized on that, if you attempt to run, they forget about you and concentrate on those who don't see them as a threat at all.

They applied simple psychology, knowing full well that those who refuse to run can easily regroup to fight back. They deemed it necessary to lock them up.

Patience, Ani called. "Where are you going to" Patience moved here lips indicating at the man following her. "Is Alhaji in the office?" oh! You've not heard? The Jackboot officers have arrested him. Patience stood still, "oh no this

Jackboot men have knocked my job." Her mogul stood far off not knowing he was being discussed. Take heart we can still manipulate him. Ani reassured her. "You see that girl Ani." her job is most risky as she coordinates the girls in Uzuko area; she is a no nonsense breed, she operates with charm. Her male friends suffer terrible cause she obtains money from them forcefully. The traitor said. Your fallow officers have tried to arrest her in the past. "These girls behave like men their only difference is their gender. The Jackboot officers was inspired by the traitor's increased it's aggressive on the people. "Bring down every door," the commander said. Knowing that the art of burning must have originated from Uzuko; majority of the youths in Uzuko part of the town are jobless; they are prone to all kinds of immoral activities, a saying that an idle mind is the devils workshop. The Jackboot's belief was that Uzuko youth's base on idleness must have championed the art of rioting. They mounted roadblocks. People could no longer leave nor enter Uzuko community. The Jackboot men penetrated all the compounds along the major road. Most youths apprehended were adamant for they wanted to continuously see the action. The situation at hand was based on information the section of Jackboot team that unleashed mayhem knew were to go at any time. The whole area was agony redden. Along the Ukuraibo old road, beginning from the bank down to the market area, harbor jobless youths of the town. Who on daily basis think of what to do to help them? The houses in the surrounding were shades of mould, which were plastered with cement that have caved in obviously due to age. Also the youths of the area are used to nucleus life where they sit in the most popular guys place and descend on Kana snukor AK47 which is know also as "Ogogoro" the usual illicit dry gin brewed locally. Not very far off is joint were Indian herm called Igbo is sold the richest person introduces the

Indian herm and a bottle of 'Ogogoro' and the whole house will cheer. The traitor explained. The crowd on seeing the Jackboot officers advancing dispersed.

Unconsciously, a teenager walked into his compound, to his dismay he saw his mother lying on her back while the Jackboot were treating her like a common criminal. Weeping profusely she called. Help, am almost dead oh! The boy could not restrain himself, he rushed to rescue her but was halted by a near by neighbor who was watching from a far distance. "John it is of no use leave them alone since, they have taken the law into their hands we have no choice but to pray to the living God." He will for sure come to our aid." He leaped forward but was held back by the firm grip of a neighbor who led him away from the sight. Will this ever stop? He wondered, as he was being led away?

Nicolas was most disturbed because he had not seen his kid brother. He assembled all the members of his family. Please, I want you all to know that this whole thing is motivated by an external force as such you all have to be wary. We don't know where this will lead us to but for all I can smell is trouble brewing faster than anticipated." Watch out for Samson, I don't know if he has been arrested." He strolled leisurely out of their mist, signifying he had finished his address. Everyone knows he does not talk much but he sees from afar what is to happen.

Maxell, "I can't believe this?" "Of all the people whom are suppose to protect us from the menace of the societies are the same people causing us pain. 'Don't mind our situation.' If we complain about this minor incidence, what of Nido Laseyab state?" Where, a whole village was wiped out simple because they cried for their right." Don't forget that was masterminded by the first citizen. Nicolas said. Here you have mouth to complain; we pray ours will end at this." "I pray oh!" Kingsley chipped in. Nigeria's situation is always the same, I mean comparing the military and the democratic era. "If you flash back to the post colonial days, you find out that the people that fought for independence were so entangled in the struggle for power. They got the power and became power drunk." What do you expect? Mark replied. They never expected power to come cheap as it came from the British colonial masters as such, to relinquish that power became a difficult task.

'This is a country were truth is hunted down. Nicolas said. Why do we expect the jackboot officers to be friendly when politicians choose violence in all ramifications?" Nicolas said. Yet they go against cultist in higher institutions, whereas their act is even more vicious and deadly, than cultism." "It is a shame." Mark pointed out. "What about examination malpractice? It has to be legalized. "Don't you know these elites as they are termed pay so much in bribing their lads into higher schools of learning? Gilbert added. That means legalizing malpractice is in the making. Mark said. It is what the people want. Gilbert replied. Our politicians have set a bad precedence, such that, their control over the Jackboot is stemmed towards continuation of their set goal." "My brother I blame late general Aguiyi Ironsi for putting a halt to the 1966 military revolution; that would have brought sanity to the country thereby putting a final full stop to nepotism. "Today we have a Prime Minister that does not have sympathy for his subjects and you expect the people to gain from his rule?" No way! "It is the same man who betrayed his people because he was scared stiff thereby relinquishing power to a dishonest set of people." Now he is on the match again, good or bad he wants his name to be registered in history good book. Well, if he wants that he had better start dislodging the bad elements in government. Sure bet he will achieve his dream. "Gilbert, If we discus the problem affiliated with the country, we will be cramped by this hoodlums of a force called the Jackboot." Mark said.

Hundred meters away from the market a bricklayer headman was screaming at the top of his voice. 'I can't find the workers, where have they gone to?' "You had better look for them because I want this job completed in the next five days." As you can see, we can't afford to pay for another extra day. Do you comprehend? Be informed the chairman is coming to inspect the building by weekend. "There won't be any explanation to give." He did not finish his last word when the Jackboot force stormed the site. "Wait a minute, you can't do this to me" he said. "Who the hell do you think you are?" the Jackboot commander shouted. 'I'm on an official assignment in this site.' Both the site engineer and his supervisor were arrested, what for? I don't know what you are talking about." "When you get to the Jackboot station you can explain yourself."

CHAPTER SEVEN

At Akarba Jackboot station Eddy pleaded to see the DJO who refused to grant him audience, he was locked up with the boys who were arrested initially from Ukuraibo. The people knew no peace not until the last batch of Jackboot left Ukuraibo at about 8pm.

The whole community was in panic, this extended to the night hours, which was more complex for the people were ridden in fear of the unknown. A swift drive through the old road portrayed a community in disarray. The entire drinking joint, in town were as if closed shortly, prior to the sudden attack by the robbers that saw the entrance of the Jackboot force into the town. All joints were given an operating time of 10 pm maximum every day. But as if an order was passed the whole drinking spots were all closed unceremoniously. The main scenarios were busy gossips gathered in several groups discussing the day's attack. "This Jackboot officers will surely pay, what bits my imagination is the complexity of the conspirators." Bats! All in the name of a force, if they come back we shall resist with all valor. The emptiness of the people created room for more gossip.

"Had they tempered with any of my family members, they would have known that the khaki they wear is not leather. Others kept calm and listened to the conversation of the armchair analysts.

On reaching the end of the town Edmond pulled up at a shabbily looking bar. The place looks deserted, all the customers failed to visit, the palm wine seemed untouched and the cups remained in an open bowl filled with water. The cups were completely out of use while the benches used for seating were pushed upside down as if in a struggle. "Who is in here?" there was no answer. The light was very dull. As he stepped further into the bar, he saw a man lying with his face downward. The man was dazed. "What are you doing here?" He enquired as he tapped the man. The man woke with a start, fidgeting at the same time and was very scared. 'Where am I?" He asked in panic. His voice not audible but at close range, Edmond read his lips and understood his question. He did not bother to answer him for he knew his problem. "What happened?" Did they take them away?" He asked. Who? Edmond was edger to know. The Jackboot came and he staggered backward but was held back by Edmond who was a stone throw from him.

"Never mind all will be taken care of. Edmond said." "Where is your home?" As he came back to his senses he pointed to the direction facing him. "You're sure you stay there?" Edmond asked. "Yes Sir." "Go in peace." "Thank you." He greeted without looking back. Edmond concluded that last bus stop the owner of the popular joint has been arrested. "What can he do to be of help?"

Nkechi did not give in by the treat, she patiently waited by the window and at interval she checked her timepiece. 21:00 hrs she opened her door midway, as if waiting for one person to take the lead most joints owners opened but the people were so scared to patronize. Mathew, Jorum called had they attacked when we were around Uche, would you have stayed back? Uche laughed. "We would have known if the weapon would fight for them. The older generations were sitting at a palm wine spot sipping left over palm wine. Madam how come you did not bring this wine to the house the first day? Papa Mark asked. "Listen everyone, the announcer shouted. "Tomorrow at 17:00 hr every adult male should assemble at the Onotu- Uku's place. Cluster of people gathered at a compound "dutifully ignore the Jackboot officers act, since, the law is the Jackboot as the Jackboot represents the government. 'Any act might be termed instigation. Better we leave the struggle at the hands of our government representatives.' They in turn will fight our cause for us' explain Mr. Inyama, a dark skinny looking 6ft, 4nch tall bully who forced himself into being a chief. "Anything we do will amount to taking the law into our hands." "I know by tomorrow things will be settled amicably. His family is the most popular in town. Among his family members are lecturers, Lawyers, High court Judges, Pilots, Navy commanders Engineers, Bankers, Chief magistrate; Members of parliaments and presently some were in government. Name it. He knew his compulsion for he just did not speak. He didn't know Ukuraibo's case has drifted beyond his capacity as a village elder. He eventually went to bed but was very uncomfortable.

Ania studied her husband for a long time before she made up her mind to speak out. She knew from their years of marriage that he fidgets at sleep only when he is having problem breathing or when something serious is bothering him. 'Chief what is the problem again?" she said. "Oh nothing." "I just got tired because of the days meeting." "He never shared his problem until it degenerates to a headache." In his mind, he saw blood all over the whole place but could not picture what objects it covered, as he came back to his senses he knelt down to pray, no word suited his moment Lord set Your people free, Amen"

He was astonished at himself knowing that he was not a Christian neither was he a pagan. He looked at the ceiling as if a solution was going to come from there. His stare was so intense that tears began to accumulate in his eyes, he felt embarrassed because his wife was staring at him. 'Chief I know there is something bothering you but you don't want to talk about it.' "I just had a bad dream to be precise, a nightmare, "I pray this town problem will stop at this." "Considering the Nairegen government who takes delight in seeing it's citizen suffering I fear the unknown." With that he went off to sleep again.

Stella's family was not that lucky. She got home from the market to see that the house was disorganized and she could not see any body to ask what was wrong. She quickly put down her load and rushed out. As she was leaving the compound she met her cousin Angela who was coming to see whether she was back from the market, "Sister Stella." She called as she turned to see her face; it dawned on her that she was crying. "They have arrested Uncle." Where is Mama and little Nat?" "They went to see them at Akarba Jackboot station." She in turn could not restrain herself so she joined in the act. Both went back to the compound, as there was no one to console each other. 'What time did they arrest him' initially they did not arrest him, oh it was when he tried rescuing uncle Samson's Son 'Tim' that they left Tim and arrested papa." "Oh!" "I can't imagine papa being arrested for no just cause." It's shameful for the leadership of this community to see it's citizens being arrested just for burning of a Jackboot station: If they arrest every body, who is going to champion the course to raise money to rebuild the station?" Stella said, dripping in tears. Do you blame anybody replied Angela. "Of what use is our legislators, we attribute these to our lawmakers who went into government just for their own selfish interest. They don't legislate anything worthwhile. They are after erecting buildings and drive on expensive cars which they never dreamt of owning. Stella said. Sister, it's a crazy world don't they think if the youths were gainfully employed they would be busy with their work where would the mobilization come from? Is it men that are retired and tired as well? The country is sick and what do you expect from a sick society aguish, trouble criminal act and all form of lawlessness?

At the other side of the town known as Emusumu, a peace loving part of the town believed to have a heritage of Opkoize on the contrary descended more on illicit drink. The Jackboots stormed the neighborhood hoping to take some hostages, but were highly disappointed when they saw only women. In range they rushed at the middle-aged women who helplessly succumbed to high standard intimidation. "Where are your men? The Jackboot officers shouted. You think it is easy to be a DJO? Common pull your cloths and stand in single file. The women gaze at them knowing that they had no rescue they faithfully obeyed. Oh! You want me to show you example? The Jackboot officer said, he rolled his trouser to his kneel level revealing his manhood. The women closed their eyes. Now pull I say he raised his whip the women hurriedly removed their wrapper the officer shake his head oh no. Remove to your pants, lie down and face up the women obeyed he squeezed the tear gas into their female organ. "My mama oh, the women shouted.

On leaving the scene the Jackboot officers met some group of women including some young girls, whom under pressure were harassed into pulling their cloths. Revealing their nakedness; in amazement they were asked to dance makosa dance, a highly corrupt dance, because of the manner at which young girls and boys shake parts of their waist to the musical lyrics it is acclaimed to be for promiscuous people.

"I hope you will stay with me Angela you know I can't sleep alone in this house. " No problem I told daddy I would pass the night with you, "you are such a darling how kind of you." I forgot to tell you, the Jackboot men almost arrested brother, Gabriel. But he beat them to it. You know he was a 100 meters goal medalist, in his schooling days. He swerved the short Jackboot officer and jumped over another off he escaped. They tried but could not catch up with him.

Teddy woke with a start he intended going to Irraw but for his younger brother who came from Abasa he had a change of heart. They both went to the expressway with the intention of stopping tipper drivers carrying hard-core stone from Auchi; a town located in the northern part of Edo state in Nigeria. The people's culture has close resemblance to that of the northern part of the country who is pure Moslems. Teddy waved his hands, the driver as if expecting a stop over slowed and packed in front. The first vehicle they stopped was conveying little dust chippings, used for road construction only was let go. "I don't approve of these small size hard core chippings I think that will do" Teddy said as another vehicle parked. A Jackboot van zoomed past, more vehicles in convoy followed the Jackboot officers hung on it displaying their riffles; followed closely were other Jackboot van filed to the brim. "Hanging as if they were going to quell a coup, the flow of vehicle continues for about 10 minutes. The new road as the express leading to Elepas, Robga is popularly called. Charged like an atomic reaction, the people were taking cover right lift and hub.

They branched off at Iama road entering Ukuraibo town; few stores were just opening for the morning business. Few of the traders on seeing the Jackboot vehicle locked back their shops and remained indoors. Teddy decided to buy any of the stoned for he was tired of selecting; time to go, he informed his brother. They both joined the tippers and drove through the express to Oloni Street, which terminate at the old road. The street was a clear picture of an un-kept village. Galloping terrain terminating at various pools of water, if not properly accessed sinks all cars that passed. But theirs was a tipper so they didn't have problem passing the street.

They got to the old road through the link road and negotiated into Clara Inene's Street. The street is newly carved out in erosion prone area; the topsoil is gradually given way thereby uncovering the sub soil. The building, which is situated towards the end of the fence, has a common boundary with the street ends. On your right hand side is a massive fence painted white with a black gate and security house by the gate. The gate was opened and it reveals the well-arranged self-styled bungalow. The men in the compound rushed out to witness the arrival of the Tipper crew. The crew highlighted from the truck to meet the supervisor. He greeted Teddy who seems to know him. "Oh boy you've refused to come and see me why?' Don't take offence I've had a tight schedule replied Teddy. 'I don't know if this is the right stone for this flooring job.' Teddy enquired from the supervisor. 'Never mind stone is stone countered the supervisor.' What we are going to do is to mix these very big ones with the smaller cheapens. He was pointing at smaller granite at one side of the fence. You got it. 'So how is Abuja or Abasa?' "For I don't know where you're coming from? They both laughed. I'm fine answered Teddy; 'I have to pay this people off so that they can go,' Teddy said. Yes! 'You can see we can't' Teddy beckoned on the drivers. 'Take up to 5 trucks.' We have cash flow problem unless you people have to come down on your price. If not the deal is off.

'Samuel pay for these 3 trucks' The drivers followed Samuel to a corner where they all counted the money to be sure it was N93 thousand Naira. After counting they all separated the money into three places, this yours, you and you. Each took his part and thanked Samuel; they left without going back to Teddy. 'Please sir, consider us' the remaining two pleaded with Teddy 'you know the distance we have covered to come here.' Wait let me talk this out, 'Supervisor' he called. See how much you have got to spare, so that we can pay for these extra two trucks. He proceeded into the inner room came back with a bag and handed it over to Teddy. Pay for them both cause "I'm not sure if the five trucks in all, with the one extra stone heap will be enough to floor this compound. The last truck was still reversing, when some boys ran towards Teddy on noticing him they stopped and greeted. "What is the matter?" The supervisor asked.' Oh! It's the Jackboot they've started again this morning. Mathew said. We were in my house eating and all of a sudden they burst the door open.' We all rushed out through an outlet they did not know existed in our house. "Bros you can't believe it they even followed us to this street junction before going back." He explained. He was still panting. It is like the whole exercise of yesterday has started afresh. Paul confirmed. "It can't be." The supervisor said." don't underestimate the Jackboot people; they can go to any length in achieving their goal." Teddy said. "From what I saw yesterday they acted as if they were upon an order but what will the person stand to gain be he a government man or not if he kills the body can he kill the soul? One of the boys asked.

Mathew narrated the incident to the supervisor who did not witness the previous day's episode. I advise you to leave now that you can senior bros' this town is not safe any more. "Personally, If I can go back home, I will just pick maybe a shirt and trouser and go to a safe place to rest my head. The boy said. "You mean the Jackboot officers are breaking into peoples houses?" the supervisor asked. Bros is like you are learning how to talk? If it's just breaking into it's a good one then, the harassment and intimidation that follows is enough to scare you if you're not arrested. Paul said.

Niggers, but the people are not fighting so what do they need, the supervisor said in ewe; you can tell that to the marine the young man said and walked away.

CHAPTER EIGHT

I can hear the voice of a town crier, what is he saying? Edward asked a young man that just arrived at the scene. He hung a towel on his shoulder. Obviously he was just coming from the stream. "Oh! He responded. "They said all women should come out and dance to plead." What for? Teddy asked. "That they don't want trouble but peace, even some young men were ready to join in the dance." As for my family and I, we cannot join in such provocative dance' Teddy said. "It is not safe Godwin said. Teddy and his brother Samuel left courageously amidst the fear that shadows the mind of the people. All they care was how to reach home. As they approached the Elepas Robga road, the quietness that greeted them made them uneasy. They began to feel like they were sitting on a volcano, if erupted there wouldn't be any safe haven for them. No soul was seen except older women. They quickened their footsteps. "Samuel, Teddy called. "What is this staring all about?" It baffles me," Samuel said. We cannot see one person to ask question. "Let's get the hell out of here." They moved on ensuring their compass was not leading them astray. As they got to a street before Ekidumu their street of residence, they recognized an elderly woman. Sam she called, "what are you guys doing?" Every youth in the town has hidden for safety, if you know what is good for you, you had better find a way out of this town." "Thanks, we're on our way to the house." "I feel it is safe enough, bye." As they got to Ekidumu Street they both exclaimed "oh!" 'That is the house but I told you I'd direct you to the house." Samuel said. "You must have had a perfect geography teacher in your school days. Teddy said. "You're right he is the current principal of Abmonibo grammar school." Not long they both settled at home.

Neye was busy by the river side chanting he was invoking the spirit of the gods whom he so believes would come and rescue him from his present predicament. Women, little girls and grownups watched from a distance, symbolically even the ardent native doctors would not function in the public but Neyes case was different. He assumes the posture of a youth and a child who is motivated by an unknown spirit. Youths of different age groups lined up and received their share of the traditional medicine one after the other. "Won't you join? Hector asked prevention is better than cure. This charm of his will wedge off any bullet. Even when it is directed at an individual, he inherited this gift from his grand father. He continued in his bid both old and young hailed him for bringing the saving charm to their doorsteps. Normally charms like this works if one is extremely lucky. But in a situation whereby every Tom, Dick and Harry knows you're wearing a charm, I wonder how it will work considering the wicked world we're in. An old man watching the scene told a group of teenagers. He shook his head and left; closely some women were discussing." "But for crying out loud, why would charm be displayed openly. Agnes said. By so doing the users are placed in other people's mercy. She left in a sober mood.

"Forget this boy is undefeatable, when his father was alive he use to fight with witches of all background he was crown king of the witches, before he died he transferred all his powers to Neye. On hearing this the youths rushed to receive their share.

You must not fail to arrest that chief I told you about. The DJO said. He lives at no 5 Agnabga street." "His house is at the back of the old Jackboot station and it has a brick wall veranda where his guest sits down." The veranda looks quite modern" You can't afford to miss it.' 'As a matter of fact, a new order, arrest any chief you see." They have to pay dearly.'

The women gathered a distance from the shrine, as they were about to proceed 'wait' someone spoke up, 'let the youths join us in this dance. Chidimma, why? 'You always want to be in the mix of the male folks.' Helen said, 'it would be more honorable.' They all laughed. This delayed the procession.

Neye moved from the riverside followed by his fans. He carried a native pot on top of his head, chanting all the way. He got to the traditional shrine and got intoxicated by the powers of the spirit! As if possessed by a demon, he ran back; "my gods" he shouted, all of a sudden pulled a leaf in front of the shrine 'oredo.' As he turned to proceed, the leaf tree cut in half and fell off without him noticing. Neye was not observant any longer, ha! The oredo has cut into two; he must have observed the bad sign synonymous with a falling 'oredo' had he turned. Nelson observed. He moved on and the people follow suit. He at interval poured native choke, blew it and chanted all the more; at close rang he was follow by youths who tied leaf on their fore heads. They were not left out of the act of show off. They vigorously danced to the tune of the song as if they were going for an intra tribal war. The women felt secured by the closeness of the men behind, forgetting that bitter or no taste precedes any sweet taste.

The manhunt was aggravating, the Jackboot on noticing the tick smoke slowed down; "so it has gotten to burning of buildings," the commander said. The Jackboot officers adjusted position on seeing the assumed protesters in front, fear gripped them, and their guns almost slip from their grip. The protesters were dancing towards the Jackboot truck from the left wing of Iama road junction while; the Jackboot team was at the right wing coming from Akarba.

Adams on seeing the green 406 coming shouted 'all hail! The local government chairman is coming.' The gathering that was very cautious of their plot started jubilating as the car; "a tinted glass 406 green Peugeot car" pulled over and stopped by the Jackboot squad. He wound down the backseat right window, a heavily built dark man in his early 50th, his height is an average of 5ft 10 inches. He wore a bola hat, which gave him the look of an outlaw. He had a brief coded discussion with the commander of the Jackboot team, and drove off. The protesters were disillusioned on seeing their hope vanishing into the thin air. The Jackboot team got awakened and instantly started firing directly at the people. Neye on noticing a whistling bullet spine past his ear, he turned and was dazed to see a pregnant woman in blood as the bullet went through her skin. As he turned to move on, another bullet hit him and he slummed. He was dead in the hour. The crowed on noticing their mentor and motivator dead dispersed. The Jackboot inspired by bad spirit started firing indiscriminately aiming at people who were not protesting, as they shot, the bullet believed to be an experimental specimen imported into the country hit more innocent people.

Monday heard the constant shattering of gun shot at his farm 3 kilometers away from the scene. He dropped his working implement had a quick change of attire and headed for the village. "Can you imagine, a whole community is being shot at without fighting back?" Andrew said as he gazed at the scene. Though he was walking along the Iama Road, his concentration was altered. He almost fell as he stumbled on baker's wood. 'Look where you're going' Jennet said. As he turned he said. "Why wouldn't I fall, when one sees his own people suffering as a result of the Jackboot cruel brutalities' 'I wonder if their immediate boss has a people, if yes, it baffles me that he really ordered this cold blood massacre by the killer squad.'

In cold blood the people were murdered they were all seeking for help which eluded them. They ran for their dear life. Worrisome they were, for the government refused to care. "How bad can a government humiliate and maltreat its own citizen, it boils down to the fact that Nairegin is been governed by the peoples antagonist. Andrew lamented." Stray bullets hit most people running for cover; a girl was hit as she was about entering an open compound. Someone shouted 'keep running oh!' He said as the bullet hit a man going to his place of work. The man believed to go every day to his place of work at Irraw refinery, the bullet did havoc to the blameless. A stray bullet hit a lad and he died instantly. Oh! The man took in a hard breath and said can we survive this? 'The Jackboot are going to pay, if it's going to take us twenty years to bring this hoodlum, of a Jackboot force to book we shall definitely do that for this great injustice and human right crime and abuse on the people of this community.' Barrister Nat whose brother was hit said as they carried his brother to the hospital.

All stores along Iama Road closed at once. People started running 'in a confused state to different direction' the final onslaught on the people, there was a general wailing, and the people were seen crying in all hidden corners of the town. Oh! My God! What has gone into these Jackboot men' brain? Alfred thought this is real genocide, harmless citizen were slaughtered in broad daylight and nothing is done. Little did Alfred know of the hellish task the people were encountering He lived in an exclusive area of the town across the new road where, both protesters and the Jackboots find it difficult to reach. Couple with the bad condition of the road it was completely avoided. He got up from his bed check the time and was amaze he was late for his Irraw appointment. He quickly rushed to the bath since; he was trying to conserve time he never bothered about steaming the water. He quickly had a shower rushed out of the bath and started dressing up.

Teddy in his residence remembered his appointment with a pal but felt all the same that, he could quickly cook something since he was starving. He rushed to the kitchen and carefully brought out his cooking materials. He placed the pot on the gas burner, which he lighted at once. He measured 3 cups of rice and started per boiling. Normally he would have waited to wash the rice but this time around, he wanted to be through early enough. Subsequently, he brought down the pot and just sieved the water and added more water to it, with small quantity of salt. As he left the kitchen the blearing of the horn attracted him knowing his friend's car, has similar horn sound. Based on assumption, he quickly went to the bath, 'Mr. Ted' what is happening?' Alfred asked as he entered the house. "I'm almost through with my bath,' Teddy responded from the bathroom and came out to greet him. "We have to leave at once for we are out of time." Alfred said. "What of chief Okeson is he not going with us? 'He is in the car outside.' Teddy picked up his pair of trousers and was getting dressed when the chief showed up. 'Good day chief.' How're you?' 'I'm fine.' Teddy answered. Remembering his brother was traveling, he said. "Samuel you can't go to Abasa through Ukuraibo, while not join us to Akarba from there, you can board a vehicle to Abasa. 'That's okay by me.' Samuel said.

It did not occur to Atti's family the extent of the damage done. Atti reluctantly gave in when asked to close the garage, as he was about to come out of the garage, he noticed the whole area was over taken by smoke. All of a sudden there was a gun shot in the air some square meters apart, he noticed the people rushing towards his direction with the Jackboot on their heels. Instinctively, he needed no further warning but joined in the rat race. The Jackboot officers were shooting directly at the people, while they ran for their precious live. The unlucky ones where wounded. A young boy of about 12 years suddenly fell. As if the bullet that hit him was not enough to harm him, another bullet whistled past him. Instantly an onlooker acted in no time to rescue him. He was taken out of the scene and was rushed to a nearby clinic; where he received treatment. The Samaritan said, as he was about to leave the doctor. "Please Dr., take proper care of him.' 'I'll be back and good lock.'

"You see the young doctor was not bothered about what he was going to make, but of the injured. The Samaritan said. This character was not common amongst most old doctors, who would first demand for an effective bill to be paid, before commencing treatment on the injured; Forgetting that delay could be very dangerous and could lead to the loss of a life. Jonah said. The doctors are mostly interested in the money they intend making not considering the life they are about to save or loose. The Samaritan added.

The boy is in good condition, what he needs is rest which of course he is already getting. The doctor addressed the nurse on duty. He strolled out of the children's ward he met the Samaritan, you came back! Guess, all this shooting would be over soon. "Me too," my fear is the after effect.' The Samaritan replied. 'What, I don't quite figure out is the indiscriminate shooting of lads.' Does this mean that the 12 year olds joined in the demonstration as the Jackboot claimed?' 'I strongly believe that the Jackboot were ill advised'

'Oh! My God' Teddy exclaimed, 'what is the matter? Alfred asked.' It just occurred to me that I did not put off my gas burner. Teddy said. I had wanted to boil rice before you came.' I should have put off the burner but as you came, it escaped me.' 'So what are you going to do now?' Alfred asked. I don't have a choice but to go back. Let me not waste your time further.'

"I will stop here to take a public transport back to Ukuraibo," Teddy said. Alfred slowed down turned to the right and packed the car. Teddy came down and hailed his friend safe ride, his mind was racing, "I pray the rice does not get burnt before I get to my house "he though. He crossed to the other side of the road to wait for transport back to Ukuraibo. It was not easy to get a vehicle to Akarba but luck was on his side. He saw a motor bike which took him to Akarba park. From there he joined a vehicle to Ukuraibo." What is going on at Ukuraibo?" The driver asked. I heard the youths burnt the station." If it is that, the story is old and stale.

As the driver approached elf filling station, the fumes of thick smoke covered the whole area, there was an unavoidable hold up on the express way, "there is usually nothing like holdup on the Ukuraibo express road" Teddy thought he strained his eyes; the smoke was so thick. "I strongly believe a filling station is on fire." The driver said. In front, all the vehicles were reversing. His driver did the same; he turned just like his co-drivers. Fear was written on their faces, every one wanted a fast exit. Teddy decided to get off the cab. He noticed human bodies mutilated, a lifeless teenage boy with tattered shorts under wear shot lifeless was lying as if some couple of minutes back he was not full of life and vigor. Also in front was a young girl of 21 years with bullet wound.

She was continuously rolling in pains. Teddy was completely disillusioned; he felt pity, moved as if to go and rescue her but was halted by a call from across the road.

"Brother" help, a voice from the blue on turning he saw a young man across the road 'what is happening?' He asked. They shot me, the man said. Please help me, okay cross the road quickly; as he joined Teddy he explained "the Jackboot came on direct confrontation with the natives and shot at random" that was how I sustained this bullet injury." This time the whole expressway was deserted apart from both of them there was no one in view. It was a sight not to be remembered. Every body within reach was panic ridden. In a confused state the driver of a blue 504-salon car was about to take cover before the man sitting at the passenger's seat noticed Teddy. He stopped by Teddy's side. 'Please, is there any way out of this place? 'He asked. "Sorry I'm not familiar with this neighborhood" Teddy said. He drove off as if Teddy never existed. Teddy felt a sense of fear for if people with vehicle could be this scared, he needed to be more careful. With this belief he figured out that his bearing would be altered if he does not move along at once. He traced his way through the dirty house corner. Most of the people mostly women who saw him passed, were all position as if they would run off. It took him more time to get to his destination, simply because at that critical hour one could not reason properly but, all the same, in no time he was at Ekidumu street: the street was deserted completely; he did not hesitate but to jump the fence and was right inside the compound.

On reaching the chiefs apartment, the scene was as if the whole town was having a town's meeting. The chief's guests were all seated while drinks and cola nut were being presented. A young man arrived with his brother, who happens to be a co chief; both were welcomed and were offered seats. The man was restless; he stood up. "Odogu Abi Osa Aje Aje, Ndum Of ne ebewedi oyebune ekene oh!" do permit me I have an argent call" he said. The chief spokes man said. "You can go and be back" Driven by an unknown force, an urge he could not resist, he followed a part leading to his female partner's.

Less than 2 minutes of his departure the Jackboot squad stormed the area, some of them position ensuring all access to the compound was completely sealed. Opposite the chief's house the Jackboot men started firing at random, no body moves a young man was apprehended; he tried to pull away from their grip and the Jackboot man held onto his necklace as he pulled from his grip. He ran like he never did, the Jackboot in need of what to do started shooting at the ceiling.

'What is the matter?' questioned the chief who rushed out of his house as he saw the confused state of his guests; it dawned on him that the Jackboots were not friendly cause the Jackboot had guns cocked pointing at the people. 'Where is the chief?' asked the commander. On hearing the speaker, the chief moved across to him. 'Yes I am the chief is anything the matter?' Instantly he was pushed by one of the Jackboot officer standing nearby.

Arrest the whole men here the commander said pointing to the men present, an act to humiliate the chief. In the adjacent compound some Jackboot team invaded a block building opposite the chiefs. "Where are your children, madam? One of the team members asked. 'Oh!' 'They have all gone away.' She answered. One of the team men raised his koboko to flog her, stop! One of them barked. He was halted momentarily; the whip swigged through an open door and tore the curtain half way. Another set captured a man that is ill health. "Where do you dwell?" "I will show you," he said. On the way they started flogging him, "please sir I've been indoors for a while; this fever nearly rendered me useless. Nevertheless they kept flogging him until they reached his house that didn't have a wall. Their action was halted on seeing the house without a wall at the front entrance. The entire Jackboot wanted revenge. So they never bothered about the man's situation.

At the extreme of town, a middle age legal practitioner of 5ft 11+++ inch tall, ebony black in complexion came out of his apartment well dressed in sport wears, a short sleeve shirt, white trunk and a canvas to match;" he got into his mothers 280 Mercedes Benz and Cruz round his area. As he drove past he acknowledged the Jackboot men but he had his defense mapped out if eventually stopped. He wasn't a law breaker he told himself therefore has no reason whatsoever to fear. On the way he met a friend who informed him of the mass intimidation befalling the people. Oh no! the Jackboot men did not come because of me; if they dare me we shall meet in court.. He was about to engage gear when he saw two men walked up to an elderly man, what really attracted him was the manner they greeted. "So humbly unlike Ukuraibo youths" who sees disrespect as being wise? Morning Sir "they prostrated,' we are across the river' the younger one said. "Please sir we are starving," the dark skinny boy said. The elderly man burst into laughter. Please sir, the younger boy said. Help us with little quantity of garri; we had barely eaten since last night. Ha! Ha you guys cannot bear it a little longer? Remembering what the bafrian soldiers passed through during the bafrian civil war he said. It is too early to start asking for garri when the struggle is just beginning. He said as he laughed on showing no sign of sympathy. "Be strong, hunger does not kill, it will only enlarge your head portraying your ill health," He advised. Then the young lawyer realized he was only the lonely. He quickly accelerated and droved straight to the house got out of the car and went inside with the intention of remaining inside until the Jackboot war era elapse

CHAPTER NINE

Oma, a man of the people, resides in an enclave were most youths go to for relaxation. Oma a man in his late 30's dark in complexion, about 5ft 11 inch tall, with broad shoulders giving him the form of a lion, always wearing a clean shave which keeps his face as dark as ever an, ardent political juggernaut. 'Who do you want to contact? He is your man. A brilliant young chap but for fear that his dream and ideals does not elude him, he is constantly at war with the opposition especially the local government chairman who he intends unseating by all means. As such the local government chairman sees him as a threat to his position. An anti local chairman he remains; inspired to do his own selfish will, he is always at the fore fronts instigating a rivalry against peace loving people who naturally depict good leadership to their kinsmen. As the crises erupted he knew he was a target no doubt, he quickly enhanced himself with few of his belongings, which he normally packed ready for a journey. He called his mistress "take care of the home, I will be back as soon as this is over. "Ogawu" he called his aids all rushed to meet him. The chair, Ogawu called. "Have you heard?" what again? He said eager to know what was latest in the gossip arena, for he is master of gossipers. The town is finished; the Jackboot officers have killed almost everybody in town, the fortunate ones have all absconded into the forest.

When I get back from this journey I shall see to their plight. He said and entered his vehicle and left.

Norbert propelled to help his people thought of a way to help his people out of the abomination, his bag fell of his grip.

'What!' He growled. Instantly the spirit to help invaded him, "where're the people." He asked. They are across the river, the informer said. Being a practical man he just did not want to believe rumors: he really wanted to substantiate the fact, he drove to a shopping center in a neighboring village.

"Let's go" he did not mind the gully created by erosion on his road the car stopped suddenly jerked forward as he slammed the brake, automatic braking system held his tyres back from projecting down the valley. He drove straight to a neighboring village.

"Madam" he called organizes foodstuff enough to feed a large crowd; I mean to salvage a work force.' What 'kind of food do you want?' She asked. 'Anything so long its eatable, cooked food could be bread, rice, beans, butter eggs name it. The woman knew what he wanted; she packaged cooked rice and beans in two different container, loaf of bread, Queen of the coast 'Sardine' and some pure water. On ensuring the items were well packed he paid and was on his way to the camp settlement.

This time he needed to be very careful he said to himself, on that note he had a change of heart as to which access way to follow, remembering the railway construction, he reversed and turned right into a road which terminates at Robga Ukuraibo express road. The road being a link one way to Nineb City, always very lonely, apart from farmers and a few villagers from neighboring Edo speaking towns, it remains very lonely making it a one-way road because of neglect. He prayed in Italian language 'kashuraman,' made the sign of the cross. The route seemed to be out of use. The bush has succeeded in taking possession of the road, giving it a track road status; the hazardous nature of the road compels most drivers to abandon it. Since on coming vehicles are not seen from a distance, bad still, the road is associated with series of curves. The only good thing is that the villagers did not abandon the road, a likely helpful way for farmers as their only root to farm called reserve. "Government own reserve land." Which Belong to Atled and Ode State Government having boundary with Edo State Government; he negotiated through a driveway after Akarba, Umehe junction. Before the bridge he turned right into an old track road leading to Ukuraibo as if going through the railway line a road directly at the back of the settlement.

The refugees rushed out as they saw his car, "a gulf inscribed 'peace" he was held in high esteem for coming, the youths called him "pastor" even the chiefs who abandoned their domain were not ashamed of their act instead joined the youths to call him "pastor." One of them said it is better to run and regroup to fight another day because only the living bawl, he who fights and run away at times of danger is a wise man. Andrew retorted.

Norbert, felt a slight wave of pained to see his kinsmen in their present condition. He wept internally. "Be strong it is only when we are strong that we can win our enemies he encouraged them. The reassuring words made the whole camp settlement to jubilate. "Norbert! They all shouted. As he entered moved to his car he shouted; "the process is almost complete I know the Jackboot men would be withdrawn and punished accordingly. He Retaliated, the efforts of the youths, who have ensured a peaceful coexistence within the camp. "Please help yourselves, with these food items," like a hospital visitation or prevail of an accident, each victim recounts his lucky moment with joyful heart, the memory of the nature and life style of the ancient early men who lived in the past, where items were shared among families. Owning of large property was not an issue to cause problem among brothers or neighbors; insinuating the actual love binding the human race existed then.

Recalling the word of his mentor Prof Noncester "Justice is a still birth in Nairegin" we as individuals are bound by wisdom to enhance a lawful input Jackboot force. Arthur, one of the refugees said in consonance to the message delivered.

Pastor Norbert left the people seeing the phase lift they had within the short visit, he repeatedly told himself "Abasa has to do something" we can not run or be shielded from our homes for this long.' 'Unless we are not Nairegins then, 'we can call for foreign assistance against this oppressive government in power.' Being driven by fear and optimism knowing his family was still in town, he was full of hope and consolation believing his wife was capable of handling situation. He prayed as he drives on "Kashuraman, "he prayed again and did the sign of the cross but ending at the Father and our Son

"My children what is happening today is not different from what happened at the time of Biafran war, when the federal troops met here in Ukuraibo: chief Benji said. 'It was on a market day like this,' the whole women were in the market; all of a sudden we saw troops allover the town, but our luck then was that we had a leader in the town, "late chief J.O Efad" who stood firm and defended his people to the latter.' 'He made the federal troops to understand that

Ukuraibo was not an Ibo speaking tribe, renouncing the claim by a close by village, who had betrayed Ukuraibo by feeding the Federal troops with heinous lies leaving them with the belief that Ukuraibo was purely an Igbo speaking tribe with an interior motive of acquiring the latter's land when the town is defaced.' Can you beat that the women were made to come out en- mass to dance in solidarity, signifying the town was not in support of the biafran led war.' Why should we support biafran when Ojuka did not wait for other ally instead moved to liberate a people without problem.

The fear amidst the people is "supposing the Jackboot as they are called were sponsored to perpetrate havoc, then they are bound to remain indoors and be steadfast in prayer to God Almighty who is the only recognized helper we have; Him alone can intervene at times like this.

Men, both old and young gathered as one family across the river, the community drift encompassed a new eating habit. There was not much to eat; anybody's food belonged to all. They shared all what was available just like the time of our Lord Jesus Christ "the only son of God" when love was still handy; they invaded the farms in search of uncooked food, which was, transforms into food.

"Who among you will go to town with me?" Asked Chinedu, if no body that means I will go alone. Erick and Tim followed him. Chinedu's intention was to go and see what the situation it is in town, they crossed the bridge, which shows complete absence of the Local and State Government of Atled, an old bridge, constructed when Hardwood Company was still in existence. The plank which is the main material used in the construction work is mucus ridden, It's color has turned black conspicuously out of forms, the water has so soaked the wood in that most part of the wood is just hanging on its support not strong enough to withstand stress. In the days of farm activity farmers find it difficult to ply the road without bringing down their goods from their bike then to transport the goods by hand carriage across the bridge before they can finally proceed on their journey back home. They were able to maneuver the bridge to the other side of town which is an erosion ridden area called Akabgu. "It's synonymous with an un-kept part of Sogal called Esaleko of old," the erosion has eaten both sides of the road if not check on time will drastically affect the stability of the road. Invariable the road will be minus one.

As they approached the main junction, they stopped to see whether it is safe to proceed further, unconsciously it happened like a flash of light. From the opposite side of the street, the Jackboot officers moved at once to action on seeing the three young men coming. "Stop there!" they barked in unison, if you move you are dead meats.

On hearing this they all knew the threat was good to be real, with self conviction that if they catch up with them their faith will be like, that of a cockroach which ends up in an untimely death. "Run now" Chinedu advised, they ran like they had never done in their life time; the street they knew very well was of advantage cause they were able to channel their salvage ran through several house edge which gave them leverage over the Jackboot. What? We've missed them. Bats, you should have waited to see what it takes to burn someone's property.

'Let's trace them to the river you know they came from that direction.' The commander said.

The groups informed themselves in "aboh on the ethiope" an isolated part of the town, an outstanding compound that shows Ukuraibo in the hearth of civilization. "Own by late Esidi Efad, one time finance minister in the then midwestern region and first chairman of Nigeria Airways after the departure of the colonial masters," they rested by a dilapidated glass building. Bombed by late Mulitala

Rahmat Muhammad. "One time military head of state of Federal Republic of Nigeria:" his military troops invaded Ukuraibo doing the Nigeria Biafran war; an old glass house with a transferred design from England by Alex Ekwueme a renowned Architecture and one time vice president of federal republic of Nigeria. "A man of repute, integrity and strong will"

"We cannot wait here for long. Chinedum said. My instinct can't be wrong, I've a strong feeling this mad cow can trace us to this place." "No way, we must leave at once." He voiced out as if inspired the two guy did not argue with him. They all passed a bypass at the back of Ethiop primary school, which saw them to the bridge side.

The Jackboot team was so upset to have missed their prey: they never relented "We can catch up with them if we hasten up." The Commander said. "I think this is where they must have followed" Since they were new to the environment they all agreed to follow a narrow part in front of them, hoping it will lead them out of the area. As they proceeded they saw a shadow in front and stopped. "Who goes there? Barked the commander, on hearing the instruction the old woman in her late 70's readjusted, all her life apart from aged days of terror intertribal war" she had not had course to fear in this track road she had been passing since she was a kid. "Danger cannot be in the village," she whispered to her grand daughter who was withdrawn in fear as she stopped and waited. "Where are you coming from old one?" Jackboot officer 2 asked. "My pickin, I am come from farm" she said in broken English language. Where is the farm? Is it very far, you have to cross the bridge. She responded. 'Oh! there is a bridge in front?' "Yes but is very bad now," she answered. "Okay mama you can go" She continue her journey back home not aware what had transpired since she went to the farm some couple of days back.

They moved cautiously along the narrow part till it led them to Ethiop primary School. Directly in front of the school is Aboh on the Ethiop. '"There is a building over there" Jackboot 4 said. "What is going to stop us from going over?" said the commander. Let's see if those braggarts are hiding out there. They entered the compound through a small opening in the fence made up of aged wood combined with Babb wire; because of age most of its part had given way. Facing them was an old dilapidated building built before the civil war. Unlike must recent building that does not have enough space, it was well spaced. The outstanding rumor that the wife of late chief I.O Efad "the British national" saved the chief of losing both of his houses when the federal troop invaded and wanted to destroy the building, she stood her ground as the owner of the house.

They moved further into the compound passing the bombed building as they noticed another building. "My instinct can not fail me this time. The commander said as they reach the house. The commander said, "we know you are in there, you had better come out this moment. If we come in and get you it will be worse" he repeated, there was no response.

Inside the house, a young girl with her little child was home alone, she quickly moved out of sight as she heard the commander's voice praying her God would not fail her this time. She did remain in a sit tight position, sensing any neither shake nor movement will attract the team. All of a sudden a stronger force over powered the team. "Your saving grace is your little kid, we are going." The commander said on seeing the baby napkin.

The commander moved his men to the waterside on seeing the cloths by the riverbank shouted fire. The constant firing on the river shake the water table, the fishes deep dived. The men dipped dived holding their breath underneath the water.

“If I don’t die, this once never will I die at the hands of the Jackboot crime.” Eze went below his intention was to crawl following the grass as the shot came in. fire the commander shouted. “I can observe bubbles in the water, the men out of fear forgot the magical power they all had the bullet hit them on the back and bounced back. The water bubbles as they moved underneath they swam to the other side of the river knowing that the jackboot men cannot swim. Eze was first to speak as he came of the water. “Thief, come and get us if you can.” Had they seen something to steal they would have soft-pedaled. “Yab these Jackboot men for me” Chuck said.

CHAPTER TEN

Ever since he was told of his keys, "Eddy" wasn't himself as if driven by the unknown spirit. "I am off to he told his wife as he came out of the house. "I'm off to Akarba," he told his wife. What for? His wife demanded. To collect my store keys of course. "Neighbors please come to my aid oh! My husband wants to kill himself." She wailed. "Oga Eddy, wait till the crises is over after all no body will open your store" Samson pleaded. For all I care this key must be with me today. He was out of the sitting room unnoticed. His lucky day as he observed his wife was in the rest room his car started on first attempt. Thank God he said knowing his car with kick-starter problem. He increased speed, as Elepas Robga road was free of traffic he slowed at Akaraba town and turned left facing the Jackboot office. Eddy walked straight to the desk officer. "I want to see the DJO" wait a moment he will be back soon. The officer said. Someone from the DJO's office came out he wanted to decongest the station asked. Does anybody want to see the DJO? Eddy raised his hand. Yes can I be of help? "I want to collect my store key." "You're from where? The Jackboot officer asked.

Ukuraibo town he replied. There you are let him join his people the DJO said as he approached the deck. "But I 'm not a rioter' protested Eddy." Oh you have mouth to complain. One of the Jackboots raised his gun and hit him on the head.

They quickly crossed the bridge "thank God Eric said; this is my second escape from these Jackboot operatives, you see, I did not want to go out for the dance but Neye came and told me it was going to be peaceful, even he promised to bath all the protesters "male," with his native concoction to prevent any mishaps. Unfortunately, he got entrenched by his concoction and it failed him he died nobly in active service for his town. May his soul rest in perfect peace; he concluded.

"Maybe I should organize a prayer section when we get back to camp;" Erick said. I can't imagine how this whole thing started. Jokingly we've lost more than 19 citizens of this clan. God knows how many more will follow suit before the end of this emergency.

'I wonder the kind of government we have. Look at you Tim said. "What would you expect of Abdul's man?' 'The business is not new to him, my joy is being safe more so, the people's initiative to desert the town.'

Blood was allover the whole place in a minute. "Oh! My head! Eddy wailed." He was forced into the cell in his present condition. The prisoners crowded round him as if they could be of help. 'Chief take heart, it will be over soon.' 'Sorry we know they are out to do more damage.' 'We all here are in safe hands.' I 'm happy to be here even' James said. The boy by my side died on the sport when a stray bullet hit him. He lamented. I remember running in the direction of your store all of a sudden we found ourselves in the hands of the enemy.' 'That's how we got here.'

"My life as a young man I've never visited the Jackboot station not to talk of being in a Jackboot cell." Eddy said. Well it is an experience worth remembering.

At Mandela hotel, she came out of the storeroom; the foodstuff in this house is finish she said. We had better drive down to Akarba to buy some foodstuff. Chief Ekure said. You know this crisis can continue for a while.' I remember the story of Tiv, women stayed at home without food for many days.' 'Now that we can, let's go before it's too late.

Papa Edwin refused to leave with his family to their hideout. He took for granted that his being an old man is a guarantee for safety, not knowing the sets of Jackboot deployed to Ukuraibo did not see age as a factor for consideration. He came back from the farm and was about to settle down when his little son rush in "papa" he called. The Jackboot officers have arrested aunty Anna's son, every body is running from the town. He simple ruled out being harassed. "Nduka," at my age no one would want to hurt me" you go with the kids I will be safe. She reluctantly left passing through a filthy access road that leads to an old bridge called "Ata" the bridge was made and structured by the natives which enables the farmer's easy passage to farm; the river was very quite no trace of a single individual. Unlike days before the day break massacre, where space was a problem for passerby. The river was always over populated. They crossed the bridge to join their fellow deserters.

"I'm tired of staying without something to eat." if one continues in this manner we will all die of starvation.' There was pricked tension among the listeners, Ken did not wait for anybody contribution he picked up his bag and left without mentioning it. He traced his way through a narrow path, being a track road for farmers the only mobility applied on the route were bicycle it's shady nature makes it convenient for farmers as a resting point. Most of the bush being virgin land housing rubber trees that has stopped producing rubber latex. It took him 25 minutes to reach the other side of town where hardwood is. He did not stop but continued through widening road, now open because of the railway line construction across the river, terminating at Akarba/ Nineb Road. On the way he met other homeless community members, "you people are close to Akarba, you can't stay and starve yourselves to death?" "Please join me to safety." He said. They gave it a taught and without further delay joined him. 'Where have you been Patrick? Nicolas asked as they proceeded.

'Man! 'Trouble,' can it end?' 'It is a tell tale story, we all had it rough but my greatest concern is my father who refused to come with me even with all my persuasion. 'He was adamant 'I made him to understand that; staying at home alone was suicidal for his age, he ignored me still. Anyway I hope he will be fine.' 'So where are you going to once you get to Akarba? 'Because I 'm not going there.' 'As soon as we hit the main road I will start looking for a vehicle heading to Nineb City.' Emma said.

On a second taught, Chief Ekure said. 'Do you have to visit your Mum all the time?' "Let's just see her, we won't stay long." She pleaded. 'Okay,' 'if you so insist.'

They drove past the Jackboot station to Belinda's Mothers house. "I hate this road' chief Ekure said. 'I don't know why the state government does not want to come to the people's aid; whereas come 2003, the politicians will want to lobby for votes thinking the governance of the people is hereditary.

You forget how it is to convince your people Belinda said." I pray the enlightenment campaign propelled by the whole youths reaches the grassroots.' Belinda added. Why not, the youths are doing a perfect job.' 'My only prayers are response by the people.' They were busy discussing the problem at hand not knowing the extent of havoc the Jackboot team had perpetrated within the hour

"Welcome in-law" Belinda's mum greeted as they were ushered to a double seat; they exchange pleasantries. "Bring me kola from the fridge" kola nut was presented and wedged with money to prevent it from rolling off, as it is the tradition of the people to present Kola nut along with money. The money is believed to act as a wedge according to the custom. Presenting of kola nut to one's guest is important while in absent of kola nut in some part of the country; money is used in its place. 'What is going on in your town asked Mrs. Robinson?' We had resolved to send someone to check on you, is it true that the whole town was set on fire?' "Well he paused some unlucky ones were killed while, others were arrested chief Ekure replied, perhaps on my way out I will stop over at the Jackboot station to see them. "Ha!" Don't go oh! His mother in-law said. We learnt the people are being maltreated there oh!" 'Of course "that is the reason why I have to be there to stop the act. Chief Ekure said. His expression was that of a man concerned over the annihilation of a particular race, he was in no mood to discuss the matter further. 'If by tomorrow this incident is reported obviously, it will be proclaimed by all who hear that Ukuraibo does not have leaders who can address this matter amicably.'

"Enough is enough "I cannot stay in this house to watch things deteriorate John said; after all, the short cuts in town are well known to me. He rolled out his bicycle, greased the hub, which has been his problem ever since he was knocked down by a hit and run cab. He gently tied his "Ghana must go (four corner sack which was mainly used by the Ghanaians in the early 80's) bag in the carrier. He watched to ascertain no- body was in sight knowing his exit route; he pedaled like he never did, passing an opening that brought him close to the bank. Since he knew his map very well it was not difficult a task to avoid the old road, he channeled, side by side houses occasionally stopping to roll his bike through some very narrow hovel edge. By the time he reached the end of town, he stopped watched carefully on his right hand side. After ensuring the road was business as usual (safe) he turned left facing Abmonibo, a neighboring village in Ukuraibo. On the way, he met Stanley an iron bender identified mostly by his metallic hand "Can you imagine, "It was immediately the commissioner of Jackboot left Ukuraibo that the daybreak massacre occurred." Stanley complained, "So you mean the governor has not commented on this, Anslem asked. "How can he when the people voted their conscience in 1999 general election." "Don't forget he is bias over Ukuraibo." "That means he is not a democrat, he still has the spirit of dictators in him." You speak as if you are from the moon; for a young man to spend so much money in installing a transformer in a community, yet the people were ungrateful! Justify yourself speak up if you were the one won't you do worst things?

Mr. Ekure got to the Jackboot station with the intension of consoling the DJO over his property, as he entered the station he parked his car behind a station wagon car. He came down from the car, as the DJO was about to leave, 'Oga DJO' He greeted, we are very sorry for the property lost. Please accept my sincere unlimited apology, once things come to normalcy we shall compensate for all that was lost in the process. "Oh!" "No problem God is in control." Replied the DJO Surprisingly, as he turned to greet his people the DJO passed an order to the desk officer "don't allow him to leave this station" who? The officer asked, he pointed at chief Ekure.

Just be calm, I will see that everyone leaves this place as soon as possible. Thanks for coming sir. As chief Ekure walked towards the door he was intercepted. "Please sir you will have to wait a while it's an order." "Just feel free; you will not be molested like others." You "can sit down." Thank you corporal, Chief Ekure said.

At the Jackboot base the Jackboot commander sat on top of a wooden chair he felt weak and tired as such he knew he was not fit for the operation at hand. He beckoned on his assistance that hurried to his side. "Listen carefully as you go on this assignment endeavor to apprehend not just commoners but those you know who can bail themselves with reasonable sum. Be warned we must send returns to oga commissioner.

In a discreet area a lad came out of the house without knowing the team of Jackboot officers were close by "way them" he said. "We are here' replied the Jackboot officers; on seeing them he ran into the compound, he called for help as he entered the house, this attracted his uncle and family members. 'Etim what is the matter?' his uncle asked as they came out of the house. The Jackboot were ready for action; One of the Jackboot followed Etim into the house, Etims grand parent tried to stop the Jackboot from chasing Etim into the bed room he narrowly went off balance as a result of the push from the crazy Jackboot man, he held on to the chair support. The wild Jackboot went still to fetch Etim from under the bed. The Jackboot men went further to arrest a young lad, who was in form two, taking him to be a rioter!' 'His mother rushed after the Jackboot she was whipped consecutively with their whip. She insisted "do you think he is a rioter too" the noise attracted her husband who came to her rescue, this aggravated the Jackboot who fired 3 times directly at his foot, but as luck would have it, he jumped up, as this was mere reflex action. You think you can challenge me me in a physical combat the man said. Look at this miserable beast I will want to know who gave you this order.

"Les's leave this place now," ordered the acting commander. The family gathered to thank God for his mercy knowing He has saved one of them from gun shot but prayed for the arrested boy. "We can no longer stay and see our own community extinct. We must see the legislator at Abasa so that the house can intervene promptly. Both parents hurriedly put on their cloths gathered the children; it was like a video clip of school children rushing away from the principal, the man in the house started the car but did not allow it run as usual.

'Honey, let's leave we have no time to waste.' 'I'll be with you' she shouted from the room. She quickly hurried the kids to meet the husband in the car. Get inside quickly the man said he put the car on drive position and being the longest street in Ukuraibo he wheeled off through the bad road, on a good day he will not drive through the watered road, he was at the end of the road terminal by Iama road, he viewed to his right leading to Iama road junction, the Jackboot team was station at alert. On seeing them he increased speed crossed Iama road to the other end of Efad road. "Did you see that? The commander asked. He turned right not bothering about safety.

The Jackboot on sighting the green V. boot appearing on the express quickly embarked their truck and went after the V. boot. "I know it's that family!" the corporal said. We should have arrested the man," complained the acting commander." They chased the green V. boot but, the driver of the V. boot knew he would be followed. He never reduced speed not until, he was quite certain they had retreated.

He continued along the express road though he was in no hurry to give up the lead. He was sure his friends at Abasa would respond positively. At Ovaba town he met a Jackboot check point. They simply requested him to slow and later passed him on self-recognition "I don't know what went wrong," he said. "The Jackboot men are so hostile," "naturally I wonder who must have given them such backing to invade Ukuraibo in this manner?" "Someone must have instigated those Jackboot officers that shot at me, I bet by the time I am through with them they will willingly request for their dismissal from the Jackboot force." He slowed down as he approached Imoru junction, turned to the right and moved on towards Edenumu. "A town of the night life, traders from far and away stops over to rest. He slowed down to buy bananas; how is it that your banana is so small?" 'Sir, it's the season, we are approaching scarcity period? The seller said. 'So how much would this lot cost?' 'Sir just gives me N100.00, it's a good price.' He paid her the #100, "give me groundnut #40" this will complement the banana. He said. As he preceded, his wife said "darling you just have to watch out for this luxuries bus drivers." "No problem the last course I attended in SPDC is "Defensive Driving," We were made to understand that an on coming driver is termed a mad man on the high way because he can lose control over his vehicle suddenly; as such one has to be at alert at all times." He turned into the Ogwachukwu road as he was explaining. "Anyway, since you reminded me, I had better take this road," "Edenumu/ Ogwashi Rd" we have for some time now reached conclusive agreement that this is the safest road to Abasa, though very lonely from Edenumu axis.' He continued through the lonely road avoiding bumps occasionally. Not long he was at Ubuluku. Kids uncle Henry attended this school in the 50's he said when he was here they used to trek long Kilometers to visit in the neighboring village on their outing Sundays." In no time they were driving past the Jackboot's headquarters. One of the kids said. "While not we go and complain here?" No it's of no use, "remember, the order to shot at sight emanated form this office." If we foolishly stop over to lodge any complain, our aim of coming to Abasa will be defeated, trust these Jackboot officers they will delay or detain us. On hearing the word detain from his mouth he quickly accelerated so that he would not give it a second thought. He was at Asubi junction in less than 10 minutes. "Where do we go from here?" He asked.

Fear gripped the family members across the express a stone throw from Ukuraibo grammar School a building on the right hand side when coming from Akarba town; they had witnessed the shoot out all day long, they patiently waited for their daughter who was involve in the dance. "I perceive something mysterious has happened to her" please brother why not go and look for her. "What is the matter with you?" sergeant Paul said. I promised going to look for her then why the constant reminder. Just like I said it will be of no use if we all sit down at home day long without venturing out side to see for ourselves situation at hand. He rose from his chair." Let me go at once to look for her." She has stayed long enough. I expected her to be back by now but she is not. "Big bros why not you go and confirm the girl with the bullet wound." Nkem said. She's been crying for help all day, that way we will be able to ascertain our faith. He put on his army camouflage laced his booth then he stepped out of the house. "I will see you all in 15 minutes time." He said. It occurred to him that Jackboot encounter is always like this, as an army officer, they were trained to always protect the civilian. "There is no way as an army officer you will have face to face confrontation with civilians."He thought. As he reached the girls position she was unconscious. On seeing him the people watching from close doors now hard courage and moved towards him. "Let's move her to a safe place." Alex said. They quickly carried her to the house and at once started administering first aid treatment. Notwithstanding the treatment going on there was constant wailing in the home

Commander, Sir! The chairman said this man will continue the task of taking you round town, he was pointing at an averagely dark in complexion young man with lip wide enough to be used as rapper for gift item. His conventional nickname is Oyeke Amanma (meaning man has no reason to be fine.) The man followed the instruction given by his boss to the later. He called the commander who was downing a bottle of Gulder beer. Yes man, shall we? The commander said. "Listen to me, all we want from you is to show us the house of those notorious chiefs and the bad elements in town. "But Sir, they will know I brought you to them." Okay, show us the houses then we drop you off before we come back for full operation. Along the express, not quite three different places he showed them he met with instant pay back. Oh! No! "This cannot be" "my boy he wailed! My boy! He jumped out of the vehicle, as he was about to carry the boy, the Jackboot moved in on him "Kiminini" this one is among too. A fling of koboko tore his shirt; he was lashed with Koboko. For the fact that he wanted to save his son his sense of feeling pain was dead, he ignored the Jackboot action on him. Knowing that he has to save his son, he did not feel the impact of the Kane. All he wanted was a restoring home in the name of a hospital, where the boy could be treated and brought to life immediately. Corporal let him go, he has finished his job. Some poles adjacent to Mandela Hotel the people watched with keen interest. "What an irony," Victoria said "he was busy at the rear implicating his relatives, can you see?" She pointed our God is a Living God; he did not hesitate to endorse of his sons death. Elton said the man did not know prior to that time if not he would have had a second though when given such an obligation. God of our generation is God of host. Peter concurred. Can you try God? No way! He did not hesitate to approve of his sons death. Because he is evil so that he can experience in whole the agony of losing one's child without warning sign. Austin said

All along the atmosphere was calm, no sign of any soul, unlike when the crises started. Teddy really wanted to confirm from his dad, if they and their tenants were the only person living in the area. His mind was playing tricks on him. He never wanted to go out of his compound, a fenced compound, with flowers serving as coverage protection from external invasion. He put on his trouser since he had his shirt on. He was by the door, he unlocked and locked it was out in the open, it occurred to him the risk of being caught outside his territory. Though he was not convinced by his own imagination he moved on. Down the road he met with one of his small uncle. Because of his non-involvement in financer obligation of family business the name small uncle originated. He was first to notice Teddy's presence by signaling him; Teddy observed that most people who had courage to come out never took for granted the privileged they had, for they did not want to make their presence know by making noise. Consequently when Adams saw him he beaconed on him by a mere wave of hand. Teddy called him as he approached. "Uncle Adams" he was very sober he quietly announced. "There is problem." "What has happen again?" Teddy quarried. Uncle Ekure has been arrested. "Did they go to his house?" Teddy asked exasperated. "No he was arrested at Akarba Jackboot station," you know he is always at the forefront when it comes to matters concerning his community. He might have gone to actualize the release of those arrested persons. Adams said. "From what I leant, they said he went to visit his in-law from there he left for the Jackboot station." The DJO himself gave the directive "detained him, was his word. I wonder when this crisis will naturally end, Teddy said. If uncle of all people can be detained then who else is safe. Don't talk like that Adams said it is not over until it over. Look, you don't have to be fooled with all those sayings that does not have practical base.

"Is that not John Hends, why is he not with his aid this time? Teddy asked. John Hends is a grown man who sees only at night making him a nocturnal animal; he carried the buddle of wood off his truck into an open hovel he distinguished the wet ones from the dried ones simply convincing Teddy and Adams he was in order.

Hends how is the job? Adams asked. Well as you can see, I'm progressing. Adams moved over to him and whispered. Hends moved out of sight and was handy with a brown rapped paper, he handed it to Adams who happily received it with a thank you smile. Teddy's reaction was dissuaded for the incoming family, once out of sight he ensured they were out of earshot he said, you can't continue with that stuff. Forget what you have seen, it does not count Adams said at any given point in time I'm wary of my environment.

"Please yourself Teddy said.

What will we do now to be of help? Since we can't perfect his release, why not we go and inform his brother Teddy said, who eventually is Teddy's dad. The moment they entered the narrow part that housed Teddys fence they saw some boys who were running, they breathe profusely. What again? Teddy asked. They answered, the Jackboot team are at the street end, we narrowly escaped them; "they are coming" one of the boys said without waiting to explain. He hurriedly left running like a displaced rabbit in the daytime. Teddy and Co did not wait further, they took to their heel luckily the fence was close by, without hesitation all they did was to apply skill of old (western roll.) a stylish way most athlete apply in high jump practice. With a finger on the block itself, in one moment they were right inside the compound. Teddy was almost in shock, his breathing rate increased; he tried breathing in and out until he was back to normal. They both went into the house together. Once inside Teddy had to knock for his dad who was inside the room, he came out in no time. Dad uncle Ekure has been arrested, how do you mean? Teddy's dad asked. They went to his house or what? Benson Sage asked. Not at all, he went to Akarba to see the detainees, Teddy replied. But who sent him that one, complained Sage. He should have known the tension is on the high side, with killing here and there anything can happen but we reject it in Jesus Name Amen Teddy and Adams said.

So what do we do? Teddy, Adams asked. Nothing of course if any one goes there he will be arrested as well Sage said, that will further humiliate us, we have to stay and watch but if you can why not check on Samson at Abasa. He suggested I've seen that the mobile Jackboots are not cultured, they don't respect your status or age, and it is a pity the orientation is very poor in this country. The most annoying part is that he went there on his own, what a pity.

Once Adams is safe out of sight, Teddy considered going out but had a change of heart he was not far from his bed the latest vital foam product he slept off as the bed implies, he suddenly woke from sleep he jumped up was still very restless. He left the house again on a fact-finding mission forgetting his uncle was not yet back. This time he journeyed through the same lane but moved straight, unlike the first time. He terminated into the next street by his right. Since he was used to the track he followed it to a street called Agnabga then turned left, took another short cut, an apian way he passed a house edge with fencing work going on, obviously in a short while the fencing will be completed. He repeatedly told himself. "Cautiousness is the key to such business" as he walked he listened to hear footsteps from far but there was non-to his imagination. As he was at a close range within Iama road vicinity, he peeped through an opening in-between two store buildings, built at close rang. Side by side he moved further, was satisfied he was the only one on sight and was able to view towards the express.

Right in front of him he noticed a covering, he inquisitively tried visualizing what it was, instantly he retreated as he had a close look, "my God!" he exclaimed; a lifeless body covered? Oh no! He was disheartened: the body was covered with vita foam wrapper. "A body that was full of energy a few hours back" he thought but "life itself is meaningless and useless according to the philosopher David's son in Ecclesiastes.

"There is nothing that will happen now that has not happened before life is useless, all useless. All you spend your life working, laboring and what do you have to show for it. Generation comes and generation goes but the world is still just the same. The sun still rises and it still goes down going wearily back to where it must start all over again. The wind blows south; the wind blows north round, round, and back again.

Every river flows into the sea, but the sea is not yet full. The water returns to where the river began, and starts all over again. Everything leads to weariness, weariness too great for words, our eyes can never see enough to be satisfied; our ears can never hear enough. What has happen before will happen again. What has been done before will be done again as such there is nothing new in the whole world. He was deeply pained, "any evil done by man shall be redress, and if not now certainly later for the wages of sin is death." For sure there must always be a corollary. The sight saw to an end of being inquisitive, he followed a part, which terminates at Efad's Street. Further down, a distant of 3 spans of conductors he noticed a shadow his pace was drastically reduced, he waited for a while as the person appeared. On seeing the man was no threat to his subsistence. The man greeted him as he reached his position. In his confuse state the man does not seem to fidget. He was surprise or "could be this man is not aware of the development," he thought. He moved closer, "where are you coming from." Are there Jackboot men in sight? He asked. They are there but I avoided them. The man answered. That's all the man quickly added, the fear of the unknown is gradually subsiding. The people having the guts to move was impressive, can you imagine street once deserted is springing up to life. Teddy laughs. Teddy bid him fare well and "safe movement" the man replied, and continued along Efad road, his fear subsided as he now had a stone heart; walking along the road he met a group of young men in a fence compound. Mere seeing them depicts confidence. "Mr. Teddy, where are you coming from?" One of them asked. Before he could reply Ken the most carefree among them said?

"I suppose you are not going to the other part of town, you know we can't afford to loss you." The older boy said. I've seen too much, with these little eyes, of mine. As such I don't want to step out an inch. No body can take me away from this house. "Can you imagine? Those "nincompoop" rushed into our compound, some of them scaled the fence to show how callous they certainly were ken said. But T for trusts what happened, they went out the way they entered. At times I begin to wonder if the gods are unhappy with us. Simon said. Look at you; better hold on to your bible before you talk of gods. Teddy said. Never mind you've got to take heart the problem would be addressed in no time. Let's hope so, Simon said. All I know is that this cannot continue forever if the president is involved is he not a mortal man? Forget, there is no fire without igniting element. Teddy said as he proceeded

The DJO walked into the station instantly all the Jackboot officers stood at attention. Inspector he called! Yes sir, remember whatever happens don't forget your duty call he said. Yes sir! I suppose the number of arrestees is affecting our normal business, we have to decongest the station. You are right sir!

Radio Napke Jackboot station and inform them that we are sending the prisoners of riot (POR) for safe custody. Also signal the truck at once to convey the people to Irraw; I don't like the way this station is jam-packed he said.

The truck, conveying the chief and his visitors arrived Akarba Jackboot station. The driver care freely galloped to a corner and parked. The tail board was open "listen everyone; it will be ill-fated for any mishap to happen to you here, you just have to adhere the rules in here." Get down everyone; the Jackboot had already position. All the speaker did was to remove their thinking from the surprise. As the people both old and young descended from the truck, the Jackboot men started flogging them at random, not minding the receiver of the stroke. "What a humiliating sight." A legal practitioner who came to bail his client arrested for wondering. The chief was so courageous; he was not bothered since he was the hub of attraction. He didn't blink nor block as the younger generation did, signifying the kind of breed he is made of. The people were very helpless, 'so these people don't have a government representative? It goes to insinuating prominent people are short of the town." Patrician said. "As you come in pull your clothes," the Jackboot officer at the counter said. "Write down your name; another Jackboot officer said. The Jackboot officers were more than exited on seeing the number of detainees. "Move" a Jackboot officer backed at the chief. The people were susceptible, as they had lost all hope. Before the Jackboot could resume with the whipping parade the first set had entered the cell, "come back everybody," the Jackboot shouted. The people's behavior altered as they conform like zombie. The Jackboot officers whisked them ceaselessly after which they were officially allowed to re-enter the cell. The Jackboot stopped the group and asked them to go in one after another. As the chief was to enter he was halted, 'this man! When we are through with you, no one will advice you to act like an elder." The Jackboot were very relaxed, they mercilessly flogged him all over his body including his head. He turned and faced the DJO who was smiling. "You will surely pay for all this" this act perplexed everybody watching, he simple walked into the cell without altering any pleading sign. Portraying himself as a fearless leader

The sound outside his house made him to panic, he knew the enemy were allover the village "it is better to be safe under the bed than to be caught" he thought as he bend to relocate under the bed spontaneously his door was broken and the small room was stocked with uniform men. "Oh! My enemy" he said silently. All he did was to raise his hand in surrender. "I surrender," he shouted. The Jackboot nearest to him gave him a kick that swept him of the floor, he landed like a child of kindergarten "let me go" he shouted as he was carried away. He was joined with another chief who was arrested as well. How did it happen? He asked I was leaving the village with my family near Benson's compound, along the old road. "We were stopped, then it was not this serious; maybe they wanted to keep me hostage." Anyway I thank God they left my wife and the children." They were both interrupted by the heavy footstep that preceded their discussion. They remained numb as they came back. "You sent your children to burn down the Jackboot station old men?" Jackboot one said. You forget that the Jackboot station is government property, "you shall never see your children again." They were driven to a nearby bush path. "We are going to kill you here, right now. You had better say your last prayer, now consult your oracle. As the Jackboot finished his speech chief James started crying, "You cannot do more than a dead rat," chief Ada a known native doctor said. "Try what ever you want to try; if you want to test your faith, then you will know we have been silent over this issue." Feel free cock your gun and shot at an old man, if you will live beyond this moment." His face portrayed stiff hatred. His treat did the magic, the Jackboot lowered their gun and he along with chief James who was crying nonstop were pushed back into the vehicle, they were driving off when another set of Jackboot officers stormed the bush "leave me alone the man cried" let him go chief Ada said peeping from the truck the Jackboot tuned and fired at chief Ada at close range the gun spilled out fumes along with smoke. Chief Ada jumped down from the truck and held the Jackboot officer "I said let him go" the Jackboot pushed the man back inside the truck and they drove straight to Akarba Jackboot station.

CHAPTER ELEVEN

The prisoners were informed of the movement to another destination, this caused panic among the young men and boys. "I will resist being shot at like a slave if it means to die standing in the process I rather die a noble man than being shot at from behind." Your reasoning is unpleasant Paul said. Why won't I, contested Obi? What do you expect from these heartless lots? Imagine the agony chief James must have gone through. How on earth would you want to kill an old man that means you don't want to get old? Edem said. Had chief Ada not administered wisdom and little magic no body would have known what transpired.

"Single file everyone, your names will be called in numerical order. Once you hear yours come out and join the truck." Discipline was the order of the day, the best was gotten from them as fear implant discipline in them; they felt threatened, the faith of a man led to the slaughter without any form of resistance; apprehension caused them pain transfiguring to derision; written allover their eyes, the cell was confusion pricked and their faces were mask of sadness. "It engulfs the whole place" like the time of harmatan, right from the first man to the last was wearing a heavy face which humbled them. To further cause them more pain and grieve, they came out to see chief Ekure sitting as a detainee in an angle just by himself. "I can't believe this" chief Ekure is arrested? Austin said when he is the one suppose to be at fore front to actualize our release now the reverse is the case. The bounty was not finished for them as they got out of the station they saw chief Nelson; with his clutches a marginal pain was felt as Akpor busted out "take my life and let it be yours," Lord I can't notice any change between Ahcaba tyranny government and this fascism of a democracy." These people are operating in a close circuit such that the right of the plebeian is at jeopardy simply because the rulers are deep in crime that they have less control over the Jackboot force, Nairegin rulers are the replicas of the slave masters. The executives are enshrined in putting a puppet as the legislatives mouth piece in that the legislators are entirely frustrated in the whole process. Maxwell a 3rd year student of law emphasizes. "Mami" the only chance as a citizen is to vote in a labor party were everyone would be given equal right to dialogue to achieve positivism in the actual sense. But we don't have a labor party do we? Samson reminded. Then we had better look in that direction.

Boarding the vehicle took more than expected cause most of the detainees were busy collecting their various items deposited before entering the cell. This crowd is too much the DJO said as he walked up to the counter decongest this place now, move out every body he barked the people struggled to be at the front thinking they will repeat the flogging spray. They eventually left abandoning their items; they embarked the truck and were carried away as prisoners of war. (POW) Inside the truck the people started rejoicing praising God, an attitude synonymous with man only when in difficulty. "It is our duty to praise the lord. Working in the house of the Lord, Johnny sang oh walk, walk, walking in the house, walking in the house of Lord. They all echoed. I tell you brothers that our suffering will not be in vain; our tormentors will only succeed for a short while. Remember that when God says yes no body can say no. Don't forget my brothers and fathers that this is as a result of our sin, which has grown in us like a tumor. Repent for the kingdom of God is coming on us, for the rate at which we are drifting apart from the right direction is so alarming that I'm so scared. Suddenly the truck became a convergence for prayer section some inmate led them in prayer, someone shouted halleluiah! It is well with us. Johnny said. All praise the Living God, halleluiah they did not know when they reach Irraw town. The driver stop at PTI junction, "I want to ease myself he said." He jumped down; he was in such a hurry that he didn't know when he urinated on his trouser, "look at what you have down" the Jackboot escort said. "Please don't mind me" he moved without looking to see if there is an incoming vehicle a typical Nairegin driver's orientation.

Jackboot, why? An Agbero shouted, a man sits in his own house and orders for a driver's license without going through normal driving test procedure. Where do we take to the station he asked as he negotiated the first drive way. You should know that the hold up would be tense, along PTI road by now. The Jackboot escort said. He turned right towards Nuruffed roundabout. An okada rider lost control and was in the driver's front. Before he could slam the brake the okada maneuvered was almost knocked off the way, "you stay and smell your nose," shouted the Jackboot driver.

The holdup at the roundabout was so tense, in that all the incoming vehicles speed was altered to comply with the slow pace nature of other cars. In front ahead was a broken down trailer, its crew members help in controlling the traffic "thank God if not for these boys it would have been a disastrous situation for all," not what they bargained. "You don't look at were you are going to, "ode muumuu, I'll drive myself" the Jackboot driver barked. The man in question was fuming with sweat after narrowly hitting a bystander, who helped in controlling the traffic. Gradually the holdup eased off and most of the crowd dispersed into their cars and drove away. With the Jackboot trunk in view the people cleared faster than anticipated, the driver raining abuse at passerby cursing he branched into refinery road on the right hand side from the roundabout.

Napke Jackboot station is off the refinery road, it is famous in crime busting but has a lot of defect base on corruption; the escort on reaching the station ordered, one by one until the last man came down from the truck. "No rushing this station will accommodate only 20 persons." A heavy mouthed Jackboot officer addressed the new arrivers. A private moved close to the detainees who were disillusioned by the sudden change of event. "Look as you listen" he said, "you will all be fine as far as you don't constitute nuisance to yourself." Ensuring he was through with his speech a young officer in his early 20's stepped in, "follow me" he said. In a single file he ordered, "No don't rush." The detainees felt they will unleash same treatment melted on them at Akarba Jackboot station, fortunately this was a different ball game; they need not fear the Jackboot but the inmate of the cell. The victims were distributed into various cells, which housed about 20 persons. The whole cell was congested a typical Nairegin certain. An onlooker will assume from surface view, that detainees are treated with modesty since the act of crime is not confirm yet, but for law to take its course they are held in custody to prevent obstruction of justice. A crime against the poor, since they don't have enough money to pay as bail bond considering the corrupt nature of the Nairegin Jackboot are kept in custody against their will.

The Jackboot cell is a small room of about 6/6, in an ideal situation normally it is meant to occupy just 2 or 3 inmate at a time, but the reverse is the case where each small size cell house more than 30 person. It has a small opening at the upper end of the wall with an iron protector and the door leading to the cell is a hanging wood nothing to impress with. Stained wall must have been painted last when the building was erected, the dirt on it have lasted over the past decade. It's all colored in dirty brown due to stain, some noticeable changes were the inmates wrote their years of being detained in the cell. The inmates have a worn out look, owing to the fact that malnutrition has dealt a great blow on them. These ones cannot set to punch not to mention hitting someone as the detainees feared when they were to regroup with the prisoners. They quietly shifted position to accommodate the new visitors that has the cell as their new abode.

The one with tick set of teeth was the first to speak up, "welcome to joint one" I'll give you guys a tip if you would listen to me; his spoken English is hardly accorded value. "It is a notable rule not to shout at the warden unless you want to visit papa shango cell" (papa shango is an iron fist old man who sees himself as defeated in life,) he bites like a baby; a very brutal man he is with his feast, thereby supporting it with the teeth. He is a complete monster in human form couple with being alone for the past 2 years in solitary. He spoke happily, with a sense of humor; thinking he was impressing his immediate audience: "his crime as was speculated is not enough to keep a man for more than two days in isolation but the reverse is the case." Are we not Nairegins nothing good comes out of a corrupt system? Festus said. Could be he is acting out of frustration "you mean he's just all by himself all these years? Akpor asked.

"I've just explained that; he never barks nor talks unless provoked. But he eats asked James. That is when the warden remembers to give him his ration.

Eze Oke junior said Papa shango's problem started when the day's ration was served: he seized the whole plates to himself and made do with the water too. When the wardens were alerted, he fought everyone including the warden. Lastly he was over powered. Naturally it took almost the whole wardens strength to calm him; He was handcuffed and led to the isolation chamber: He receives food through an opening, "I'm surprise we've not heard his voice today, at times I begin to feel for him to the extent I don't mind them releasing him in place of me" Johnny, who is due to be released in three days time said. "You're not kidding!" Not at all, they all laughed even those that have not contributed to the discussion.

Copra yes sir! "How many detainees did you bring?" The desk sergeant asked. In all sir are 45 but the others will be distributed to other stations in Irraw town; I did leave 25 detainees in the vehicle, all right! Ease yourself he said. One more thing sir what! One chief is among the detainees? I detailed the desk officer to allow him stay behind the counter until a release order comes. He walked back to the truck "I felt pity for that other chief, so I left a standing order that oga said he should stay behind the counter, until a release order is sent across. "That is kind of you oh!" The driver said as he reversed and drove out of the station. Since he was familiar with the road he drove straight cutting across Jakpa road and Napke town, straight on through a bridge constructed to ease the drain terminals, the drain terminal being a golly, were all eroded material assembles as a result of flood. Not withstanding there is a free flow of debris because of the water carnal, terminating at interval with solid bridge capable of withstanding upsurge. He passed NNPC housing estate further down the road leading to

Shell estate. Finally the road terminates at Airport road; he turned right towards Kosini breaking through the holdup caused because of road maintenance, along airport road. "Dem this red sand deposited has metamorphosed into mud as a result of constant rain, he hissed. "Everybody wants to be a road contractor including lawmakers, how won't the work be neglected. The Jackboot said.

"Ralph you mean the Jackboot men is still terrorizing the people at Ukuraibo?" Rtd Capt. Ogene said. Sir if it is at that it is good, it is getting bad on the hour, "sir, from what I saw the whole community would be wiped out in no time." Capt. Ogene hailed a bike "take me to Ukuraibo" the bike man moved towards the direction of the crises zone; he rode through the express and was at Iasso petroleum inches away from the Jackboot checkpoint. The Jackboot men on seeing the incoming bike sprang up from their seating position. "Stop there!" They barked! The bike man before getting to their position reduced his speed, his leg was on the brake pedal as he gently tapped it twice and stopped, "where are you going to?" The man was about to answer when a low rank officer walk up to him and slapped him. What! He said. Not minding the consequence of his act he retaliated and pulled out his shotgun simultaneously. If you make any force move, I'll release the trigger, back off he screamed. On seeing the pointed gun and the man's fierce look the Jackboot man withdrew, "sir may we know you?" a superior officer said on reaching the scene. "That is what you were supposed to do in the first instance." He pulled out his identity card and said, "I'm captain." They all stood at attention before he could call his name, "feel free but don't exceed this limit, starting from the filling station backward is another community, so stay away or we shall be compelled to attack back." Yes sir, he left with a sign of relief unknowing to him that some set of the Jackboot team were at the other part of his acclaimed territory. Along the old road the people drifted to the riverside as the Jackboot men embarked on massive assault on the people whom the captain has given protection. "This is it! Here we go aha! The Jackboot man said. The truck parked along the road adjacent to a fence compound. 2 kilo meters from Abmonibo town, they disembarked and headed straight to the fenced compound; the fence compound recognized for it's uniqueness notably a compound of three bungalows built in form of an L shape the front has some structural art work, displayed as if in wait for exhibition. The fencing not high making it venerable to all sort of invasion. The team of Jackboot men capitalized on the low nature of the fence and in one swift was all inside the compound.

"We know you are all indoors" the team leader said, he proceeded, "let me warn, we shall not hesitate to deal decisively and ruthlessly with anyone who fails to obey a simple order." I hope my being polite would not be taken for weaknesses. In panic the whole occupant of the three bungalows open their doors wide enough to the Jackboot view; jubilating the team rushed into the house, "out everyone" move they ordered. In a confused state the occupants both old and young were forced out of the house. Mercilessly the team tortured them, they were made to roll on the rough floor "kneel down and craw" the people tried to comply but got stock as the gravel floor hindered smooth crawling. "Please sir, we are" we what! The commander shouted. They flogged them with all enthusiasm; the punishment was so hard on them that the families cried like babies.

Inside the house Abel was most disturbed under the bed, he initially wanted to comply as the treat was initiated but on a second thought resisted being fooled as he listened with his inner self. He remained under the bed until he heard Samson scream as he was hit on the head. He rose from his position and felt not secured still he peeped through an opening. The state at which he saw his people made him scared, he tip toed to the double bunk bed and position himself, ensuring he won't be seen from outside he climbed the bed in turn opened the ceiling cover without hesitation. He eased himself inside the roof and covered the ceiling back with the cover.

The chief on reaching the station snick out by the power of voodoo magic, he hastily pulled his trouser and deposited it in a refuse dump close by, he thought the safest place to hide his money beside his trousers inner pocket is an obscured place. "Who will imagine there is valuable cash in a refuse dump," considering the known fact that in his youthful days the best way to hide something then was an obscure place; were the mind will never drift or think towards. Once satisfied no one saw him, he entered the tiny hall, which housed the detainees unnoticed as they were being led to the cell. To reassure himself of his plot, he spoke out that was when he was seen. Ha! Elder they brought you here too no noise he spoke in a tone, which signified more of fear than brevity, but to reassure them he said never mind we are in it together. We must all pay our due he voice out but that does not term us fools; the only difference between us and our brothers at home is the inherent confinement in this small room he continued, within a shot while all this will be a thing of the past he added.

Elder how is our town before you came? My little one it is of no use answering that question. Have faith all will be well in God's Name he tactical avoided question that will make them sad. "I must not fail to let you know that our community members at home and abroad are not sleeping over our incarceration, it's saddening but we can't stop its course the channel has been modestly created before now." They are doing everything humanly possible to effect our release.

"The government would have been able to avert this crisis had they applied wisdom; it's very unfortunate that we the ardent of democracy have not yielded for us leaders but same rulers. As if in a dream we have lost more than 13 of our relatives." As he spoke his eyes was dripping in tears; it poured like a flood of water running down a new found tributary.

The boys clustered round him in embrace as one family "elder don't cry."

He remained in the ceiling for close to two hours, to his astonishment there was no sound from or within the compound; fear overwhelmed him as he drench in sweat, his body was walking as if he was poured with a bucket of water. He was so scared that the courage to open the ceiling and come out to see for him did not exist. Right inside the ceiling he found new companion; some rats accelerated towards his position. Unknowing he was there suddenly stopped and took a u-turn back to where it was coming from. In amusement he almost lost his grip to the wood that protected him from leaning directly on the ceiling. His concentration was bashed, he was no longer in the mood to think and his only concern and most of his greatest problem was how to leave the hot ceiling now a prison to him. He solely praised himself, for it is better to be in the confine hot ceiling than to receive the inhuman punishment he would have gotten had he not played smart. He was in a deep thought which metamorphosed into slight sleep, suddenly as if pushed from one end before he could readjust himself to hold on to his grip, there was a crack; it's vibration affected the ceiling's stability, Abel's weight on the ceiling was enough to loosen any strong hold, consequently it gave way and Abel was on the floor without a warning sign. He was lucky to have narrowly missed smashing his head on the iron bed, which aided his accent to the ceiling. He no longer cared as he expected the Jackboot to rush in and brutalize him, but to his astonishment no body came to attack or to rescue him, then it donned on him he was only the lonely. The house was deserted; his memory was blurred. He could not virtualize what has transpired. In the light of the same agony he slept off, only to wake up in the hospital.

Jackboot drive had eventually driven the whole community into panic as a result the helpless being more confused than ever, the community was relocated into the neighboring villages. The man was in a state of total absurdity, in a neighboring village called Utumu a small town situated on the hilly part of the Ethiop River. A village on the major express linking Ukuraibo and Robga with an access road called Ilego road, an inlet root that serve as link between other villages. The smoothness of the major road differentiate it from other villages round Inauwku, confirming the claim as true that the traditional council of chiefs is very stable. A highly populated clan and has similar life features of the Ukuraibo people, with same traditional council making it an enabling ground for the start of festivity since high number of its occupants are mainly specialized in farming thereby making it possible for abundant food supply. He is known to be in control of a callus team by name team 28; he sat in front of a supermarket with white chair arranged for the sale of alcoholic drinks, he was submerged in thinking as if in a trance a message was being related to him he jumped up oh! "Emma my son" he exclaimed, "I left him behind, out of desperation oh my regret these are his age group playing ooh!" he pointed was panting. My God! What have I done," he moved to leave but was held by his associate. I can not imagine why I had to abandon him in the midst of this crisis. Here I' m all alone in the world." He was reproach by some close observers. "Take it easy, whatever, he is save any where he is: don't put yourself into unnecessary tension." Roland said. Be warned you cannot go down to that unsafe town of yours alone. Edson added. He eventually calmed down by the consoling words of neighbors around him

CHAPTER TWELVE

"Utumu community can not condone this mad rush from Ukuraibo, the people with their known rascality If given full support to stay in this town, will turn our town into little China, in a matter of seconds. Remembering the bad influence of an exploration company that had its base at Utumu: what do you intend to do about the situation?" Mathew asked. Let's go and see the Ogbuemi, so that an announcer can go round to inform them to leave Utumu at once. Manuel said. We cannot fold our hands and see our town in total insurgences, they moved straight to the Ogbuemi's place

The elders in council were going through a critical state simple not out of fear because of the young men but decision that is bound to affect relationship between two identical communities of same origin "one has to be extra wary" the Ogbuemi said. I disagree with you completely on this issue, why not if not we are of the same parents. It insinuates trust and protection at time of need. As such we cannot be the ones to betray them, are you aware that our people "Utumu indigenes resides in Ukuraibo? Chief

Dick asked. "Are you saying we should do away with them, or their neighbors whom they must have invited? Young men be sensible, think, if no, then their associates from Ukuraibo who came, as refugees cannot be sent back, as such I degree they should feel free to partake in activities of the town, period.

With all respect sirs, he addressed the elders in council on standing up. Our coming to seek your opinion does not mean we cannot do it on our own, but all that culture demands we are fulfilling to get your blessing. "That my gentle man you can not get from me or my subordinate," The Ogbuemi said. He rose and his second in command excused himself as well, they both strolled out of the meeting leisurely feeling accomplished. "What a tempting young man" the second in command said. Don't mind him he is a daft, the Ogbuemi said.

Out in the open Mathew the instigator said, "We can actualize this thing without the Ogbuemi and the elders." how do you intend to actualize that without arousing trouble for us, Manuel said. Who will be able to pin it on us? Mathew said. To hell with that Ogbuemi and his elders Manuel said. "To hell with their none compromising believe." Added Mathew without thinking of the offence and the outcome of neglecting the elders, they walked towards the T junction terminating at the village announcers house. "Who's at home?" Manuel called out as he knocked at the door. Is any body in here? Yes! "Hold on I will be with you in a minute." The village announcer strolled out from the house with garri-stained hand, "you guys have met me well," he said as they greeted him. "Come on in" he pulled the curtain to reveal a six spring iron bed positioned at one end of the parlor which serves as both room and kitchen at another end an area carved out to accommodate the cooking implement; he arranged the items just at the entrance of the house, replica of a house without children.

"I don't know your mission but all I know is that a frog does not move in the daytime without something pursuing It." we greet you elder. "You know too that the bird that stands on top of a rope is ready for a dance." He laughed who teaches you young men these words of our fathers?" go on I know you are of a good tidings, let me know your aim of this visit for I know the bird does not stumble without being chased." Thank you for your concern, we shall not waste more of your precious time if need be. We are here specifically to inform you and give you as well the money necessary for announcement. So what is it all about?

This people from Ukuraibo constitute a nuisance in our town as such decisions have been reached to do without them, Manuel said. That is why we have come. Elder, here is the money needed for the assignment #300, please you inform them to go back to their town, for we do not what an extension of their problem in our town, period. You don't need to explain because they don't deserve it. Mathew said. He collected the money placed it on the table, his main interest was the money not the gravity of the announcement to the people so to say more earning to his pocket enticingly money is the root of all evil.

Contrarily to public opinion, he washed his hand and assembled his gong and a metal in stick form in preparation for the mission, unknowing to him the mission would terminate just as it started. He stepped out of the house. "Attention all, this is a message from the elders in council, if you know you are not a native of Utumu by birth; most especially those refugees from Ukuraibo you are advised to go back to your town in your own interest. Utumu is not a dumping ground for all sorts of people. This was continuously announced as he walked along the Ilego road.

In a drinking joint along the main road some youths gathered in drinking spree, "what was that? Festus I heard he said non-Utumu indigenes should go back to their town for peace to rain. "Did you hear that, I think the man is in sane? Nelson said. Festus drag that man here. Festus always wanting to foment trouble stood up as if injected joined with a group of young men, who were getting drunk on the influence of their host quickly rose and went after the announcer. "Stop there! The boss wants you informed Festus. Before he could resist, Festus signaled his men, they picked him up like a luggage, and his legs were completely suspended of the ground until he reached the big bosses position. Mr. Man do you know you are an accuse as well as an accomplice? Nelson enquired. Who sent you to make this nonsense announcement? What is your name? Bob asked. Where do you stay Andrew asked. He was bombarded with series of question some were abuse from the impatient ones who want treatment order to be issued without delay. He stood dumfounded, speak up ape or you'll be made an experimental goat for all to see.

Evil goes with evil, since you have refused to speak up and for playing part messenger of doom! Boys teach this man a lesson of his life so that he will not partake in such evil again. Nelson ordered. Gently he was hauled down, deal with him for his bad countenance. He is not fit to exist in our mist, more so for his evil utterance. Nelson ordered. Please sir; oh you can talk now! You should have said something instead of pleading. Festus quarried. What do you know you are pleading for? The village announcer was in a deep shit, he reasoned out his mistake for he did not bother to confirm from the appropriate quarter. If the message was from the elders, this set of youth can be stopped; he knew he was in trouble immediately they accosted him. All he wanted was to go back home to complete his meal. He was dazed his hands were in surrender position. He was absorbed in thought knowing he had to carry his cross all by himself, by simply obeying all instruction passed unto him. "Sit down stand up, and roll," Just like military drill, his adversary devised every tactic to humiliate him. His mind reflected to the 60's, when he was challenged to a fight by a group of friends; who were known terror in the community; being his youthful days; he fought them to a stand still and defeated them all. That was before his accident, which has completely disabled him. He could not even fight a group of children not to talk of grownups. He resigns his faith to that of a woodpecker who promised to peck down a palm tree in his father's funeral occasion, but was ill luck to have had swollen mouth a day to the occasion.

"Allow him to go" Nelson ordered, his condition might degenerate if you continue with him at this rate, "let's not bring his doom on us" that saw to an end to the announcement which almost tour the whole place apart.

"Come and sleep in my house, I know you must be tired" as he came back to his senses his mind was clear off thought of his sons absence, he was convinced to leave with the convoy from Abasa. Along the road music of Dennis Osadebe was played, this agitated the boys who sang along the beat of the music with bottles of star in one hand, forgetting their sorrow. Signifying that pain is only for a short while; "these are people driven from their community by an unknown strange force, invariably they do not have home any more but in less than 24 hours are jubilating as if it is an award winning night. An elderly man, who has all the while stood and watched in total bewilderment thought, what a challenge the elders are made to pay for crime committed by the entire youth. An act of bondage, it is synonymous to the sin of the father were children suffer as a result of sin committed by their offspring, which is vice versa. Parents are receiving physical punishment based on the crime motivated by their lads. That is why the most painful part of the body is placed near the fire to heal it as quick as possible. "Leaders of tomorrow, you people have failed in your responsibility." Andy said. A time of happiness repels sorrow or vice versa. Both are two different orders of life that cannot be interchanged. Is like walking before crawling, which is non compromising. When then do you feel inconsiderate? He said.

CHAPTER THIRTEEN

Nelson retired very late in the night after the nights clubbing he attended with a couple of his pals he's doing business with, he got home very drunk in that he could not open his door after consecutively struggling with the keys for no avail he had no option but to sit by the corridor

"Hi guy what's up? What are you doing outside all by yourself at this unholy hour? Christian who stays next door asked. There was no response he walked close enough to see that the man he addressed was far asleep, man he tapped! Tapped him to his feet, instantly Nelson waked and was fidgeting, what's the matter with you? Nelson was still dazed he ransacked his trousers pocket and found his house keys; he did the opening himself and helped him to get in. Once inside the house he staggered to the bed without pulling his shoes slept off with his shoes on.

The clock ticked 12 noon as if an in built alarm was in him. He woke with a start, his mind racing on how he can get home. He felt a chronic headache, knowing he has to leave for his village he rushed to the bath and had a complete scrub. In no time he was putting on his cloths, at exactly 13:00hrs he left Sogal thanks to the fact that his house is at Ojota, he did not have problem of traffic jam, which is the main bane of Legosians. He was, and acted like a true Nairegin on the way. Each Jackboot checkpoint he gets to, a bribe of #100 naira single bill passes him, without having to check his particulars and receipts of the electronics that were contained in his back seat and booth. He continued with the induced spirit on him after a whole year of being away from home. More so with his latest purchase he is cooler than the gang, he want to truly display it. He had some bottle of hot drinks as a tradition washing of the vehicle is mandatory as he drove on he opened one of the gin armed himself with a pack of Rothmans he lit the stick of cigarette occasionally sipping the gin he kept on steaming from one stick to another. He drank like a man drinking to his grave. The rate at which he manipulated the wheel, he would have hit Nineb in less than 3 hours if not for the constant stop as the road was in a deplorable state. "A death trap "he rained abuses on the persons in charge of the road repair, he lamented "even without the oil wind fall other products are more than enough to execute projects in the country without it citizens complaining, if a country like Cotovoa can sustain it's economy with cocoa I wonder why Nigeria with all its oil can not lead a unify life of self satisfaction."

Not minding the bad roads he was able to make Nineb in 3 hours time. He was very prayerful as he reached the tollgate, asking for God's favor so that the road will be free of hold up. Just as he anticipated there was no trace of hold up. "At least in the next 2 hours I'll be at Ukuraibo," he thought. He drove through new Nineb road to Hawe road. In no time he was entering Abopki slope, which took him to Abopki hill. He had a brief stop at a petrol station to have a refill. Unlike the Odno, Nineb road Robga/Nineb is a smooth tar. The doubling of the road made it traffic free: he remembered his last trip to Benue state the road was a true replica of this one. He increased speed as he progressed into the road to 160km/hr as against 130km/hr, not considering safety rules. Since there is no outstanding monitory body to implement safety, Robga was breathing at him within a short interval, man! He exclaimed. What a smooth drive. He thought. He was so happy with the road and was almost forgetting his road home as he passed the turn. He lamented, "How I which the Ukuraibo Robga road is like this. "He negotiated through the Emahela road to college junction, he turned right was on his way to Ukuraibo through Abavo; "a town well known for wholesale of yam, new and old inclusive." He reduced speed a little below the usual 130km/hour to 100km/hour only increasing speed at regular interval where he feels is not safe; mainly when he reached Ebginoru notoriously marked for armed robbery cases. He was happy he passed the bad sport before it was dark. The Utumu Bridge exited him so much that he screamed on getting to Abmonibo he checked the time, 18:00hrs. meaning he made it within 5hours 30mins.

On reaching Ukuraibo he saw Jackboot checkpoint, he felt it was normal considering the recent clamping down campaign on armed robbers in the country. But he was so observant that these set of Jackboot men mounting road block were so much that he from experience knew it is only crises prone zoon that such number will be meaningful. Well, he took for granted that any thing can happen so long the government really wants to function but to his dismay the Jackboot men were joined by another set coming from patrol making the number alarmingly high. He reduced speed, as he was about to turn back but on a second thought declined base on ethics. Why will he go back without finding out what is going on in his local environment? Before he could reach the checkpoint, he heard a gun shot from a distance followed by a stop order. He stopped immediately knowing that the Jackboot orientation round the country is so poor. Their pervasive nature makes them to shot indiscriminately as such, so many innocent people have lost their life, simply to the stupidity of the Jackboot force in the country; couple with the government inability to control the unholy development he was on guard. As the Jackboot walked up to him, yes! Where are you neither coming nor going to? Barked the Jackboot and what are these things in your possession? He asked non-stop, do they have receipt? He smiled, now to answer your questions one after another. I'm chief Obeufo, and this is my town, I'm on my way from Sogal state, as such this is my end point. As you can see these consignments are my electronics and the receipts are in tact. On seeing how compose he was the Jackboot man said carry on, meaning that he should go on. He was so relief, he moved and left them turned into Ukuraibo town, as he entered, he observed the quietness of the town, which is very unusual of his town. To further alert his imagination the whole stores were locked and he could not see any body to confirm from. He moved further into Iama road he was dazed on seeing the corps lying lifelessly on the road. His hand shook on the steering as ghost pimple appeared on his face. The town was in complete isolation. He was demoralized, an instant attack was imminent but he recovered almost the way it came. He wanted to stop but from his side mirror he noticed the Jackboot men were watching him. He drove to his house still dazed; he was still wondering what was happening when a small girl ran to him "uncle," she was panting every body is by the river side she said. As an old and retired cowboy he understood what has transpired, maybe there is intra tribal war in the village. He hurriedly unpacked his items to the house had a change of dress he was still thinking of what to do when he was visited by some set of Jackboot among whom was the one that interrogated him. "Chief you have a fine apartment." They complimented him.

He got up to give them seat, "as a chief the tradition must be fulfilled." Once a visitor come visiting you must present him with a kola nut, this I must do without hesitation. He brought out his root bottle and filled it with the refined illicit gin he brought from Sogal along with kola nut while he added #200 in the same plate with the kola nut. The money acted as a wedge so that the kola nut does not roll off and fall to the ordinary ground. For he who bring kola nut brings life, ironically he presented kola nut thereby bringing life to the people that took away precious life of the indigenes of his town. They all drank and charted, the young chief was absent minded, he said. "Officer may I ask a question?" "Go ahead and ask your question," the team leader said. "What was the cause of the desertion by my people?" Don't bring that matter here one of the Jackboot men said, no he needs to know so we must let him know countered the most senior among them.

Chief your people revolted and rebelled against the government by burning down the Jackboot station and the DJO's personal properties. Is that all? He asked. Officer the truth is bitter but we have to acknowledge it. The government owns the Jackboot station, "I'm I right," the team answered. Yes! Who are the government? He asked. "It's you and I." They repeatedly answered. More still the station was built with taxpayer's money. Note that the DJO's property can be replaced but can you replace any life that was lost during the struggle? As he spoke the Jackboot men stood up knowing that they have over stayed their welcome. The team leader said "chief see you another day." The chief did not reply, on his part he was ready to excuse them but they took the lead and left.

"Austin your friend will not come in the fun of it to deceive you, don't you know? He is acting as an informer now to civilian because he is a co Jackboot man. Austin pretended not to hear. She persisted, "You're not safe in the town understand that almost every man your age has left the village," before he could respond she started crying. "If they come here with you at home definitely I'll be arrested and maltreated too, "what if they don't stop there?" On this note he felt he was no longer man enough he changed his mind to leave with her to her apartment across the express, an area exceptionally devoid of attack. Since the area is not easily noticed unless one is told. They left the house virtually the whole compound was deserted. He was surprised not a single soul was along the road they passed Okufi Street down to the new road, as they crossed the express, a road newly constructed because of recently built houses was discovered to ease their entrance into Opkoize road. Instead of taking it straight he advised they channeled through off cut to avoid being seen. The compound was built in such a way that it does not have access to the road, unless through the backside of the house.

With the kind of design you can quietly access your house without fear of being seen, they needed no ceremonies to check into the house, which they honorably did. Austin acted as if he was being remote controlled, it was worse than ever he got up from bed picked is pair of trouser and shirt, he started dressing up a man whom the gods destined for punishment would be disillusioned then will be made mad. He left the house without warning to buy cigarette. 'Cigarette smoking is dangerous to your health, not just health but kills" he was reading the sticker as was placed in front of the small store called last bus stop, before he could attend to his choice in the store he saw a woman and her little daughter running frantically towards him.

Brothers please run ooh! "What is the problem?" He was at the verge of asking further as he turned in his left flank, some mobile Jackboot men were onto him almost abandoned running after their hunt; two were coming in his direction he did not wait for any further advice but joined in the rat race out of Jackboot reach. He ran without looking back to know if his aggressors were still behind. "The road being a narrow part more so a strange pathway but he kept on going praying God there would be an end point. He followed the narrow part till it terminates into a farm settlement. He took in breath of life, as he felt relieved on seeing a host of immigrant he was familiar with.

'Austin what brought you here?' Someone called. His attention was focus to get the actual calling point as he passed by a hovel; he was invited to a cup of palm wine, 'a whitish liquid in form of water, which is gotten from palm tree.' How are the people reacting? Dick asked. He was among the first set of people to leave town so he didn't have a clue to the events; knowing his involvement in the protest and a key player in the property burnt he had to be on guard.

"I leant that the death toll has increased," Nnamdi said. Friend "maimi" replied Austin you're not far from the truth, what I despise most is the present assumption, which insinuates Ukuraibo as a town of violent heritage. Austin I think it is proper for us to know our faith concerning this matter. Challenge Samson, if you may recall Udi, massacre was purely an invasion caused by lack of understanding and knowledge by the brave youths who were armed and possessed quality of maiming the anti riot squad, unlike Ukuraibo youths who are lily-livered. The soldiers sent to quell the fight acted purely on instruction, which was wrong in a democratic certain anyway. Ken countered.

In comparing our case with the Tiv Zango Kartaf Zaki-Biam stands as witnesses to the present's short fuse. In the communal crises there was mass killing of civilians and military officers sent to quell the riot. Ken said.

What of Okosi crises that emanated as a result of dispute between two factions in religious groups crises didn't the group burn down a full truck of Jackboot men, what happened? Or is this revenge in disguise,' they should have gone to those areas to revenge then. Samson said. In our case Ukuraibo was sleeping when the Jackboot men stormed our quite neighborhood and stole from us our hard earn peace of old, they killed maimed and harassed, did all sort of questionable things. Did they stop there? Austin said. No they succeeded in driving the spineless presumed able bodied men and women, children, even babies to the bush all in the name of burnt Jackboot station.

"I feel insulted, how can this happen to us, when the common environmental robbers terrorizing in the area, cannot be tamed by the Jackboot. Arthur said he continued, Look my friend for posterity sake, we must not fold our hand and see the crime itself "Jackboot" destroy our set goal, enough is enough: they all listened without interrupting the speaker. He did not notice her when she passed, she walked into the mist of female immigrant toward a small cabin housing the palm wine drinkers association, the cabin is made up of red sand 'lactrite' at the base which is supported by wood cut from tree branches while the roof is made of raffia palm. Her concentration was solely on how to find him, as she approached the Cabin in front of the one they were in. she saw another Cabin similar to what she was standing beside. The vibration of loud voices attracted her. Inside the Cabin it was as if the people were quarreling. She quickly made up her mind to see the people inside. "So you're here drinking and rejoicing, then I'll be the one to have high blood pressure." She said

What's all this about? Her eyes were red, "you mean I'm not worthy to know your movement." Chidimma! Please guys help me explain to her the circumstance that brought me here, "as if propelled by an unknown force I found myself in a strange certain, if I had listed to a second thought or given it a chance, Austin would have been history by now." Can someone rescue me out of the situation? Andy you're good at story telling, lets here from you, "Elliot added."

Austin took leave off his friends and headed for Opkoize town they had to take the bush path a hilly part, which is the main road to the town, the convert were by product of the 1st republic politicians the road was in a state in the right sense is termed a foot part highly water log with sizable ditches the hill terminates in a flowing stream the water has greenish color which makes it unique unlike every other river that is pure white. Mr. Brown

Opkoize town is little bit of a remote vicinage, the people being local businessmen and mainly farmers to serve their community needs. The village is separated into three parts making it impossible to have the kind of population Utumu has. The kind of houses found is mainly built with sand which is smoothening with cement giving it a perfect outlook: they were thinking of the way to the second Opkoize when they saw Tablet an old acquaintance of Austin. He offered them accommodation, but for his girl friend he declined and moved on to the second Opkoize where she had contact. The village is similar to the first one, as she knows her way around it did not take long to locate her friend's house.

Vicky was frying garri in the kitchen built so that anybody coming into the compound would be seen on first entry, she could not believe it "Austin in Opkoize" as for Chidimma its no news she rushed out to welcome them. "This must be a dream it is unbelievable. Vicky it's a long story, where should I begin? They had to put up with her, she sympathized with them, "so what can I prepare for you?" Don't worry yourself Austin is okay. Austin could not sleep he had nightmare he turned from one corner to the other. "How can this befall him, as early as 5:30hr he was up Chidimma! He called I'll leave through Umukwata he had his trouser on so what he needed was his shirt by 06:00hrs they were seeing him off. Austin you can find your way from here at least it is bright now and you don't have to ask question for the road is straight to Umukwata. He thanked them held his friend, "don't worry, I'll come over once this is over." Austin can't you stay until the crisis is over? Victoria appealed. "You mean you want to trek, what if you don't get bike at Umukwata?" Never mind I'm there already.

Since the inception of the terrorist attack on Ukuraibo the smaller villages has a lot to contend with, more inflow of traffic with less possibility of transport facilities. Austin trekked to Umukwata town; the journey which started as early as 06:00hrs ended in the afternoon. Due to bad road he was force to remain in one position till he made up his mind to adapt, he jump most of the bad sports as he walked.

Eze waited at Umukwata longer than expected for a motorbike, for most people drifted to the town to have an access to other village. Unfortunately his wait was prolonged because the bike was not regular, which prompted the rise in lawlessness. Fight almost marred movement; okay "I'm no longer going, please stay away from my bike." Austin advanced, "let there be orderliness please first come first serve basis." Naturally it calm the whole place as in crisis time every individual was forced into being humble. There was an emergency road transport union, which helped to coordinate the people. This reduced the rush since any new arrival will book first and would be issued a number; in this bargain, the elderly ones were given preference for it would have been hectic for them. Austin finally joined a bike when it got to his turn the bike took him through Iama to Emugo he was not aware that such bad roads existed in the state. "Rubbish! So what is all this campaign all about good road, when in one local government area there is no good road? He was relieved as he entered Awkodu west out skirt of Emugo, the road was uncompleted as the first phase asphalt laying is gradually giving way both smooth compared to others.

Stop lets give this people a helping hand Austin suggested as they saw the family. The bike-man complied and slowed to a halt "let us give you people a helping hand, come over. One of the kid and his elder brother joined them. The ride to Elawk town was a smooth one.

He arrived from the farm, his usual was served him 'beans and garri' as he sat to make meal his children came in, papa! They called; you're still here when the whole community has abandoned the village. He left the food and was on the run, papa wait and wear your shirt they called running after him but he kept on running till he reached across the river called Ata "an area not been habited leading to the boundary between Ukuraibo and Ebginoru." As they caught up with him his shirt was given to him. He sat down on top of a storm was breathing profusely as a result of thorny breath; normally the speed he controlled was enough to win an award in the incoming all African games. What a relief he felt, a man as the Onotu Uku being his staff of office would have been in the fore front especially for the emancipation of his people. Instead is subjected to running thereby abandoning his royal throne, on hearing his community was finish. Without asking to know the extent, this goes to prove the style of naive rulers. His eldest son thought. In the town meeting he will be in the rear when it comes to meaningless issues that will eventually set the town back. He slept off as if in a dream the earth was un-ravaging under his sit slight movement was felt but for the scream he would have slept on, he was on his feet in a moment. "Papa you were sleeping on top of a snake, it folded in form of a dead wood." Agnes said. It crowed away unnoticed. Peter concurred. "I should have known that it couldn't hurt;" you know why you saw it that means it's not harmful, he boastfully said.

They got to Abasa he turned left facing Robga but turned right through an access road to the legislator's quarters, his horned alerted the security man who came out to meet him. "Sir may I know who you want to see?" Is Hon Pius Okpala around? He asked. Just a minute sir he moved out of reach, with the aid of the intercom he was able to confirm? "This way sir" as he opened the gate, do you know your way? "Don't worry" Mr. Felix said as he drove to the apartment, they all came down from the car the door was slid open while they were ushered in by the steward who informed his master of their arrival. The legislator on hearing his people were around rose from sleep to attend to them, he was in the parlor in a moment, they exchange pleasantries. "Where is this boy" he rang the bell, instantly the steward was within reach. Bring some drinks. Leave that one first Felix said. But as custom demand I must give you something to drink he insisted. "Our mission is a life and death thing we don't want to get to a cross road." "But no body is dying here? I must first present you with kola nut before we can get talking." They all laughed.

"Jonah" he called get the matini with Champaign he presented the drinks and wedge it with # 1000 naira explaining, "times are hard, please bear with me and accept this small offer," the drinks were accepted without formality.

Yes to business you have not heard of the crises at Ukuraibo? Oh yes! I was informed but was waiting to see the commissioner of Jackboot. What for? Felix quarried. "He is not important; all that is important now is that you're our representative as such the man takes order from you not you taking order from him." He can be invited on your normal sitting in the house; compel him to inform you of the security report at Ukuraibo which is in your immediate constituency, and then the lapses will surface. He moved to the bedroom collected his shirt and was at the door, lets go and see Hon Osiji he said. They were lucky Hon Osiji was at home as they sat down they told him not to bother about kola and went straight to business. After serious deliberation Hon Osiji N Osiji suggested to raise the matter as Ukuraibo motion in the house for deliberation in the subsequent days meeting.

Dad the death toll has increased don't you think it's high time these menace has to be checked, by whom? He asked, you forget so soon your environment, with the senator from Awkodu, house of representative member and chief liaison officer to the president on house matter from Ukuraibo we can't be crying wolf. It is purely when you're not truly represented that you can tell it to the Geese, could be they are taking their time, maybe till when Ukuraibo is erased from Nairegin map then the peoples obedient servant will be forced to act, then they will not have a constituency to represent anymore. But the people have right to recall their state representative who failed to perform? Of course, the only problem is lack of awareness, these 1999 legislators are all opportunist. Take a tip from me come 2007 there will be mandated stewardship where issues would be properly handled.

You can save the situation go to Abasa and intimate the state house of Assembly the problem your people are facing. I'll do that right away.

Teddy made do with his clothing since he had already had his bath it did not take long he was ready for a trip to Abasa. Ukuraibo was still in darkness, he had to take the bull by the horn, it is a two way thing either he sits down at home and see his town removed from Atled state map or he take the risk of not being seen to the outskirt of the town, the same feeling Nairegin soldiers had during Major Gideon Orka coup got hold of him, as most of them from far north were tactically removed from Nairegin. Based on Major Orka's pronouncement; As lock could have it, on reaching the gate he saw a bike as if the bike was sent to convey him, he joined the bike to start of Abmonibo. On the way he confirms if the bike man was harassed as he came by the Jackboot men, the bike man replied, "I avoided them which I intend doing again." 'He took Efad road straight to the express. He safely was at the outskirt of the town, was too step from the bike when he saw a Mercedes Benz 230 coming from the town, the man on the wheel was fidgeting: an abnormal condition he had no choice but to stop him. An urge to help was totally in control of his action he stopped the man who was at the verge of stopping. "Please, where is the way to Robga is" man you're on the right track Teddy answered. "Sir if you don't mind we here" Teddy pointing at others said. "Re going to the same direction Teddy said. Come in at once he said. They hurriedly got in and he drove off. "I came to town 2 days ago and we have been indoors ever since, the man said. I didn't know of the daybreak massacre," you won't believe it my friend and I stayed two days in fear; I belt you I was the happiest man on earth when his neighbor informed me to leave immediately" Since the Jackboot had left this position, we are; initially they had a check point at this junction.

Well, "you're in a safe environment now, as for we the fight for them to leave our community is still on." Teddy said. "I pray your people will get their freedom soon by the special grace of God." Since they were in deep conversation, truly touched by the suffering of the people they did not know when they arrived Robga town.

Teddy boarded a car going to Abasa without wasting time he really want to meet the house sitting, so he paid for two seats.

The days meeting started with a motion raised by Hon Okpala on Ukuraibo matter, which was seconded by Hon Osiji of Awkodu west. Jackboot has been our problem in this country Hon Okpala said, it got to a climax as it was argued that if president Obedient can go to Udi after the crises to sympathize there is every need that the speaker sets up a committee to go on fact finding in Ukuraibo. The speaker being the head of the committee headed the delegation as such the house process was halted and members hurriedly vacated their seat. They all rejoined in the car park as they entered their vehicles, among the group were some members of the community who came to report the incidences, and men of the Nairegin press followed closely.

The car was not convenient for Teddy but he wants to get to his destination on time he adjusted; he was not concentrating on the traffic but when he heard the siren he looked up, "oh it's the legislators" he thought I hope they're on their way to Ukuraibo. "What's going on at Ukuraibo?" the diver asked. Please that matter is disheartening, real crime on humanity is being committed and the government is exhibiting a charlatan attitude. "You mean they have not visited the town?" Barrister Hector asked. I pray that is where the siren vehicle is heading.

"I'm just a driver, what do I know" driver please concentrate and leave Ukuraibo matter for politician, Mary said. Why? Teddy asked. You know why if you continue till tomorrow there would be no end result, it is all discreet. Madam you know why it's good to always talk on politic. Teddy said why? If I may ask, It goes a long way to checkmating these people, If you look at the generality of Nairegins the enlighten ones 're 100 in a million but with constant conversation like this in the car, store, beer parlor, palm wine joints and bus stops. You would have succeeded a great deal in driving home the message to the average populace, who will in turn do the remaining work of spreading to the low breeds. Teddy said. Don't forget that the food you eat is all about politics, health, transport, Education, Social ware fare and housing EST.

At Abasa Teddy took a taxi to the state house of assembly as he got there it was unusually quite, he enquired from the security men who informed him that the speaker and a set of committee members had gone to Ukuraibo then he confirmed his initial assumption.

CHAPTER FOURTEEN

At the Okpala Uku's palace the people gathered awaiting the convoy, among whom were indigenes that came as a result of the crisis; unlike days before the crisis, when a general meeting is scheduled the place is always very crowded but the reverse is the case hardly were the seats occupied. Presiding over the meeting is an aged man who governs by the aid of his subordinates. The drive to Ukuraibo was precipitated by speed cause the believe was that the Jackboot were still maiming, unarmed citizens of the community as the speakers entourage reached Ukuraibo, the speaker ordered the whole cars to stop while the pilot vehicle was asked to put off the siren. He asked the members present to come down, all came out of their vehicles for effective fact finding. They took a walk from Iasso petroleum, down the old road as they approached the market the Jackboot on seeing the crowd, assumed shooting position waiting on their new prey. The speaker was disgusted, oh! 'Look at them he pointed, they are positioning to shoot at us." He said. "We need no further confirmation, this proves it they are bloody killers, and he turned to face his colic's "is like the whole villagers have left the village for them." They walked through Iama road and saw for themselves the unlawful killing of helpless citizens by the said mobile Jackboot force. "These officers are meant to protect the citizens from enemy attack but have turned the people's enemy." One of the legislators said.

"I wonder why the state delayed its response." Nnamdi on sighting the legislators said. "For sure in a democratic rule like ours, the governor of the state has been empowered: he is the overall chief security officer of the state, he is in position to stop the act, "these men you see are just playing elementary role of an android since the commissioner of Jackboot issued the order it is expected of the governor to issue a counter order. "But the governor is no were within the state." Dominic said. "Must he be in the state all the time? Why then does he have a deputy? "Don't be fooled, some school of thought have it that he refuse to perform at the right time since the town disappointed him during the 1999 general election; after spending his hard earn money to install an outdated transformer in the town the people voted their conscience, the people are enlighten since their conscience could not be purchase by gift. Ben said.

Information circulated like wind the people who had faith were the first to respond, Emma! Anslem called how many people were killed at Araho? Being the governor's home town when his bodyguard was killed, instead they went to sue for peace but in our case, we did not kill anybody yet the commissioner of Jackboot visited and as he left harmless citizens of this community were massacred in cold blood, most excruciating nothing is done about it, or was his visit a mission accomplished. Who knows Emma answered.

What do you people think you're doing? Enquired the speaker, where is your commanding officer. Sir! "This is an animalistic behavior, how can you open your eyes and shot at people without arms; in cold blood, dam it's high time the government stops recruiting illiterate in this your so call Jackboot force. "What has gone wrong with you? The commander was speechless. You people have no fear of God; you think you are dealing with animals forgetting that it's the same blood flowing through your veins. At the Okpala Ukus palace, the people's number increased gradually, elders of various age groups nonetheless a scanty crowed, if not for the day break massacre; the people would have assembled as if a banquet was going on. The speaker was received by the community spokesman and was led to a seat along with his entourage. The community spokes man stood-up The Okpala Uku and "we the entire people of Ukuraibo welcomes the honorable speaker and his entourage from Atled state house of Assembly for visiting Ukuraibo at this critical time in our life time, not minding their tight schedule."

The speaker lamented, "it is saddening to see you in twinge, I do promise with the assistance of the state to unravel all that is connected with this assassination attack on the Ukuraibo clan. "Please kindly send the list of the affected persons to the state house of Assemble, as this will enable us a prompt response as we reconvene."

The community spokes man commended the speaker on behalf of the Okpala Uku and his kinsmen promised to deliver as requested by the speaker the number of afflicted in the community. And promised a peaceful existence of his community as it was before the day brake massacre as far as Atled state is concern.

Samuel is that you? Who's this? Samuel asked what's been happening to you. We have expected you all this while in Port Harcourt. Brother it's been tough; work pressure has made me stay out of circulation. Samuel answered. "What is this we're hearing about Ukuraibo crisis unlimited?" Runic asked. I learnt that my old boy has been arrested, my information source was not specific she said both your old boy was arrested as well. You don't mean it? "It means I'll get across to Elliot in Irraw so that he can confirm it," Samuel promised. "But I left Ukuraibo a day back, I presume those people are in sane if not why would they arrest at random." Do you blame them? Replied Runic, we are indispose, do you think the government of today is better than the dark days of Ahcaba and his cronies. Don't forget Ahcaba is dead but his cronies are still much alive and are willing to perpetuate in disguise the same rule. Can anything good come out of an evil plant? Samuel asked. No way. "Take heart my brother all will be alright soon, they can try but for sure they are bound to fail. Nothing can deprive us of our hard earn freedom; remember that delay is not denier. Runic said. I feel for the less privilege a great number of them are backward, the few enlighten ones are displaced for they have lost focus." Samuel said. Why would a minority Jackboot force intimidate a whole community as big as ours? Runic asked. For posterity sake, we must do something no matter how long it takes to bring these evil perpetuators to book. Versed Samuel See you don't fail to contact me when you're through Runic reminded him.

The phone rang at number 16 Osagede Street in Irraw town. Elliot was far asleep, the sharp tone of his Nokia 3310 phone woke him; he was about to pick the phone when it went dead. Not quite 30 second the phone rang again. Hello, P J? Bob that you, "Ukuraibo is on fire, is like the Jackboot are doing random arrest; I was just informed of uncle Ekure's arrest along with popsi Runic said it casually not too sure. On hearing the names mentioned Elliot no longer felt sleepy, From information gathered we are yet to know their where about. Samuel reminded him. But I just left Ukuraibo yesterday, he reassured him so I wonder when this whole arrest thing took place. Even popsi was advising Teddy and I. "be very careful" he said, you know his misgiving about the Jackboot force. So where do we start from? Elliot asked. Since you're in Irraw why not check 'AB' division and Napke Jackboot station to confirm. Elliot did not bother to take his bath, he put on his trouser and shirt since he was alone at home he quickly dropped a note for his wife acquitting her of his where about. He took a bike that conveyed him to 'AB' division as a result of hold up it was not easy to get to 'AB' division, he caution the bike man as he started the carefree non charlatan attitude, which at the end of the day leads them to collide with in coming cars. On the opposite side the bike man stormed the road not noticing when a middle aged girl crossed, from the right hand side; before he could redirect his drive wheel, he was on her. He pressed the brake pedal, the bike lost control and hit her, and she fell with her head hitting the sandy edge of the tar, 'how lucky her head narrowly missed the coal tar.' Gabriel said. The people rushed her and hastily she was taken to the hospital.

The number of detainees has gradually increased; you said, "Your uncle was arrested as well. His case is pathetic, "a light skin Jackboot officer confirm." what really happened? The first day the Jackboot stormed Ukuraibo. 'Wait,' the Jackboot officer said. Meet that other Jackboot officer, Babson he called 'please attend to him.' He was not interested in the story but unhearing his uncle is among the newly detainees he slowed to enquire, "please who did you say was arrested at the station?" Alfred asked. Is one bros who went to collect his store keys?" Alfred needed no body to confirm his uncle's arrest. So what're you going to do about his situation? Teddy asked. Couple with this incessant arrest that the Jackboot had embarked on, I wonder how you can see him because once they get wind that you're from Ukuraibo. Hook or crook I'll go and see him tomorrow. Then look me up on your way out; we have to know the numbers of detainees. Teddy said.

Teddy slept off with the light still on, the time was not yet 05:00hrs he woke up as if he has a fix timer in his heart. He quickly went to take his bath; not minding his routine of steaming a habit formed, the water was so cold as a result of Hamattan wind. But on this day he had to forgo his hot water if not for his job order he intends collecting it was enough reason to postpone the trip.The dressing time was as good as bathing time, he was on his way in no time, roughly in 20minutes on the dot he was at Alfred's gate due to water being part of the road.

Who is at home? Alfred came out yet unprepared. "Why is it a habit that you've to always wait for me before getting set all the time? He quarried. "Sorry I over slept," Alfred apologized he hastened to the bath and came out with the same speed.

Unpredictable Alfred's dressing time was altered unlike the days he was not in a hurry. "Let's go" he said, Teddy was taken aback "We have to go over to Agnabga Street to carry my brother's wife." He said. She should have been here though she is never cautious of time. He was in a state, which affected his composure; he came to the car and slammed the car door. He finally left at 08.05hrs and made it to Agnabga within the hour. She was still not ready as he came down, "what is all this? "You think I'll spend the whole day waiting for you." he quarried. "I'm very sorry," she said as she approached. "You don't keep to time; you know I have my business to contend with." I'm sorry, for what? "I had to prepare his food, if not I should have been up and doing," she explained. This is not the first time you've made me to come looking for you. Alfred refused to be misinformed.

Good day sir, yes can I be of help? "I want to confirm if Engr Ekure and Chief Benson are here both of Ukuraibo. Oh! Rioters, none in this station for now, why not try Napke? Cause I over heard a radio signal that a truck is approaching the Jackboot station. Thanks for your concern; you're welcome. "What a kind hearted Jackboot officer" he thought. Elliot had to take a bike to quicken his movement to Napke as directed, he moved to the desk Sergeant as he turned left he notice someone sitting all by himself with his back facing the entrance. He was so calm even in mist of enemies. Elliot recognized him within a second glance, 'then where is popsi 'he reflected as he met him.

Uncle what is happening? He said as he approached, it would be over soon: how soon he lamented. Never mind he calmed him, "I thought you were arrested with my dad." Elliot enquired. No, that was wrong information. So what can we do to get you out of this place? "Do me a favor call this number; inform my friend of my arrest okay." I'll be back as soon as possible, Elliot said as he walked away.

He left the Jackboot station half satisfied since only one person was arrested it will be easy to effect his release until all was set for hearing.

CHAPTER FIFTEEN

Most villagers were skeptical on listening to the announcement, at times of crisis it entails a lion heart to function properly. She knew her role as a councilor and her position cannot be looked down on. She had no choice but to yield to the call of her chairman, the road though too quiet for comfort she wanted to prove a point as the town crier specifically informed her of the meeting, scheduled to hold between community leaders and the council executives.

At the council secretariat, most representatives were present including elders of the community. The local government chairman stood up, I greet you all my elders, it'll be a bad precedence if we start by apportioning blames on ourselves thereby discussing the cause and not finding a lasting solution to the problem at hand. You're all witnesses to the ills that beseech our town. May I put it across to the house in seeking your opinion?

Mr. Chairman if you don't have an agenda for this meeting let us know. Nelson responded. "How can you say that Jackboot officers will come to your domain without informing you, being the local government chairman as the chief security officer you must be kidding? Don't put words into our mouth please. Chief Benson said. You had the powers to quit the Jackboot officers from your constituency but you failed, instead you encouraged them. What are we talking about? Apologies before we can move on. If you still insist why are the Jackboot men not attacking your people? Chief John asked, or is the attack coincidental.

Mr. Chairman, who are the men on white t-shirts? Andrew enquired. The crime committed against the people cannot be measured. You mean you seek the peoples mandate to slaughter, or massacre them why then are you chasing them round the globe to eliminate them all.

The meeting that attracted few village head ended up in a roar, members of the chief's entourage were lead back in to the town. Mark and Mathew watched the selected few as they returned from the meeting. Brother, this people seem to be working freely. Mark said. Oh you are still in the wimp of deceit, the whole thing as portrayed is sectional and politically motivated. If not, how some few would be allowed to walk without harassment?

Teddy and Alfred arrived Alaja town; a neighboring Irraw village where Aluminum steels is processed for export purpose. The Jackboot station is along the express, as the car pulled over Alfred intones called Teddy, you know the crisis at hand. It will be good we fake our identity. Good afternoon sir, yes what is it? The Jackboot officer asked. We are asking after Mr. Eddy Eseronwefe, one of those arrested from Ukuraibo. Teddy said. Go and buy one toilet roll and a medicated soap, a woman Jackboot officer requested. They went outside and made the purchase from a caravan. They handed the item to the Jackboot officer. What do you want to give him? She pointed at Eddy's wife. She brought out the food flasks. Pour that in a rubber bag before you can go in, no spoon is allowed, she said. Why? Teddy asked.

It is for their safety since cutleries can be used as tools the prison authority issued an outstanding order. Please as you pour test it, she did as was told. You can come in the Jackboot officer said. The counter being an open hall with an entrance, "please we'll only accommodate two persons at a time" Eddy's wife was given preference since she had the rice and bread in her possession. Alfred was allowed next and when it got to Teddy's turn the Jackboot man said, "please this will do" but I'm the last Teddy complained in exasperation. We have tried in our little capacity or you don't know? We were asked not to allow any visitors at all he stated. "Look what have I done?" Teddy complained. This people will not know that I visited.

So what did he say? Teddy asked. There is an Alhaji who wants to help him out of this mess.

The man rose from his hideout, knowing his sole responsibility as an honorable councilor, was to play an instrumental roll to put a lasting end to the crisis. He was running against time, all he did was to alert the man. Both in the quest to do a good job agreed on a mission terminate.

"All we have to do is to contact madam as fast as possible." The councilor said. What are we waiting for? Let's go Austin said. Robga Park was unusually crowded the passengers waited patiently as the only transporter crawled out in a snail pace, the driver reversed his bus; given benefit of a half life monopoly instigated by fear from the general public, the driver loaded his vehicle forgetting all ethics of safety rules. The eager passengers were not in the mood to complain as they squeeze themselves into the waiting bus. The driver a fragile looking old man, with sets of hand that must have done more walk, than required in his early days. He positioned his seat pillow to fit in perfectly and held on to the wheel. Speeding, a habit of the youth solely reflected in him, he made the bad road as if he was driving along Sogal, Nugo express road; if not for the continuous Jackboot checkpoint that altered his speed occasionally. "Pack there!" a Jackboot officer commanded, "You mean I'll have to introduce myself everyday." He voiced out, showing sign of not being happy.

"Oga tender for the overload charge, 'we're not charging for the tollgate, our usual normal fee." A junior officer explained. He reluctantly parted with his hard earn #40.00. He screeched and the bus jerked with a moving force of a double engine.

No! I can't contribute any longer please!" he said. On reaching another Jackboot check 2 kilometers from the first one. He walked to the car started the engine the Jackboot officer hit his vehicle with a large stick as he drove off, roughly 5 minutes drive brought him to Imoru junction; the most populated park in the town. They joined a waiting taxi, to quicken the flow they had to pay for an extra seat, which was later occupied.

Along Nineb Abasa road sudden hold up built up as the road construction team annexed the bridge diverting all road users to a one-way part, gradually the holdup built on the hour. Once off the hold up the driver accelerated to a high speed, forgetting all safety laws binding all road users. Do we have to see B-man? Austin asked, as the driver pulled over at Asubi junction Austin said. "I don't think it's important, all we do is to contact his mum on phone." They stopped a taxi: "take us to any business center nearest to this place; as fast as you can drive." Austin told the driver on entering the vehicle. The driver accelerated, was in a breathing speed, he curved on reaching ministry of works gate and pulled over. Sir there is a business center over there he pointed. Austin willingly paid him #200 for a good job accomplished.

"We don't have to travel together, so that I can cover this end as you will communicate to me Hon." Mission partially accomplished they joined another vehicle going to Robga. Austin paid for an Abuja ticket, while the liaison officer joined another vehicle back home.

The member representing Inauwku/ Ndokwua constituency in the federal house of representative, chief Hon Mary Eseri was not in the country when the councilor Arnold visited Abuja. Arnold none the least was relieved when he saw the eldest son knowing that he has played a greater roll in the politics from the closed door. Arnold did not wait to be offered a seat; he briefed him on the extent of damage done. Godwin a skimmer always in the right direction contacted his mum; once contacted she briefed him of what line of action to take until she come back. She said "get in touch with the chief liaison officer to the presidency on house matter," "you must see senator Osanebi in person, so that you can brief him in details as you've told me" she requested.

She put a call to her agents terminating her appointment. She also requested for a flight scheduled back home. She felt nervous as she finished communicating. Owning to different images appearing to her; from experience she knew stories are not rightly conveyed to someone outside the scene, which increased her fear for the worst.

Information carpeted on line communication network, the managing director was informed of the mayhem that besieges his town. "My God!" he altered. He picked another of his cell phone and dialed "Hello" this is the governor's office, how can I help you? "Can I be on to the governor?" who is on the line? "Tell him Bradon Bank MD." Your Excellency what is happening in my town? He asked. Your constituency is on gun smoke. That I learnt from the Jackboot commissioner. "What is the Jackboot scrap that I'm hearing?" he queried Well I'll be in Atled state with the next available flight.

She hurriedly ordered her escort jeep driver to get ready for a scheduled trip, more so she picked her handset and dialed. "Your Excellency I hear my constituency, precisely my town is on fire." Please do something, from what I gathered the indigenes have abandoned while the town remain deserted, apart from the warlord Jackboot patrolling the town as the town's custodian. She contacted top government functionaries within the federal capital territory, roughly 30 minutes she was busy dialing / connecting until she finally called for her personal assistance who moved her bags to the waiting vehicle.

The delegates from the state capital left the palace at exactly 17:00hrs. The assurance that the state will look into the matter reduced their worry especially when the honorable speaker affirmed the state government position on the killing. "The estimated exalt death toll and the injured report should be submitted to the state assembly for confirmation purpose;" he also scheduled a meeting of hearing at the state house with the community leaders on the 23rd of February 2003.

Sanity returned to the town eventually, when a group of teenagers championed by Emapko and his group of able Nairegin youths embarked on cleaning exercise, they went round the community ensuring the bodies of the deceased was removed from the main road to the mortuary. Devoted young men joined in the exercise as they returned to the town from their hideout. This made the work easier. Gradually a ghost town actively became very busy while the number of people patrolling the area increased on the hour.

"Oga you will accept this as my widows might please." Peter said. The man looked at the bundle of #50.00 denominations and removed his face. Unless you don't want to maintain our good relationship Peter said; as he squeezed the bill into his hand. Okay for your sake, he grudgingly accepted the #5,000 from Peter, who was paying for his younger brother 'Andy's' release arrested along Iama road.

"Big bros I'm grateful, it's an experience worthwhile." If ours is like this I wonder what the real prisoners will be going through. I feel sad on a daily basis; imagine what most inmates are passing through. "Do you believe that most of the guys arrested for crime are mere victim of circumstance? He explained Come to think of it they are kept in an unhygienic, condition in that if one is not lucky an attack is his before vacating the home. Whereas in most cases the detainees do not have affiliation to the crime A tradition of the Nairegin Jackboot force that one has to bail himself as long as he's been arrested guilty or not. Otherwise the person languishes in detention. "Our case is of the good the bad and the ugly; most people did not witness the crisis while others partook, with a view of replaying the act if given the same opportunity."

The word of Anslem the cricketer "we meant no harm to the Jackboot force but look at the grave injustice it has done to our community" "Where is justice in the eyes of tyranny? When citizens of this great nation can be brutally murdered in cold blood and no body is acting upon it.

She did not complete the work as proposed but started making some contact as soon as she was through she picked her handbag and left the office. Outside the presidential villa were combat ready mobile Jackboot men who waited patiently, the commander was signaled after brief consultation; he ordered the Jackboot men to embark on the truck explaining 'madam is ready, move now.' She got into her own car, the drivers all waited for the pilot vehicle to take the lead. He moved and they all followed with minimum speed controlled by the pilot driver. She was very moody knowing she has to get to the village as soon as possible.

On like every other trip the Abuja / Lokoja way was a bit longer than usual. She seems to be liberal with the driver who increased speed knowing she was in a hurry. Partly due to her not concentrating to know the speed at which he was driving. She persistently prayed for less casualty as her informer had no time of briefing her, in details the exalt casualty rate based on poor communication network in the country. Even with the GSM service providers the line went off and when she tried calling the same number it never went through, all she heard was, 'the number you dialed is not responding please try again later' She abandoned.

The crested Jackboot killers blocked the road, as she reached the junction. The federal squad she was with gave her backing. "Now pack all your belongings and leave the town she ordered. "Can't you see that the people were not rioting? How callous you have become over the years, how can you open your eyes and shot at defenseless citizen, when you should have easily devised a means of quelling the peaceful protest if any." The Jackboot complied sensing her authority. "You can tell your men to function now. She told the new set of Jackboot men

The people were reassured as they saw the masked killer squad leaving the town. The youths on hearing she was in town flocked around her compound. She came out to address them, she brought out money to present to the leader; "use this to buy casket so that we can proceed to bury our dead. Madam, "I don't think this should be the first step to follow;" the youth leader said. We are talking of our dead patriots whom the government is treating as common criminals. Adam added. "Justice is all we need; the crime itself should be brought to trial, because there is no amount of compensation that can bring to life this lost. "Brethrens, we are all in this mess, so please don't take it down on one person." She explained. "I know the pressure I went through before getting here; I mean no harm for the plight is on us all. The youth were so adamant that they refuse to see reasons with her. They left the house premises grumbling with a prejudged stance without consideration of dialogue in achieving meaningful success on the matter.

He became very tense, as he listened "the whole town gathered in her place to take a final stance on your involvement." The informer revealed to him on entering his compound. "What can I do to stop the gang up?" the chairman said. "Why not go and see her, so that she can hear your version. She will not judge by one standard alone." The informer urged him.

He drives through the express road, avoiding the town since he does not want publicity, as an offender number one. He got to the house along Aboh on the Ethiop "a three in one" white color bungalow in form of L shape. The security man did not waste time questioning him; he opened the gate wide open depicting the fact that respect is accorded to him who deserves it, as a public savant his official car spoke for him.

"What are you doing here? Oh, you've come to do. What? After killing my people," his eyes were stone cold, he was crying like a babe. "I did not order the Jackboot to shot at the people, I swear it was a coincidence; all to discredit me.

"Well I do not need explanation from you; we are still investigating the whole matter. Since we are in a democratic world majority carry's the vote, 'the voice of the people is the voice of God', and the whole people cannot lie against you for the fun of it. You are aware we are discussing life so one has to be careful." He was able to study the surrounding and decided to take it as it comes; the compound was infested with more sycophants compared to reasonable beings as bad news circulates faster than songs of good tidings, the community in a flash drifted to her place as it spread round town. "The local chairman is crying! At Ese Udenta's residence." What a relief the people felt as some jubilated. "So the man can still cry?" Mercy asked, better go and do useful thing with your time.

Where are the people trooping? Israel asked surprised by the large crowd he saw. Don't be scared! They are going to confirm if Enext Uche is crying at Udenta's house. Alex informed him" Trust the people it's on such matters you'll see them in large numbers. When a change is preached you can't find them, especially when it has to do with the living condition of the masses. Israel reminded him with a feeling of not being impressed.

The people gathered close to Ukula Inn; a popular joint at the start of Akabgu. "My people he said the need have arisen for us to show sincere gratitude for our brutally murdered brethrens". He continued; breaths in an intake of air "we are going to fix a date for mourning. Feel free to act on your impulse as this is not compulsory a task."

Mr. Chike, Stanley called. "Don't you think the situation is not ripe for mourning? Couple with the government's altitude over this issue. We have to be mindful of what we do else people would say we are not heeding from our mistake." "Can't you see our people were massacred defenselessly which is similar to the terrorist's act of firing into the market killing as much as possible? Think brother think so that we won't fall into a trap costlier than the one adverted."

Stanley is right, the people dispersed in doubt whether the mourning rite was going to hold or not? "There was instant happiness in the cell as the detainees saw me." Alfred said. Alfred! Alfred! They called, as if the name was running away from them she narrated. "Uncle Eddy was sober; he did not touch the food, instead he invited the boys to eat with him the whole lot, even with constant plea with him to eat first he declined." "We're all in this together" was his response. The agony of being in a confine place, made him resolute on humility. "If you are mistakenly locked up in a room alone you will appreciate what psychological torture he most gone through. Teddy said. Brother Teddy considering the environment I know he won't want to eat. She continued. Uncle Eddy was deep in thought as we left the cell. "You talk too much." No Uncle Alfred, not just because I was in the mood to talk but to correct an impression. A man when aggrieved has a lot to contend with, outwardly he is seen to be sober but his mind is on a constant race.

So what are we going to do to affect his release? Teddy asked. "This Alhaji guy Promised releasing him from the cell, is that going to be possible without cash?" Teddy asked. How! Is he related to the president? I don't think so; Alfred replied. Any way what ever he spends will be remitted back to him as soon as Eddy comes out. Nevertheless we'll not solely depend on that; should he fail, the man wants to get his ass out of the dingy cell before he gets an attack. Teddy, the man is in a bad state; he showed me were he was wounded as he was hauled into the cell. Man those hired assassins don't have heart the Jackboot did not touch him it was the civilians in Jackboot uniform" Mourners in Jackboot uniform" that dealt with him. You mean those millipedes Jackboot? You've not witness where these set of cowardly Jackboot exhibits that bad attitude (B.A) of theirs. Alfred said. Nairegin Jackboot needs overhauling in that an officer caught in the act of insubordination or lawlessness would be treated like a common criminal. That will not work in present Nairegin unless we have a transferred Ednut Nobgaidi's reign. Oh! Blessed memory that was a good man; a man who single-handedly humiliated the British government Teddy said. My bosom friend once told me, "it is safer to palely with a common criminal than to palely with a Jackboot officer." That is to tell you the concept of most Nairegin about Nairegin Jackboot force. Teddy said

Fela an Afro legend in one of his sound track pointed out that your worst enemy could be your best friend and your best friend your worst enemy. While! Some will hate you pretending they love you. The song in full he was referring to the Jackboot force but most people never understood the Afro beat legend. Both laughs! I guess you all know the truth for it shall surely set you free. Alfred contributed.

"Can we check on Barrister Aike? I think he leaves somewhere around; he knows his way with the Jackboot Alfred said. Don't you think these Barristers who connive with the Jackboot should be punished in the same manner, Teddy said. They're supposed to be accomplice or what do you think? If the system can allow good work, most people will go down for crime is perpetuated more by group of people than only one person being involved. You know why? One man cannot easily cover his track but when they are more there is teamwork and understanding. "I disagree with you in principle but practically we have to contact someone." Alfred said. Why not we see the officers ourselves and hear directly from them instead of contacting someone who will connive with the cheat to get at us since we are desperate. Teddy suggested. As for me Teddy said I would have advised your uncle to stay and remain calm for he will be released in no time.

CHAPTER SIXTEEN

At Robga popularly known as college junction, the motor park was solely empty at about 18:00hrs. Travelers from different locations waited patiently for transport vehicle to convey them to their various destinations. An indefinite wait all from the blue, a Toyota car pulled over and the passengers filtered round the vehicle as the driver announced. Ukuraibo/ Akarba the back seat was all of a sudden engaged in a combat battle who and whom to enter first. Teddy studied the struggling lots and moved over to the front sit. On arrival a young man was already ahead of him. He took to the next sit by him. As he sat down awaiting the driver to emerge an irritating looking man dressed in Jackboot officer's uniform staggered towards the door was screaming at the same time. "Come down now I tell you," he said. His stability was affected by the excessive alcohol intake; instantly he pulled Teddy along with his bag towards his position. The push was so terrible that it shocked him as he staggered almost falling to the ground.

"What's the matter with you?" Teddy reacted. 'Oh he is drunk!' Teddy said. Looking at him scornfully in total disappointment, you're a disgrace to the Nairegin Jackboot force! "Help to kill your bad image" the bus conductor said. "I'll punch you," he said. Like in a play station he positioned himself in punching posture with his leg over shooting which can easily enhance his fall. He portrayed a true picture of an untamed kid when fighting. The people rushed at him let him go some pleaded with him simply because they never wanted to get on his way.

"Please don't mind him" some pleaded with Teddy "mere looking at him he is finish," someone within the crowed said. The more the people pleaded with him his spirit rekindle to perpetuate havoc. As if calming him gingered him to further misbehave giving him impression that he had more support; it gingered him to further misbehave to every body's astonishment, he attacked a man who was calming him. He continuously coursed in Hausa language

Damburuba, yowa! Lategbatawa, kabawoni he said as someone spoke Hausa to him. "They think I'm a fake, 'you don't know I'm capable of causing uproar in this place and many people will suffer." The man an average height Hausa Fulani descendent tried to pacify him, which brought the devil off him a little. But know alcoholic act cannot be subdued by a single word of mouth, the man noticed he was hitting on a brick wall, he left unnoticed.

He staggered backed and front, "who can stop my action? No body, he shouted at the top of his voice the smell of alcohol suffocated the people; couple with the spaciousness of the location he paraded himself like an untouchable. Just as the first instance he was at the front seat as the bus rattled to a stop. "Come down!" he barked! "Old man behave; the man was not ruffled unknowing the alcoholic was dealing with a higher officer. "Behave, you old cow," he said as he produced his identity card; which did the magic. The alcoholic went to the middle seat and sat down. He was so drunk that he could not recognize Teddy at the same seat line sitting by him. He cursed intermittently. The drift in him resurfaced, as the conductor demanded his fare from him. "What do you mean" he challenged, what is your problem? He said "you've failed to remember that I'm the one to clear you from various roadblocks."

"That is the man! 'He has been disturbing the peace of this place, I doubt if he is a real Jackboot officer." "He could be a fire fighter impersonating. An observer said. It was a big relief to every body present when the 2 Jackboot officers stormed the scene; in their mist was the Samaritan. Everybody responded "take him away, he has been a pain"

"I presume you're arresting me" he said, 'please take me to were ever you wish:" he quickly embanked the bike as if in panic and the other Jackboot officer followed suit; in spite of his initial posture there was sober reflection taking place in him. "He could have been a responsible Jackboot officer, but what would a responsible Jackboot officer drink alcohol to stupor. For you to be termed responsible many of these unhealthy things are not to be identified with. Teddy explained to the listening passengers.

He was informed of the community's meeting, knowing he hadn't taken his bath he pleaded with the guy to give him some time. He undressed into a round neck t-shirt, that could be termed brown if not for the crested brown setup. The shirt made the red boxers to be permanently invincible except when raised. In a short while he was by the public waterside tap system, installed to serve the dense populated area of the town portable drinking water. The tap was over crowded, empty buckets of water were arranged in a single file indicating the duration of water supply problem. "I'll have to appeal to Ester," he said to himself as he approached the well-guided area. "Ester please let me fetch just a bucket," she prevented him from putting the bucket; he could not believe it, "I have an important outing to make he explained. She ignored him insinuating the attitude of the women folks in the town. As he bent to transfer water from a close-by bucket he was whack, it infuriated him but he kept his calm, she did not stop there as if propelled by a pessimistic guiding spirit she rushed him slighting his manhood. She confidently nodded him in turn stimulating his head master's head; which has been dormant ever since Ben fainted after inviting a head bout from him. "Ben a heavily built adult of 20 years old has the look of a full-grown man as a result of over feeding and weight lifting habit, which enhanced his muscles and broad shoulders growth. His stunt nature revealed his size in height was badly retarded as an early indulgence in immoral practice. The inflow of young Phyllis girls around him is attributed to his mum's supermarket opened to their doorstop.

On a Monday morning before the normal morning devotion, Tom was busy reading a Novel when Ben strolled into the class and collected the Novel, before Tom could alter a word Ben was unto him. The girls around pleaded, "calm down" they all begged though in total support of him." All he wanted was to humiliate Tom badly, that he failed to listed to his close associates as they pulled his hand off Toms shirt; he balanced himself, Tom was turning to leave when he dashed at him with a flying kick on reaching Tom's position changed to a head bout. Blood gushed out of his nostril and spilled all over the place. "My God" the girls shouted in disbelieve. "What happened" Nicole asked, "please let's take him to the hospital?" they all shouted in unison.

The splashed of blood aroused the bystanders who rushed to the scene, his only lock was that they witnessed the whole dramatic episode.

The passengers were all seated in the bus as if nothing happed. “This is my position,” Anslem said. “But I did not meet any body here nor did I see sign of your presence.” Jones replied. You will not understand he smiled we were here, but we had to settle a row that could have bared us from traveling; the protocol officer said, if not you would not have met this bus. “My friend if you want to seat, I can shift for you not the lady.” Anslem said angrily. Maybe you don’t want to travel, an agbero (a motor park worker) who supported the protocol officer said. The man challenged! “If you say that it means you don’t travel.” Anslem barked. Teddy intruded, “please lets not create another scene here, lady for peace sake please go to the back seat; when you get to Irraw you can reunite with your guy.” She complied without putting up a fight showing the level of her maturity.

“Take note as you are all seated the fare to Ukuraibo is #150, while Irraw is #200.00,” the passengers responded by paying without any fuse.

Teddy studied the girl by his side, he memorized his key words but the girl beat him to it. “I don’t know why it is always very difficult to get a vehicle at this junction, once its past 18:00hrs.” She enquired. “Had I known it would be this tedious, ‘I would have slept at Abasa” “When did you leave Abasa?” Teddy asked. “17:00hrs” she replied. “That means I left before you.”

“My business at Abasa was just to see a cousin, he persuaded me to pass the night at his residence but I declined.” Teddy said. Once it gets dark, after 18:00hrs your chance of getting a vehicle is by a stroke of lock. Funny situation I had to sleep in an hotel on two occasion; to tell you how awful it might be “I entered a pickup van on a different occasion, we did not get home until 23:00hrs.” imagine myself sitting at the open back of a pick up van and it wanted to rain, I kept on praying till I got to my destination. How relieved I was in the shelter of my roof;

there and then I made up my mind against night traveling; alternatively I rather sleep in a hotel.

"You guys are full of guts I can't imagine myself taking such risk. She was so beautiful that Teddy did not have a stop for the discussion. "What is your name, I'm Teddy; since it is easier for someone to tell his or her name when yours is known." They were busy exchanging addresses while the conversation took a different tone, as they proceeded Teddy was not aware when they reached Ukuraibo, had the driver not informed them he would have seen himself at Irraw. She was sad as he informed her he was going to stop. "We have got to know ourselves better," Teddy said as the driver slowed to a stop. She brought her face close to Teddy's, as if to have a word with him passed on a good night kiss. Teddy could not resist the temptation for it came faster than he anticipated. "Whoa!" that is a French kiss," Dennis pointed out to his fiancés.

Teddy disembarked from the bus and said goodnight to the watching crew. The whole street was flooded, at the entrance Teddy had to stroll to the next street unfortunately the same state he met the previous one. (All water logged.) He waited for a while, was sort of in a confused state. The light from an incoming bike revealed a small portion of the road uncovered by water he premeditated properly, he moved into the street. "What a street." He thought as he preceded down the street it dawned on him he was in for hassle. The street obviously being water log was littered with all sort of debris from various people's refuse dumps, as ever the road was in a deplorable condition. Teddy automatically became a triple jump specialist; he stepped one, two, three, constantly before jumping the pools of water, carefully avoiding the water splash. Getting to an end he considered going back but the closeness to his house propelled him forward. He was so fagged out there was no time for a rethink. He took the first step in a probe of conscience but moved on at the middle of the footpath. He could not really tell but was almost on the floor, if not for the support he got by holding on to the wall; learning closely on his support he almost had a change of heart based on the slippery nature of the corner he knew he could not continue the Herculean task of crawling down the path; if the fence was not close by, he scaled through the fence into the compound. Once inside he was so happy getting home, he walked through the orange tree till he was on the main path that revealed his house door.

"The man died! Was it sheer carelessness or ignorant. Anslem thought as young men gathered to deliberate on the impact of the incidence on the town. "Please this is no time for whose property was destroyed," the speaker said. The most important today is that our whole community was not erased like Udi Asleyab state; where the government ordered the indiscriminate shooting of civilians rendering the town a no go zone.

Serially we are going to pick upon the agenda of this meeting, first in our list is a petition to the state governor, describing the incidence while there will be a reminder to the state house of Assembly since the matter is right on their desk. Further more we are going to solicit for the state governments assistant to enable the victims move on. In like manner we are going to send a copy of our petition to the State and National Assembly and to the presidency. We are going to fix a date for general mourning of the dead heroes; this will be done after seeking permission from the state Jackboot commissioner.

CHAPTER SEVENTEEN

"Papa?" her voice was tremulous "what are you doing at this time of the day?" "I just wanted to make sure brother is all right; now that uncle is gone we have to plan for his children." "Yes the children, it is always very light to pronounce but the bottom line is caring period. Right now everybody seems to interestingly want to do one thing or the other, but when the wail wind blows it carries away useful soil surface of the earth. So be it after a given period, people easily will get tired or unnecessarily fed up. A simple human nature 'I presume it's an order of the day;' an absurd culture we met and as human are bound to emulate."

"In my case I will never relent. Uncle was a very good man even in death he deserves a rite to his belongings. And assistance to his offspring's, those necessities he was denied as well as deprived of in life. "Angela your opinion is simple that of a child that is hurt, maybe some day you will understand the ethics of life. Life is full of wilderness; part of it is what we felt couple of days back. In another few mouths your uncles children will be deserted not because he was not loved but to the fact of life. The dirtiness and loneliness of this world has created a vacuum for all to experience once in a lifetime. You are bound to experience as a grown up. Never mind your uncles children will be properly taken care of; the situation is handy no one is to be left out of this obligation." He said.

The Okpala-Uku's palace was very tense, an elder who informed them of the need to be law abiding addressed the youths. He berated the government for waiting this long before coming to the aid of the people. The youth leader raised his hand to speak, "go on" he was told as he stood up a Blue 406ATHA Saloon car with tinted glass. "These legislators should stop using tinted glass car; this is exactly the same as the one the rubbers used to rob the bank. Ife said; except the number plate which varies. The driver avoided the crowd and negotiated into a packing space, came down from the car and rushed to the booth and opened it. He pulled out an automatic double barrel rifle of close resemblance to a plasma double barrel hanged it on his shoulder and walked briskly into the meeting arena with his shoulder high; the people were astonish but could not voice it out; because of the highly placed position he represent in the government.

"Okpala-Uku odogwu abi asa ajaje oyeobune oyene efa ekeneyeoh!" He greeted in the native dialect without sitting he continued. "I've come to inform you lads to be law abiding because these relief material is for a particular group of people, anybody that will give me cause to, I will shot at him and the government would not do anything about the person." Till he finished speaking the whole place was so calm no single person dared to challenge him, as a result of his barrel hung the people were so scared out of cowardice. He had a swell time since he successfully intimidated them. On his way out some jobless youths called on him; "Hon settle your boys now" "look, if you come close to, I'll fire a shot at you." He warned as he approached, the people summoned courage and gathered round him. "Ha! All die Na die, let's see how many people you can kill at a go with your double barrel." Bernard gazed at him his eyes as red as a known herm smoker. "We cannot tolerate this any more!" he said. Can the barrel fire more than 10 shots at a time?" Pablo an activist asked as he regrouped with the boys.

"Fire Hon, we want to see the end this minute." They shouted being inspired by Pablo. He was perplexed; someone among the group spoke up! "Hon you're supposed to be a man of honor but this day you have proved your not, I'm ashamed of you. You simple cannot address a small group in the constituency you seem to represent. You think it's by your power that you got to Abasa, if that is your thinking then you are daydreaming. You're lucky the system is corrupt if not we should have recalled you from representing us in the state house. Clown your type is not allowed into towns meeting since you've proved to the crowed present that you're not credible enough to represent us, well your case is pending hearing." "Or do you think you're the first or the last honorable member?" Kinsley asked. Mind you the people before you were more humble and did better than you seem to have done. Had it been you're representing us at Abuja by now you would have grown wings. Which means no body can reach you. "Be informed that you are a disappointment to the Inauwku race." Mike alerted his reasoning the man was very sober he pleaded with the young men and promised to change his behavioral altitude, the people for the fact that they were tired of being with him accepted his apology and allowed him to go.

The group leader addressed the crowed. He said. "The leaders of today are like the kings that ruled Israel long time back; who rebelled simple because they wanted to be king and at the end of the day got ruined because they didn't have wisdom and never wanted to correct their advent mistake which grows in them like a tumor."

CHAPTER EIGHTEEN

The deputy senate president walked into the senate chamber, all eyes were on him to preside since the president was not in town. He took to his seat and immediately read the prayers.

Next he announced the vote and proceeding, "I have examined and approved the votes and proceedings of Tuesday, 5th march, 2002. By unanimous consent, the votes and proceedings were adopted as amended by the senators present. Senator Paul Osanebi of Atled north senatorial district was permitted to speak. "This is a matter of urgent public importance," he said.

Pursuant to rules 52 and 42 of the standing rules of the senate I want to sought and obtained leave of the senate to inform you of the unwarranted destruction of property and killing of 15 youths at Ukuraibo Inauwku local government headquarters in Atled state by men of the Nairegin Jackboot force. "The primary responsibility of the Nairegin Jackboot force is protecting lives and property" Instead, they turned their guns on those they are to protect. For the past year Ukuraibo town had been under siege by armed robbers, who claimed the lives of about four persons between 13th October 2000 and 19th December 2001. On the 5th of April 2000 till date Ukuraibo has witnessed more than 19 robbery cases. "Let me state clearly that as a result of the Jackboot negligence, the youths of the town had no choice but to burn down the Jackboot station, having seen the Jackboot failed in it's responsibility. And the Jackboot instead of restoring peace in the neighborhood turned against its citizen. This led to the brutal killing by the Jackboot force.

The Jackboot did not stop there; they continued the act the following day. As a result, the town was deserted for three days. The inhabitants returned after the state government had guaranteed assurances of their safety. "I therefore moved: that the senate committee on Jackboot affairs and an ad-hoc committee to investigate The reason(s) for the killings of 15 people in Ukuraibo by the Jackboot; The reasons why the Nairegin Jackboot despite so many reports of robberies and killings in Ukuraibo had never responded nor made any investigation or arrest of the culprits. The extent of damage to the Jackboot station and local government headquarters; and The extent of damage to lives and property by men of the Nairegin Jackboot

The motion was seconded by Senator Edaoya Ino from Itike central and the Senate held forth for a while, senator Osanibe revelation stunned the senators. Senator Taiwo Odua from Igok west put forth the amended proposal of deleting (ii), (iii) and (IV).

Amendment put and agreed to main question as amended put to resolved: That the senates do mandate the committee on Jackboot affairs and an ad- hoc committee members formed to investigate the reason(s) for killing in Ukuraibo by the Nairegin Jackboot force. Matter of privilege: the place of the legislature in the present democratic dispensation is an issue to reckon with. Pursuant to 14 of the senate standing rules, senator Eki Clement of

Aiba north sought and obtained leave of the senate. He moved that the senate do resolve into an executive session to deliberate on the place of the legislature in the present democratic dispensation.

Senator Xela Iridak from Igok east seconded the motion. Question put and the senators agreed to resolve that the senates do resolve into an Executive session to deliberate on the place of the legislature in the present democratic dispensation.

The senate chamber was arisen once more as the members returned. In reporting the progress, the president stated that in the Executive session the senate deliberated on matter relating to the place of legislatures in the present democratic dispensation. Senator Danla Ofan S. Adifat from Anudak north moved that the senate do now adjourn till Thursday, 7th march 2002 at 14.00hrs. Senator Ayo Fajikpe from Nugo west seconded the motion. Question were put and agreed to resolve: that the senate do now adjourn till Thursday, 7th 2002, at 14:.00hrs.

The senate adjourned accordingly at 17.05hrs with the votes and proceeding signed by the deputy senate president Miharbi Uisan Utnam. On the 17th of March 2002, the senate of the federal republic of Nairegin passed a resolution mandating the senate committee on Jackboot affairs to visit Ukuraibo in neighboring suburb in Atled state. "Be informed this assignment is to investigate the alleged cases of death of 15 youths; the burning of the Jackboot station in the town of Ukuraibo; and to determine the remote and proximate causes of the above named incidents.

After serious deliberation on the assigned duties by the senate, the committee constituted a 4-men panel to visit Atled state from the 2nd to the 4th of April, 2002.Members of the panel is Senator V.K Ayetayo, Chairman, while other members are Senator Mary Umo, Senator Nakel Nugolan and Senator Demahom Ierig. Barrister F. Unosego was to serve as Secretary for proper documentation.

The Senators commenced their visitation to Atled state on the 2nd of April 2002 but Senators Nakel Nugolan and Demahom Ierig were absent with apologies. The team headed straight to Atled State Jackboot headquarters, Abasa. The state Jackboot commissioner, Mr.Nhoj Udemha who later led them to Government House, received them.

At the Government House, the Deputy Governor who acted on behalf of the state Governor, Prof Irobi, received them. In a closed door meeting with the Deputy Governor, the team briefed him of the reason for the state visit. "I want to thank you sincerely on behalf of the executive governor in whom I express the support and assurance of the Atled State government. I promise that the state will assist you in every possible way in the course of your investigation".

The senators as early as 06:00hrs were all awake and at exactly 8.00am on the 3rd of April 2002,they departed Abasa for Ukuraibo. The convoy reached Robga at 09:00hrs. "We have barely 30minutes to go" the chairman's driver informed him. They arrived Ukuraibo early and proceeded to the local government council secretariat, headquarters of Inawuku local government area.

Members of the community crowded the council secretariat awaiting their arrival. Also present was the council chairman and the councilors who received the team without decorum they led them round the building for them to see the extent of damage done during the crisis. The team noted the damage and proceeded to the 'Okpalauku's palace' the chiefs, men and women of the community received the team. The tradition was observed, while kola-nuts were presented to the team.

Senator V. K Ayetayo, chairman senate committee on Jackboot Affairs, stood up and spoke on behalf of his team. "We represent the senate of the federal republic of

Nairegin, on behalf of the senate president we register our presence. 'The news of the crisis in Ukuraibo was brought before the senate by Senator Paul Osanibe, the senator representing Atled North Senatorial District' he added 'and consequently, the senate resolved and mandated this committee to investigate and report back'. We have come to you to know the remote and proximate cause of the crisis and possible recommendations.' he stated.

Thank you Mr. Chairman, if we are to go by your cohesive speech we would have gone back without further investigation but for we to carry out our duty from all forms of bias with due diligence precision and without fear nor favor we will want to proceed to inspect the Jackboot station.

The community spokesman thanked the committee chairman assuring him of their compliance as requested. "Once more sir safe journey"

The team then proceeded to inspect the Jackboot station; from there they visited the outgoing DJO, Mr. Imuweda; wanting to get all information from the Jackboot. "What transpired? We find it heart throbbing to see this community under your care in such a mess. Sir we, we what! No point for any explanation come to Abasa and defends yourself. The Senate committee chairman said. They left for Akarba Jackboot station. At the Jackboot station they had a close look at the Peugeot 406 saloon car used for the 17th Feb., 2002 armed robbery operation at Fedson bank. Timing was a factor, which accelerated their visit. They departed Akarba for Abasa at 13:30hrs arriving Abasa in 2hours time. The hearing commenced at Harmony Hall, State House, Abasa 1hr 30minutes after arriving Abasa.

The team requested Jackboot officer's testimony: toping the chart is Nhoj Udamha who was the current commissioner of Jackboot, Atled State. CPS Imuweda the outgoing DJO, Ukuraibo spoke on behalf of himself and the

Jackboot command; followed by ASP Eledalo, Divisional traffic officer Ukuraibo, Inspector Fred Ogoma, Niregin Jackboot force Ukuraibo, Sergent Amozu Obgno, Niregin Jackboot force Ukuraibo, W/PC Akapku Idudn, Niregin Jackboot force Ukuraibo and Inspector Abanrab Mayn, Niregin Jackboot force Ukuraibo.

The committee chairman requested the outgoing DJO to come out for second briefing. "What would you attribute as the cause of the continuous robbery in your neighborhood?"

Sir the Jackboot force is doing its best but our best is short lived simply because in most cases when information gets to us about robbery we don't have immediate facility to curb the situation.

What is your relationship with the local government chairman and the elder's council? The CSP took in a breath of air 'sir' he started fidgeting "calm down" the chairman told him, the hall greeted him with wooing sound, he suddenly stopped. "That is enough," the chairman said.

After serious deliberation the committee members resolved to call it a day until the 4th of April 2002.

On the 4th of April the team of senators resumed hearing in the morning starting with Engr. Ekure a prominent son of Ukuraibo and former member PCRC Ukuraibo who happened to be detained at Akarba Jackboot station when he went to sympathize with the DJO a visit over his burnt property. Ogbuefi Nosirrah Edeja a 1st member District customary court, Iama, Inauwku local government Area and former secretary local Education Authority gave his testimony. Followed by chief Song Mahso, member Ukuraibo Traditional Council, Prof Evets Ahaceeko, lecturer, Benard Emukulo, Evangelist Iasso Heba, chairman Ukuraibo crisus management, Mr. Akuza Ekimise Frank, Mrs. Ese Odogolo, Mrs. Esther Ekezue, Neeuq Urepko, Mr.

Emuje, Mr. Wilson Elamone, Patience and I Felix, a 4 year old boy all natives of Ukuraibo community.

Ogbuefi Enext Uche, chairman Inauku LGA and Joshua Emeune, commissioner for commence and industry Atled state testified on individual ground.

The committee was able to assemble the particulars of those killed as a result of the day break massacre while the names of persons injured and hospitalized were compiled the total number of the injured. In all the injured and hospitalized are 166 names while those killed is 15 names.

The Jackboot commissioner was busy issuing a communiqué against the signal tagged. "Ukuraibo youths instigated into mourning: an intended uprising." "Dandy" he called dispatch a truck of Jackboot men to Ukuraibo immediately and stop over at Utumu base to inform the DJO. Ensure there is nothing like nor near to mourning in the town; be it good intention or not, the crisis that have rocked that town is more than enough for us to contend with. Arrest some of the youths that will at least put them under tension.

Yes sir!

To further convince the people of his innocence he mobilized his closed associates, all in a single file. He held a life cock "an Agric fowl" in his right hand. Dangling in rags behind him were teams of traditional medicine men who looked horrible enough to scare a foreigner; all armed were some mobile Jackboot officers serving as backup protectors. Should the community decide to attack? He shouted! "If I'm responsible for the killing of the people that died, let me not see peace nor happiness in all my endeavor." Amid the tension his countenance was betraying him the more he reflected an angry man not a man being remorse. He repeated this continuously until he trekked from one post of the town to another. The people stared in complete amazement. "Look whom does he thinks he is fooling." Bernard said. "Let him go and bring a native fowl "orkpa" then we will know he means business. As far as I'm concern he is a daydreamer."

Chike, "does he think these Jackboot men can protect him if he is doomed?" Please leave him to his faith. "Stanley"

"I advice you guys to go think of better things to talk or do, not this jester, who is parading himself a responsible but an irresponsible man." Such men are supposed to be banished from the community.

"It begins to prick me the consequence of civilization that a man can no longer be punished for atrocities against his relatives. Jorum said. Whom do you blame! A country where the judiciary is not functional whom is supposed to act as check is suppressed into nothing. Chike replied.

On receiving the order he called the Jackboot commander. Dispatch your men at once was his last word. The Jackboot commander briefed his men and without delay they embarked the already stationed truck. The driver an elderly Jackboot officer looked through the mirror to confirm the last Jackboot officer has embarked; he engaged gear, reversed and was on his way. He was very careful since there was no alarm signal in his vehicle. He drove to Asubi junction made it through Asubi/ Ogwashi-Uku to Edenumu road; the road being a very narrow road most transporters prefer the root cause it retains its construction standard, compared to the double lane work going on in the country. Notwithstanding the traffic the road is not dented unlike the Nsukwa axis, which has many potholes.

Manila did not wait until he got home, "Brother John, he narrated all he heard at the Jackboot headquarters. Tell your friends! I was right there when the Jackboot truck left the headquarters." The news circulated faster than a red light sensor. "Jackboot are coming on a phase II attack." the whole community called their lads and the youth leader passed a stay off the road order.

Lets stop at Utumu, the commander said: The driver turned right entering Utumu town. The commander walked into the station, "Is the DJO in the office?" he enquired from copra. Good afternoon sir he said on entering the DPO's office. "We are detailed by the commissioner sir to arrest a few scapegoats at Ukuraibo." Listen commander! I'II not entertain any more of this. If the commissioner wants to handle Ukuraibo affairs himself let him go ahead but my hand is of it. Go ahead to arrest," if you like "I assure you the town is peaceful, such arrest is not necessary." Nor does the people warrant any form of intimidation from any sector. His speech did have an impact on the Jackboot leader.

He entered the meeting; his countenance was low simple to the accusation by the community elders of masterminding a shearing formula without seeking their concept. "I've come to clear certain matter arising from the good I did by influencing the relief materials, which has turned bad." he said. What is he talking about? An elderly man voiced out. Look! Young man don't come to insult us here, if you've any information pass it on or you had better take a hike out of here. We have a serious business at hand.

The man in a confuse state said. "But I've not insulted any body? What I'm trying to put across is as simple as it is. The relief materials brought were sent to this land because of my effort and as the representative of the people to government the format for shearing is spelt out as follows." Some angry youths were on him before he could analyze the shearing formula. An out bust, which pave way for disgruntled youth members; who sees him as a complete minus in the event of things. He was out of his seat as the youths advanced towards him, the speed he applied to enter his car is equal to a lightening flash. His assailants were perturbed. "I told you to position near his car" the youth leader complained. "Look at what you've caused. The man escaped because every body wants to command they quarried among themselves.

"Can you imagine that opportunists think he can come and insult us in our territory? No way. Who does he think he is representing? If not his personal pocket and that of his immediate family members, Salem voiced out in pains.

A man in his capacity that is meant to be an obedient servant has turned a tyrant in the face of his people. Uche reminded them. "He thinks he can dictate for every body. No way! They all echoed we sent him to serve but he has forgotten. How will he remember when he has usurped all the contracts that are meant for Inauwku citizens? Ed, you have said it all. The Umukwata, Opkoize, Iama, Emugo and Ebede Umuoegeogoli Electrification projects where all half completed by him. You mean all these jobs were awarded to our house of assembly member? Why! You can't blame him all his counterparts are doing it. You can see the basic deference between the second republic legislators, and these hoodlums of opportunist, we have as lawmakers, in our nascent democracy. Stanley said. Forget nascent Salem said showing his annoyance.

Personally I don't know why we deceive ourselves, about all this big names. What is nascent in our democracy? When we have in it infested by the same old brigades." old wine in new wine skin " I disagree with you on that wise the UPN legislators that I know of are still representing the late sage "late chief Obafami Awolowo's" doctrines of an egalitarian society. Which have distinguished them from the old wine in new wine skin; most insinuating is that these minus in the political enthronement want to go back. Frank, I foresee were they will be compelled to kill the *whole* masses to be re-elected, because we shall resist them to the fullest. Wilson is it fair? With the inconsistency over the voter's registrar and the national identity card programmed. Election cannot be free and fair in this country unless the masses are truly ready for a change. Why? Poverty as a check to our mind check, we can be bought over with ease.

Order! The spoke man said, "We must continue our meeting now that he has left us unceremoniously. It is still all good, since we did not invite him. Brethrens as we have agreed earlier since we don't have powers over our elders and leaders as such the Onotu-Uku of all the quarters are in charge of the shearing. They will appoint youths who will assist them to do a good job." As he faced the chief for contribution they all nodded for the concurring chiefs were more in number compared to the outspoken ones in the traditional council. There was a brief delay in the meeting process, while a sheet of paper was passed round for assent of individual signatories.

"Okpala-Uku" they all greeted, he came in as the signing process was going on. A skinny old man with gray hair as the only remaining part of his feature; showing that he has seen more days than the one left. He is the recognized oldest man in the community. Before his arrival the meeting was presided by the number two man, "an Orkwa" the resolution that was drafted by his traditional council was passed to him for second approval. "Okpala Uku" he greeted, "we the entire house rejected the shearing formula Presented by the single individual as agreed." He nodded his head in acceptance and waved his right hand, which shows he was fully in support.

Where is he? He enquired "I've always wanted to tell that small boy not to come and insult us again. If not he will be bound from coming to Ukuraibo town." Go on with the shearing he said as he rose from the chair but was supported by an aid. Immediately he left the place the "oga" pourer resumed with the pouring of drinks, customs demands the youngest man is made to serve drinks in gathering.

"Go and do the announcement, the community spokes man said to the town crier. Intimate the people of the day of shearing the relief materials; they should all be present at the council secretariat at exactly 09:00hr." The town crier fastened his gung and make shift gung stick. Those who were still descending on the illicit dry gin heard him first at the meeting spot. A serious minded person with a crude orientation once receives money for an announcement he does not want a change in the order for his wild held belief is a crime to request for any money let out for a job. While on the part of the receiver, he does not spend unless he has reached his home as demanded by the ancestors, so that blessing will always comes his way.

Every body both old and young gathered at the council secretariat the chief in charge of the shearing were busy conversing, one of them came out to address the crowd. Please you have to be calm, we would not waste your time more than required. It's just a minor problem we are bound to overcome in a short while; bear with us it has to do with tabulations and sorting out of names.

CHAPTER NINTEEN

"Listen carefully on the arrangements," the chief said. "First on our list here is case of death, second is case of injury, third is case of looting and plunder fourth is case of arrest and looting while fifth is case of arrest only.

The first person was called; a family representative went in since its case of death. Bags of Garri, Rice, bundles of cloths were handed to the man. "Thank you sir," he said. With the assistants of some youth members he was able to convey the item outside. "Next," the chief called as the persons name was mentioned. The representative was provided with the same items as the first person. Until the last name on the fist case was attended to. The chief immediately called in the first person on the second case. He reduced the quantity of items compared to the first case. The first group was very sober unlike the second group which began to have instigated confrontation from the victims who see relief material as a means of uplifting them from their poor standard of leaving within a short sphere, unknowing that silver and gold is gotten as a result of hard work. Not by gift from a sector of the government that is meant for the whole community.

"Listen all, you'll have to bear with us, and every body cannot have the same quantity. In my list is case of plundering and looting. He called in the first person the items were handed to him. Most of the youth's members among the last group were not happy with the shearing techniques applied by the chief, they mumbled among themselves. The youths instigated by a few outcast came to the chiefs "sir for a job well done we want to get our share of the items;" not today the chief responded.

Gradually pressure was mounting as the youth were quarreling among themselves. The Jackboot men reasoned the chief walked up to the Jackboot "please help us to disperse the crowd." They pleaded. "Lets go, he spoke to another committee member." As the Jackboot men were leading the chiefs, the whole items were subjected to eye screening. Mere seeing the people portrays an urge yet accomplished; they eyed the items as people who have not seen foodstuff in their life. The bales of wrappers "cloths" available in different fold like a fold mountain, an overzealous nurtured notorious spirit awaked in them as if by remote controlled both old, young girls and boys invaded the items in one accord, simultaneously an humiliating sight; like leveling up in the dining hall "were boarding house students exhibit greed." In most cases the students are forced into leveling up after waiting a long time for the dining hall to be opened, the delay and hunger stimulates the greed in them. The food is invaded and it's so bad that the only lucky ones get enough food to eat.

Unlike leveling up in schools the items were not paid for but leveled up food were paid for by the students, which make it free from stealing, thereby exposing them to stealing process, an unfortunate act that can ruin a people.

The uproar that follows the rush made the Jackboot to turn, they responded by firing at the sky to disperse the crowd; a more sensible approach the people abandoned the items and ran for safety.

Mathew covered is face with his palm on seeing the Jackboot response. "I'm disappointed in this community! A Jackboot officer said. "Don't be, the set you see in this place are not responsible, if you go back to the town you will see that the responsible ones are in their various houses minding their business." a council staff said.

The whole items were gathered and returned to its position for safe keeping. "You were such in a hurry, why didn't you heed when he asked you to wait. I heard you, medicine after death. The people gathered in a near by store quarreling and apportioning blame on each other.

"You should have waited; you think these people can shot? Keep deceiving yourself; maybe you don't know the difference between stealing and demonstrating. Dennis is right; if a thief cannot be apprehended without force whatever he gets is his own look out or is not the concern of the state.

"I tell you keep of from the bad attitude of yours!" A council staff was reproaching his kid brother. "Turn and let me see your back as I'm watching at you, he said. The boy reluctantly left in the direction of the town. Gradually the crowd gave way to a more refine council workforce, paving way for effective working environment.

Teddy was embarrassed, he stood were he was standing. What do you mean? He asked. Whom do you want to see again and the office you are going to? The security man asked. I want to see my brother he responded. Which office? The man asked. Teddy was offended by his approach already; he told him that he knows the office and walked away.

The officers rushed to his boss, they sprinted to the office. The head of security wants to see you, one of them said. Teddy took leave of his friend to see the security boss. Don't be offended the way my boys spoke to you, he pleaded.

What did he say? Teddy's friend asked as he came back. Normal apology, he said. Where is the bags of cement going to from here he asked? Didn't you see the truck outside? Patrick asked. The cements is been sold, the money we learnt would be sheared among the victims. Why? Teddy exclaimed, "Is the cement not meant for the town's hall project?"

"Do you mind the people?" "Hedonism has taken control of their reasoning." "I can remember vividly how this community problem started, a flash back to historical lane." The disgruntled elders in 1983 moved a motion to de throne the then Onotu-uku general because of tenement rate, which the government imposed on the people. A taboo in the history of Ukuraibo kingship, though they did not succeed but the trace linger that necessitated disloyalty. Moreover when a particular clan in the community had problem of disintegration others pretended not to be aware of the crisis imminent until there was complete division that separated the clan into two different parts. Similar incident occurred in another clan, other clans folded their hands and watched the outcome, this time it degenerated into family fight that landed some of them in detention."

Teddy where did you get your gist? Patrick said, as he was laughing. To be honest, an agreement was reached by the community leaders to use the cement and zinc in the town halls building project, but due to greed from some sectors that intends to make some fast buck from the sales. They forget that ill-gotten wealth does not last coupled with problems that precede it.

"I wonder why the victims are dictating for the leaders, when the sole responsibility of running the community lies on the leaders." Teddy said. "Don't be fooled, all you see is photo tricks; they are been sponsored by some few chiefs." "Teddy quickened his step to meet Bob, Bob he called, as he wanted to cross the road. Where are you coming from? Teddy asked Palely, I've just attended a community meeting. The onotu-uku was asked to defend an allegation that he was seen conveying relief material from the council. Trust his defense he said he could not steal from a distress people. All he did was a humanitarian job by assisting the needy; those who could not afford the bill to hire a van. On listening to his defense, which is self-explicit he was cleared until the panels report is out.

"What happened to the contribution made on behalf of our brethrens abroad?" "Well I'm not too sure of the source of the information. But some says the money cannot be rightly accounted for." "Didn't I tell you this community is in shame, it needs redemption?" Teddy said. "I presume these are the set of people that what to be local government chairman?"

"That substance is stale, the latest is that this same highly influential people have devised a means of obtaining from the less privilege to release their children from detention." How did you get your fact? Ask Nathaniel whom his brother was a victim. "No body should expect good representation from a lousy government that does not have check. The time will come when these leaders would be made to pay some reparation to its subjects." Why! Are they not rulers? Can you call a man who stole from his community a leader? They are very bad rulers. A time will come for sure everybody will surely give account for his stewardship. Good day Teddy said and moved on.

CHAPTER TWENTY

He got to the meeting past 18:00hr the crowd that greeted him confirms his stipulations. "I cannot take this sheet any longer" he told himself. "What has gone into your brains? He barked at the people. Do you realize this is blood gift? Any body within Uzuko who partakes in this unrealistic sharing considers himself destined for wraths that will follow. Uncleanness is the beginning of a man's doom, when it happens he has to bear his cross himself.

"I came to this town to see our loved ones in pains, simple because of negligence of our state functionaries. To aggravate our situation the federal government decided to pacify the afflicted, which is not good enough but we are all in a hurry to receive worthless relief materials. Can money buy back our dead? You have all heard me I've spoken; it's left for you to consider it or not." The dense crowd murmuring started dispersing; the certain which resemble the market in full section became scanty.

"Mike is right" John said. "We're all acting as if a remote control is working on us all." Different groups were going home which metamorphosis into a moving debate.

Come of it Peter said. Excuse me! "Don't you know the elders are helpless simple to the fact that they are suffering from abject poverty? You know what that means. You'll be vulnerable to all kinds of bribe." Nothing is too small. "Men, the reformation we need has to come weather we are in support or not." John said. "That would work only when greed is eradicated from our traditional council."

Johnny stared at the crowd in disbelief "so there was a large turn out" he shifted base. Adams he called! Where have you been Johnny? We're just from youth's meeting. Who was the convener? Johnny asked. Mike of course, guess what? He sent a chilling message down every body's spine, within a twinkle of an eye the rowdy meeting arena became like a graveyard.

In an attempt to bust his political career he met with a few government official concerning the propose governors visitation. "Don't you think we'll rate higher if we present the governor with a chieftaincy title?" He asked. "I should have thought in that direction, but come to think of it 'if we're presenting the governor, the deputy can't be left out except you want a rift in the cabinet." "That is not a bad deal; it will be arranged, my people beliefs in me." "That guy always has genuine intention, what went wrong this time?"

"Oh no you're getting me wrong Johnny; his address was based on our representation in the sharing programmed. He was against our partaking because it was not necessary. Let me use his word "can money buy back our loved ones? No! We all knew the answer as such we left in ignominy."

Adams felt pains instantly as his mind drifted to the little boy killed by a stray bullet." When he came back to himself he said. The manner at which young men are representing this community calls for questioning. "I presume we are all living in a lawless nation, where any lawful person is an enemy of the masses. How on earth after the irresponsible killing of our brethrens the government's new target is to instigate the people against themselves. Making the people succumb to guided tricks; you youths are the sole cause of our problem in this town,' simple because, you want to deceive the people into believing white to be black because of immediate gratification; thereby presuming to be blind. "Mark it; pretence can never redeem a society. Instead it goes a long way of destroying the ethnicity."Can you imagine? Ethnic love among our people is being rubbished because of half-life gift from government. Charley voiced out.

"Please do me a favor; Christian requested. I learnt the governor's visit is scheduled to be twice?" You're right. Okay he will use the first visit to consolidate, and then we move in with the title in the second. boy! What a smart card, the people will be taken on aware.

Teddy arrived very early from a trip, he was egger to see his associates, a mapped out culture not necessarily fun fare but money sapping venture. "Who apart from your close friends is interested in welcoming you to his table? When you're not holding onto a gift as far as Nairegin politics is concern. In the town, Teddy walked down Ekidumu Street, he diverted into a footpath cutting off the pool of water in front of a fenced compound. Suddenly some people started drifting towards his direction, standing in his front are two mobile Jackboot officers manhandling a young man

"Take him to the base," another officer said. The boy was pulled along the street. Teddy asked to know the boys offence from the people present but most of them seems not to know what was his offence. He trailed along until they got to the main road on the old road. The boy was commandeered to join a motorbike. Teddy in want of what to do haled another motorbike and followed in the same direction. Teddy! Mathew called." Where is this all going to lead us to?" he was pointing at the mobile Jackboot officers on the bike. Who do you blame? Teddy asked. "Since you've refused to indicate your interest we're not happy with you."

Mathew said. Teddy explained his predicament: "not that I don't want to, but I have to organize myself cash wise. They charted about old school days and the feature. "I have to go" Teddy said on remembering his new assignment.

Teddy was in hurry to reach Uzuko guesthouse, currently used as the Jackboot base. Unfortunately the Jackboot men had completed their task on the young man; his face was covered in blood, he was bleeding from bruises sustained from the encounter. Teddy rushed to meet him, what happened? "My offense is that I beat up my girl friend." The only way her parents felt to resolve our difference was to use the Jackboot officers to intimidate me. I've lost #2.500 to the Jackboot team to enhance my release. He further explained that his action couldn't be altered. "Imagine my girl friend that I intend to pay her bride price by the end of this year was cut in the act of promiscuity. When I questioned her, she had the effrontery to tell me to mind my business. Don't you think she is feed up with you?" Teddy asked. "No way! She was with me last night;" "What would you expect? I was furious." They were interrupted by clement. "Hon the quest for peace is eluding our village, what can we do?" A young man was arrested yesterday simple because he refused to marry a girl who's well known as the public wife. Her people connived with the Jackboot to instill fear in him to write a written document agreeing to marry her. He was made to pay the sum of #3.000 to the Jackboot. "Has he been sleeping with her? If yes then he has no base of argument. "Who does he think will marry her?" Teddy said. "If a guy is not prepared to marry a girl, he shouldn't go around her."

What are the youths doing? Teddy enquired. "They are all in it, both the youths and the chiefs have sold their right as such the fundamental human right of its citizens is threatened." Charles explained. The chiefs implore the service of the Jackboot men to resolve problem perceived to be difficult to solve within them."

"If the Jackboot is invited to solve a problem that means the right of the chief is taken away." Teddy informed them. The traditional council is higher than any other body, as such it cannot take a sons case to an outsider, unless it is reporting a criminal case, which is directed to the government.

The manner in which the elders handles issues is scaring, it goes to show that they're not capable of administration, "I begin to wonder if we are retrogressing, with the unpleasant sight one see every day it gives a run down of an oppressed society. Charles observed.

The Jackboot base was suddenly crowded based on an arrest made; civilians were going in and coming out of the base just like a departmental store. One of the victims was intercepted on his way out of the scene. He narrated his ordeal "my experience in the hands of these dogs cannot be measured," he said. "Imagine I was asked to go and bring the sum of #2.000." "This money must reach our hand not later than 19:00hr today" they reminded me as I was leaving.

"When I received the message my sole solace was the community head, but on reaching there the spokes man asked me to go and comply." "There is nothing we can do as regards your situation," he said. "Based on the outcome of my meeting with the leader I had to look for the money to pay."

"So you've paid the require sum?" Teddy asked.

"Yes I have."

The place was like a trade center, most of the victims were asked to seat on the bare floor in an open hall." An abandoned hotel space used for disco in the 80's." they were drilled according to individuals offence.

The Jackboot men took advantage of Ukuraibos predicament, since it is a known fact that people benefit at crisis time the town has turned an oil mill, within a couple of days they have equipped their rooms with television musical set and video and compact disc. Just like Osubi trade fair center along Eku Effurun Road. "There the Jackboot officers are at alert to foreign vehicle numbers like Rivers, Sogal Akwa Iboe, and Cross River Kano EST. The victims are framed stylishly by unknown charges in deceit while the person would be made to pay #5.000. Cases where their particulars were wrongly documented by the licensing officer, instead of charging them to court or leaving them on the ground of error so that they can rectify it, they are threatened and obtained of their hard earn money.

"Any act committed against the people of Ukuraibo would be redress in the time to come; if Sadam Hussein of Iraq can openly apologize to the Kuwaiti government after 11 years and president Pinochet of Spain can be tried after several years of human right abuse. Ukuraibo's case will not be an exception." Teddy said as he left the scene.

CHAPTER TWENTY ONE

He was not keen on the party's primary, as true citizen he wanted to know the peoples mandate in the party. Teddy left the house as early as possible to a friend's house, an ardent political juggernaut. Unfortunately he was not at home. He passed through Iama road, "Teddy" his cousin called. He joined him in the pub. "Why are you drenching yourself in the rain" he asked as Teddy sat close to him? "Ah!"

"Oga" you are welcome, Oge said. "How is the job? I know you're getting used to the terrain." "We thank God" the new arrival who acted as the new DJO stationed at Utumu said. They were discussing when he came in; Teddy was attracted to his table because he wanted to take leave of his boring companions. "You haven't been associating why?" Alfred asked.

"You should know my plight." Teddy answered. "Whoa! "That is your car? Teddy said, congrats! Nat as he took his hand in hand shake. Alfred an old partner on stretching hand for a handshake said. So how is the new world? "Well we are coping" Teddy answered. They entered into a long unending discussion after which Alfred requested him to accompany him to see a friend. Teddy holding a Heineken in one hand left with him, they drove off in an Audi 80 car.

At the party's secretariat, the people stood aimlessly like sheep without a shepherd, as if they were being punished for crime against humanity. The rain came down on them without a warning sign, they scattered in search of a shade to rest their head. Few Jackboot officers present embarked their vehicle and drove off. Teddy remembered his initial intention requested his friend to go through the old road. At another center at exactly 16:00hr the place was deserted the people were seen on the way shivering home, their cloth was wet indicating the level of punishment from the unpredicted rain. "Reverse and lets visit the neighboring community" he said. Alfred reversed and drove to the express, passed the secretariat moved on until he was at Utumu. The people were like fowl without feather. Teddy recognized one of the victims, he called. "Why not go home? He said. Do you think there will be primaries today? There was no primary at Ukuraibo. Thank you the fellow said and left with his associates.

Every body complained of the un-held primaries, virtually all joint in town the people gathered in groups with favorable star bottle analyzing the presume outcome of the un-held primaries.

These people at the top will ruin their party "do you think I'll vote a man in such party?" Chukuma said "not possible." He reiterated. "Let them keep deceiving themselves; the game is clear as you can see." Down town the people gathered in a drinking joint. "Service lets get more drinks. Say your choice and your order will be met." "Hey! Give me my own drink. I've waited long enough:" a shabbily dressed teenager was addressing the waiter. "I'll be right unto you," she said as she walked past without looking at him. That rather infuriated him feeling slighted. He complained "I've done my part so its time for me to benefit"

"Come on she will be right back, why are you in a hurry?" Mason said. "Give me a brake; I need no consolation from any gad deem person."

"Fuck you! Do you think you are the only one here?" They were on to each other, hands tight in blow. A close observer quickly arrested the situation: "man come off it, dog does not eat dog, if it is the other camp you can go ahead and kill and no body will business what is happening." Both men were separated and each walked to different position to sit. "You should have left them in that posture, don't you think it is enough to suspend them indefinitely." Ken said. No point we shall look into their offence in our next meeting. Papa said.

As if they have been waiting for him, he walked into the crowd. Some one raised a song: "winner oh, oh, oh winner, winner oh, oh, oh winner Edmond you don win oh, winner, I say you go win forever winner. They all chanted making the place non-compromisingly busy. The shabbily dressed teenager rushed into the crowd as he smashed the bottle of star in his possession on his head. The bottle scattered and the crowd dispersed.

"Oh! My eye someone was panting," the cry became louder as no relieve aid for the hurt. "Look he is wounded, he has to be treated as fast as possible. Get the car ready:" Adams said in anguish. In less than 30 seconds he was in a fast moving vehicle to the hospital. The people rushed at him, his legs were suspended above head level until he was roughly laid down smashing his waist on a stone. "Oh am a dead man?" he thought, not audible.

"You're a lucky man, the doctor said as he finished examining the injured patient." He explained further to the people; "as you can see the cut is slightly above the eyelid, the eye was protected from the sharp object. Had it moved a little slightly downwards, it would have been a battle to see if he could see again."

"Nurse, please see to the cut, he said as he walked away leisurely feeling a sign of authority in his field. The cut was gently stitched with the aid of a needle and black thread. When she eventually finished she asked. "Do you want to go home or remain in the hospital?" "Nurse I don't mind going home" he answered. "No problem you will go home as soon as we are through with your drugs," the Nurse a young pretty girl with striking ebony black in her 20ths was full of charm. She finished her job in no time. "Just pay this bill and he is free to go with you." "Is he okay Nurse? Paul asked.

"He is, I will not discharge him if he is not," she said smiling with set of teeth as white as snow. "Thanks for your hospitality, more so for your immediate attention." Paul said. "It's my pleasure," she said.

He walked to the account department and paid the bill as issued; they were all in the vehicle driving home; instead of the gathering he was dropped off at his own apartment.

In the rough manner he was carried out of the crowd, he was dropped from the height he crashed with his face and leg engulfed in sand. He knew his offence needless to cry; the people were ready for him: he had to bear it. Time was his constant consolation, the deed had been done, now is pay back time, his alcohol intake had been very high from the previous day. "How would one not misbehave? Couple with the mixture of various brands without food." He thought. "Who will think of buying you food and alcohol at the same time? It is only when one is sensible that he advices himself on the specific intake. Knowing one's limit is determined by the flow rate, he lamented all by himself.

"Come and clear all this bottles and glasses: we have serious business at hand." The secretary general said. The group did not wait for convergence as proposed to sanction him. "Order," the speaker said. "If we don't address this crucial matter now, subsequently most people will over step their bond." "You were all here when we neglected Obi's attitude toward his brother, look at the outcome, the man now has a black eye to show for our negligence."

"Obi will be punished for sure, but what punishment will be suitable for such a grievous offence as charge. We need not deliberate to ascertain if he is guilty or not we all have eyes, he is guilty." The chair, Aike said. We have a constitution, why not we refer to our constitution and act accordingly. "You've always saved us from long debate; an award is not far from you." The chair said but in this case his crime is more pronounced.

"Without prejudice, he has to pay for Onyema's treatment. He is to pay a fine along with sharing his daily income into two for as long as Obi will be incapacitated. He will furnish us with an apology letter also." I think this will serve as deterrent to others." He concluded.

"All hail the chair," Salem said, the house was in full section of rowdiness and noise.

One year past like a shadow at night preferable a second in clock; the people awaited his arrival, nothing important was the matter but the only significant of all was the same time the community drifted. Still all good they could not remember the exalt day of the daybreak massacre signifying man's faith on earth. The word of Macbeth after the untimely death of his close associate "life is but a walking shadow, it is a tale told by an idiot." the people are up and doing, "while not allow the sleeping dog to lie instead of going through the rigor of awakening it to face the challenges of an untimely death.

A story to our beloved home and abroad, guess who is coming for dinner! Macson said. The governor and his entourage arrives the Okpala-Uku's palace; the blaring of siren activated the environment like active cinema hall, were every city boy goes to relax after the day's job. The surrounding was infested with men on black suit with hands in their pockets, uniform Jackboot officers and plain cloth Jackboot. All at alert a 5ft 9 inch bulky tall dark man distinguish by a bola hart almost covering his facial view, emerged from the car. The impart he made on the staring crowd was so severe that they were all mesmerized.

He entered the Okpala-Uku's palace and every body stood up to greet him' "his excellency" they greeted' the people without formality presented him with kola nut and wedged it with #30, 000. As he received the kola nut, he thanked every one present. The game plan was on; he was without prejudice conferred with a chieftaincy title of an "Anagba" meaning a Hiroko tree. Whilst his deputy was not left out he gladly accepted the "Onyeudo" the peacemaker of the clan.

"Tufia" kelechi spits out "a shame and a pity" a renowned drunk who the entire people see as an outcast said. "Our people forget so easily, a community in pains same time in 2002 has turned around to install misdeed itself as the peacemaker and tap root of the community. "Fear should not drift the elders who know for sure their day on earth is numbered to betray the trust be-stalled on them to accept gift of money as a means of stewardship."

"The man is talking sense," Clement said. Is like selling to an outsider that does not recognize the norms of the community that which is of the son of the soil. An outsider can only be recognized as a true son of the soil when certain issues are put in place and he scores above 75% of the total summation.

He was so calm that the people wondered, "Is this not the drunk?" He looked at them in total disbelief and scorn.

The governor thanked the people and presented them with #30, 000 equivalent to what they offered. He thanked the chiefs and begged to take his leave. The chiefs in disbelief of what has transpired in want of what to do started grumbling among themselves; no one was able to alter a word.

He rose and the whole arena was charged up, his entourage all rose. The bodyguards all hands in their pocket cleared the way for him. Every body not opportune to have seen him were egger to see him necessitating a mad rush within the low bred. The push increased the struggle, which made the Jackboot men battle ready; all positioned to dissuade the people from advancing.

CHAPTER TWENTY TWO

Steps were taken to see to the smooth arrangement of the rally arena; the people gathered waiting for the arrival of the representatives from Ndokwua/Inauwku federal constituency. Severe noise overtook the whole place making conversation virtually impossible: the senator and the member house of representative along with the house of Assemble man in the state arrived including various local government aspirants and party supporters.

The senator stood up after the introduction formality, he greeted the people in the native terms, after which he started by condemning a co aspirant for the senate position saying she made it possible for the federal government to write off the Ukuraibo Utagba-Uno road, explaining that he tried his very best. But the woman that was not a legislator was an obstacle to the smooth lobby.

"Look at what he is saying," Mark a conservative said. "It portends his mentality, instead of telling the electorates his achievements he is exonerating himself for not performing; where he would have shown remorse.

"Did I hear you right" Clement said. "You must be kidding if you will get such an obedient servant in this modern Nairegin politics of godfathers. The truth is that she is more influential than he is; know it now she is your best bet for the senate job." "You don't know that a blockhead can remain in one position without progressing:

Representatives are gifted people who need not learn to know, but are conversant with the law of the land." Mark said. A young man in native attire raised his hand as he approached from the audience. "Look he is an opposition member." Nelson pointed at him.

The man dressed in rag clapped his hand in response to the command order let out by the superior colleague. Instantly other team members were unto him. On seeing the crew the man took to his heels towards the microphone. He was accosted by one of the shabbily dressed member of the team, as he was dragged off the gathering; he tried to resist which resulted to his being manhandled. "Let me go" he wailed, as he struggled to his feet consequently he was allowed to go knowing fully well his intention was not met.

Nathan wondered if these people dressed in rags will ever learn; they are busy protecting a legislator from citizens who meant no harm, but intended asking question to know how they have contributed to the growth of the community, since their election. Before they seek can for a second term. If the answer is positive then why would they encourage this unholy behavior from their paid tugs? The guilty is always afraid since none of them want to miss coming back all in the name of a second term tagged "continuity," a word of deceit.

The truth must prevail, children of this age, why! 'Blindness you have shielded my people from the truth, now they all languish in search of the unknown. 'Fellow indigenes take a bold step, go back home and asked your parents question concerning your town right from days before you were born so that you will no more be enslaved. Johnson lamented.

Nine months after the Senate committee left Abasa Pablo sat in his doorstep. 'So this matter had died a natural death, how can we say we are in a democratic globe when our Jackboot still maim and kill innocent citizens and the government's stance is incomplete. He rose from his sitting position as he saw Nat. Felicia he called. Yes papa joy. I will be back soon let me go see Teddy he said as Nat joined him. Pablo an okada rider called, thank God you are here it is very important carry me to Teddys place. Bros 'sha! Better day' take me down first he said the okada moved the rider was so careful he avoided the waterlogged area along Umudike street and was back at Umudike street through Efad road. Pablo came down my man don't worry! You are saving your money, remember that Hon Osiji N Osiji was once like me all the okada in Elawk town knew him too well as such he gets scholarship from the all and today those bike men have benefited immensely from him. The bike man laughed and rode off.

Bros Teddy. Yes! Who's it good looking you can come in. what of bad looking? Pablo asked. Then remain outside. As Pablo stepped in Teddy said. "You know them the Jackboot men on black." Pablo laughed. How is the town? Teddy asked. Well bros as you people left it oh! It is there but if you give the command we are there already. Oh no that is not what I meant. Teddy said.

Bros before I forget how can we get the senate and house of reps reports, it's been nine months since the daybreak massacre. Teddy scratched his eyes, he thought for a while facing Pablo he said. "No big deal, I get across to my guys at Abuja. Definitely I will give you feedback over the weekend because I'm on my way to Abuja this morning.

Guys I have to get going. Nicky said. Aren't you staying for the party anymore? Charley asked. I told you Pat has to be here and she insisted that if I don't come pick her she's not coming, you know what that means 'I'm not serious' Call her considering the distance to Lagos she will be here in the next 2 hours but if you decide to embark on such journey I bet you 5 hours is just for a starter. Nicky was such in a hurry zoomed of leaving Charley as he got to the T junction he stopped came down from the car. 'Brother, help journey mercy the people shouted. He pulled out a bill of #200 naira and distributed among the beggars. God will always protect you from your enemy they shouted after him; as he approached the Lagos express way he heard a blaring horn he quickly navigated to the left the tanker held on to his brake slowly the tanker stopped with it's head light resting directly on Nicky's bumper "My God an head on collision" he wheeled back ward to continue his drive. Nicky forgot everything on safety thanks to the non adherence to safety rules by road safety agents he speeds on. A lightening spark passed through his windscreen. "My God" he shouted he held on to his brake and the car jerked forward, the tyre suspended above ground level and the car hit the pavement and flew up landing with it's back it kept on turning till it landed on a palm tree with it's tyre suspended. Nicky felt okay as he heard murmuring sound of road users. The man is inside lets try and bring him out. Nicky looked sideways my God he almost screamed but did not want to shake the car knowing a slight push will land him inside the river. The man is lucky so you mean is just this small palm tree that is holding the car from entering the river. Nicky pushed his door and it gave way, he stepped out of the car what a miracle the people shouted. Can we tow the car out of that sport? Nicky said the towing van positioned and it pulled the car, it jerked and landed with it's tyres fully balanced on the ground. "Jesus" someone shouted 'you are wonderful' Nicky tried the ignition and the car started. Thank you immensely I will be on my way.

This is the senate report as presented by the Hon senators of the federal republic of Nairegin. Teddy said, I read on. After the hearing the committee was able to deduce that the remote causes of the crisis in Ukuraibo are traceable to a few salient points: all accruing to the political disagreement between the chairman Inauwku local government council Ogbuefi Enext Uche and the leaders of Ukuraibo.

The committee figure chief Nosirrah Edeja and Evangelist Iasso Heba to be the ringleader who masterminded and instigated the chiefs, elders and youths of Ukuraibo. Latter's grievance against the chairman began when he relieved him of his job as secretary to the local Education Authority, while Evangelist Iasso Heba was Mr. Enext Uche's opponent during the chairmanship elections. He upholds the belief that the election were characterized by violence and that the results were fraudulently manipulated. A proven man of God he refers himself as such would not lead his people to violence knowing within himself that the only way for lasting peace in Ukuraibo is to flush Enext Uche out of office.

The senate committee noted that amongst other chiefs and elders, due to selfish and political motivated reasons, have greatly influenced the people of Ukuraibo into believing the fact that the local government chairman is insensitive towards the needs of the community. More so that his highly mal-administered government has led to a strained relationship between the chairman and a whole lot of the community elders. Consequently the leaders do not relate regularly nor bring him in confidence into the picture of things as it affects the community. Another factor the committee attributed is that the chairman is from a neighboring community. "Ibba Hawo " outside Ukuraibo, which the committee believes, has a greater majority of population than Ukuraibo.

The senate committee further elaborates that the elders who without success tried to get the outgoing DJO, SP Imuweda on their side against the local government chairman, accused him of forming an alliance with the local government chairman, which they accused the DJO of dinning and wining with the chairman when he was suppose to carry out his duty as the Divisional Jackboot officer to take steps in curbing the incessant crime wave in Ukuraibo. An act of extortion, coercion mortification of various clan heads were also alleged against him which made them to vow to unseat him at all costs, since he refused to submit to their control. Obviously the people of the community led by the elders were working at cross purpose with the Jackboot and the local government chairman at the same time which created ample grounds for increase in crime and general insecurity resulting to instability.

The senate committee also observed the wave of violence crimes and civil disturbances pervading the entire Atled State in general, with a special reference to Ukuraibo community in particular. Observing that in the recent past, violence crime disturbances have become a very regular occurrence in Atled Area, most of which are perpetrated by the massively unemployed youths in the area that have help in no small way to promote violent crimes. Our finding reveals youth disturbances in several areas of the state, notably, Illehgu Unruffe, Irraw, Waji areas, Utumu and most recently Ukuraibo community. Insinuating the restive youths lend themselves most times to be used as political herald to satisfy any person or group wishing to use them to achieve a particular selfish purposes, expanding their oomph vigor by frequent rioting and communal clashes rather than seeking productive means of employment.

Recalling the incidence of 20th June 2001 where some youths in their hundred took to the street demonstrating against NEPA's failure to supply electricity in Ukuraibo. Evidence on videotape revealed that they used this opportunity to mount roadblocks and extort money from innocent by-passers: taking over a Jackboot vehicle and an Atled line vehicle, including some other private vehicles; in the name of fighting for their rights. To mention a few one Sam Ekemi spoke openly inhaling the smoke of his stick of Benson and Hedges at the same time declared that he was ready to die if light; water and good roads were not immediately restored in Ukuraibo. He emphasized that he would be the first to spill the blood of the NEPA's officials.

The youths driving their message deep down the spine of the NEPA officers gave them only one week to restore light else, one or more of the NEPA officials will die declaring that without light the youths of Ukuraibo will continue to be restive as such there will be no peace.

In showing their grievance, they arrested 4 NEPA officials and detained at the residence of Chief Nosirrah Edeja. Intervening Jackboot men later released these unlucky ones.

Most recently precisely on the 18th of February 2002, the, 'oh you are back please distribute their reports round. I read.

For posterity sake something has to be done Arnold said. The culprits has to be brought to book if not now certainly in the near feature. If not the dead will certainly fight it's battle itself. Should the living fail to actualize its dream? I think the Senators think we are numb if not they will not come up with such instigated report why will they misrepresent information's, I feel their finding is misinterpreted. They have right to apportion blame but they were skeptical as if they will be blame if they represent the truth by so doing they contradicted themselves. In so many ways, else why will they say that the Jackboot according to rule 3 of force order 237 was free to use firearm because their lives were threatened. And in turn to say the era of military siege is over; as such the Jackboot cannot afford to act as the military in occupation if they are not at fault. Pablo said. Men forget the senate report; from the onset I knew it was a charade. The youth chairman said. Let us go see what is happening at the shrine.

The festival commenced on the first market day the people were not zealous enough as the danced group emerge the people shouted "Orema chanchaogone," a butch of leave carrying dances. The people all rushed out from their houses "Ochalineooh sawgarchooh orema Chanchaogone; Ochalineooh Sawgarchooh Orema chanchaogone" meaning it is preparing it is preparing it wants to come out. The people sang. The oremachanchaogene move from the starting of the town to the end and it returned to it's abode the people kept night vigil singing mostly mimicking lawbreakers and the person does not have any moral justification or powers to challenge the dancers as long as the festival last.

On the second day of the last phase of the festival effort to resolve the community crisis failed the youths in support of the elders in chiefs council denounced participation in the festival. "Enough is enough of this maladministration we are tired how long shall we continue to follow blindly? A black horse for that matter, Ken said. If we do continue in this blind wave we shall all suffer the consequence created by our own hands? This feast is none and void, no more misleading of the people. We are not partakers of corrupt practice Ekene screamed at the chief who was calming him. The whole place became too rowdy. "If you people have chosen to go your way better do that before it is too late a youth in support of the ruling class said. Don't be stymied if you people choose to go you will definitely regret it" come off your threat it no longer holds sway while will we stay on when you cannot resolve simple issues. You think it is easy to lead go try and see. The chief barked. "Oh look at you that imposed himself on the people shameless bitch. The argument continued the chief instead of calming the angry rebelling faction comprising a major fraction of the youths slotted it out with them. The youths and their leaders including the chiefs left with a perceive view of starting a fresh festivity. The Okpaluku who watched his domain being disintegrated called out to the leaders. "I wish you and your youths will yield to advice" was his last cautiousness.

Year 2005 Ekenke festival attracted people from all Works of life, the youths in preparation for the ukwata Dance waited endlessly for the Umuene they rejoined. As the designed frame in a pole likemanner with Lamplight around it called emerged. Man this Umusume People have reduced the number of light in the Umuenu. Why did you say Umusume? Jacob asked. Oh! You don't know that is its root. Wait to see the anungbunofia, how is that one? Jacob asked. If they tell you people to always come home you think is punishment look at you, there is nothing about tradition in your head. Please tell me now. There you go the Anngunofia comes out like the Omuenu the people sings hanhaan hanhaan anungbunofia: meaning double a game that was hunted and caught in the forest.

Let us go watch the Ukwuata, dance, the youth's brandished cutlass along the old Sapele Agbor road as the people awaits the major road suffered a set back as the youths patrolled to and fro in anticipation of the Ukwuata dance assembled in various groups most of them climbed different height to enable a perfect view. Gad deem it! This is most amazing Charley said as he stumbled on a group of children. In front the population that greeted him smiling as he saw a man in the mist of the crowd bare chested putting on a make shift waist gown 'an Nbenuku' the man was more visible among the people, enhancing his visibility. He held on to a suspended canoe like designed object having four edges in form of a ridge, on the mans head a flat surface canoe having a hollow boat house the top covered with a wooded flat surface with dead animal skin housing a life guinea fowl; the guinea fowl resting on the flat surface made it tint as if the guinea fowl is falling off.

The ukwuata procession trailed along with the man in their mist dancing effortlessly incessantly following the crowd. Teddy on seeing the Ukwuata advancing diverted into a small opening as the Ukwuata proceeded he continued to his sister's. The Ukwuata is in it's fullest this year, someone shouted from the crowd. What a stylish dance the people were embroiled in dust emanating from the over tramped soil. The road was locked from both sides as everybody only moves in one direction; some of the people watching followed the Ukwuata dancer as he advances making the Ukwuata procession visibly long. The man was singing and dancing at the same time and the people responded to his song The carrier dances with the objects on his head until he gets to the a compound. Holding forth while the dance continues showing the skilful acrobatics of the ukwuata dancer and thereafter makes an instant forward movement. The Ukwuata speed increased accelerating its follower's as well. They responded to his song, ' samsoye oyege samsoye' singing along the main road until he reached a three road junction, he pulsed facing Uzuko; he made a sudden retreat and started dancing back to its original abode. Simply because Uku Uzuko quarter forbids Ukwuata.

The Ukwuata is expected to go back from Uzuko as they retreated they sang: "Ebenebe Ne Okocho Samsoye Oyege

Samsoye "meaning (next year will be tougher) because this activity will not be witnessed again until the next year. The people sang the song back to Ogbe Ukuraibo "next year will be tougher " the people sang as they escort the Ukwuata back to its base. When they got to the Ukwuata base the people continue their dance back.

At Ogbe Ukuraibo quarters, the people both youths and elderly ones continue into the night with songs likes: Mejejeooh Mananaoohs Onyelanosu Nonanaooh? Meaning I will go oh, I will go home; who Indulges in immoral art will go home. Negwene ooh Negwene Ogwunneni Kani la" Anna ooh Anna, ekpele ogonogo. While at Ogwezi Uku Uzuko part of the town, the people observe an all night vigil, it is presumed to be a silent night for all. No form of light is expected to be seen outside, everyone remains in this unique state till the early hours of the morning.

At Umuedede junction the youths waited all with shielded cutlass, as the Ukwuata dance accelerated passed they pulled out their double edge cutlass and simultaneously started advancing, the people took to their heels as they advanced. Not quit 15 minutes the cutlass was raised and the people crowded him. As if the feast was an antidote to cutlass cut Degbue slapped Obiora with the sharp edge of his cutlass, the cutlass bounced off his neck momentarily got swollen. Obiora in wanting a quick revenge picked on a florescent tub and went after Degbue on seeing him coming took to his heals. Within a short interval he was accosted and Obiora didn't allow his pleading gaze from dissuading him instead busted the florescent on his own head before Degbue could take a dock the pointed edge was applied midway into his stomach determine to kill he twisted the object leaving the tub right in the man's stomach.

Mike who was among the watching crowd rushed to the scene; he struggled with Degbue eventually he was able to remove the tub from his belly uncontrollable Degbue ran hoping for a safe abode, he fell on the way, Most of the youth assemble at the shrine front called "Isunmo" meaning "Front of Juju." after helping themselves with various charms presumed to ward off any attack be it physical or psychic against the following day's activity. Between the hours of 9 am to 10 am the canon man releases his first set of gunpowder, alerting the people and a signal that the people can come out to watch the last Phase of the festival. Like Christmas day; the whole community assembled in their best of attires and to watch the celebration on the Olie market day.

The people from the shrine lead the way, as they all came out, the Onutu Ukus lead the way. Like an organized procession the people danced along the major road. The highlight of the day is the display of various charms. Individuals were usually tested to know if they were successfully protected by their witch Doctors.

The Ochu, a masquerade, made of basket like structure with feathers of various sizes designed directly inside the ring is worn on a man's head lapping on the head and the feathers protruding in that one can conveniently put gifts in-between the feathers. He paints his face with black charcoal and carries a cutlass as he proceeds he sings "Ochu-ooh Ochu." (meaning pursue oh pursue cause he has an habit of pursuing people with his cutlass. Intimidating them with his cutlass and the people will run away mostly when he gets to any shop he shop lifts as the owner runs leaving his store at the Ochu's mercy.

Outstanding youths of a certain age group brandish cutlasses, in trying to test the efficacy of their charm cut at random. Fight erupted as most boys that were not well protected became vulnerable to cutlass cut. Also there are responsible men who dress in their native attire just to show off. In most cases, depicting their opulence and achievements.After the traditional dances, comes social conviviality's. Individuals and families settle down to have a post mortem of the festivity. This is usually celebrated with the natives' oil Soup: a combination of water from boiled yam blended with pepper, potash, oil and dry fish called "enemoudo" One dead man and many with various stitches will the people learn? The doctor said as he sat in his office he reflected way back year 2002.

We must revenge, everybody we must revenge what! How can! These Jackboots that we have risked and compromised for good several occasion can turn against us, no way! We must revenge. Repeat after me, we must revenge the team mate shouted. We must revenge. Repeat kill all Jackboot be it a brother nor a sister we have no regrets; we shall kill them all. Give the men high weed we cannot wait to carry out this crime on Jackboot. Nicky said. The concoction comprising a mixture of illicit gin and weed was brought to the center. The men lined up in a single file, the teammate to quell their taste received a mug of the concoction. My spirit is arousing J D boss shouted! We shall kill them all Jackboot, no remedy to drive master. Their faces drip in tears, as they could no longer control themselves they wept. Weeping cannot lead us anywhere we have to go and have a show down with them. Nicky said. The Jackboot team by Boundary road junction were disembarking from the vehicle when the wide cats ram into them, before the jackboot men could respond One man kill released his trigger rapidly bringing down the whole 7 man team. The men moved further to the jackboot station, the station guard left his position displaying his rifle as he came out of the building, the armed men drove into the station seeing the loose men on guard took a chance one man kill pulled his trigger and aimed at the station guard the man dropped dead the whole jackboot men at the station took to their heels through the exit door. One man kill sent a shell of bullet into the station continually. There is no soul in there, let's go Nicky said. We have to go round starting from GRA. GRA was asleep when the men of the underworld stormed the neighborhood and a Jackboot van zoomed past. Reverse and follow One man kill aimed at the driver and released his trigger cutting thought the man at his fore head, the vehicle spine and rammed into a fence. The convoy stopped by the car and fired into the car spontaneously. No man must survive this blast Nicky said laughing. write this off our list. They enter their car and zoomed off along Ihama road. One man kill fired at a Jackboot walking down the road. Clean his name from our record.

Greg waved the other cars to a stop "let us visit their station" "perfect" Nicky said. They moved in rolls driving through Boundary road terminating at Ehakpen road they pulled over at the Jackboot station, as the team emerged they started firing into the station the Jackboot officers ran out through the back door the man at the rear received a gunshot as he ran before the DJO could come out of his office Greg accosted him. "I told you, never attempt a fight with a man that knows your secret." Look at your boss he is facing humiliation and you start what you can't finish. The DJO stood still enable to look him in the face. "I will spare you this moment for saving my life cause I owe you one." He left the man in an agonized state. The team drove round heading for new Benin Jackboot station. Hit that man the gun shatter peel through the Jackboots skin tearing his back open, another gun shot hit his second who was hiding behind a car his gun dropped off his hold.

Why didn't he use his gun one-man kill laughed. "so you don't know that gun can not shot a mouse."

What has turned these men loss I still cannot fathom after all we have protected each other in the past. DJO said facing his boss. Enough of these flimsy excuses. I want these men brought down I don't care how you are going to achieve that. The boss barked. Yes sir the DJO s said and walked away from his office.

Terror can only kill a man who fears terror this injustice against the Jackboot is over today no more toll gate fee until we clean our house off all these filth. Now move out of my sight and I don't want to see your back without result. At Ekpoba Jackboot station the DJO addressed his loyalist. "Who masterminded the arrest of Drive master? Sir Eze refused when I caution him on the outcome of his act but it was too late to speak to you because the governor was already aware of the arrest. Better we hand over Eze to Greg so that this assault on our person can stop. The DJO brought out his phone from the holster, the bang of gun fire awake the station all man to the armory one-man kill, J D boss, Balance and kill, Spacko. Nosy trooped out of the cars all hands high aboveshoulder the swigged their gun firing at the empty Jackboot station. Oh they could not wait, spineless Jackboot men can only outwit a sleeping master drive why didn't they go when he was awake? Greg it's all over let us go.

You mean the Jackboot is now inefficient" the governor said. It is sad but that is the situation from the security report.

The governor stared at his cheers board you can only protect the king when you have a strong army comprising of a good queen's navy and air force. He position his Knight and the Queen, no! Not the Jackboot. Contact the commandant at army headquarters along with the commanding officer of the Nigerian navy, we direly need their assistance.

The traditional rite is all over we know death has taken driver master from us but we the living must forge ahead. He addressed drive masters wife. He was a good man a crime to end this way, no word can compensate the loss but we are still team mate both in death. Thank you she said shedding tears. Here we are, you will never lack as long as we are all team mates. Outside drive masters house the group gathered. "Do you know we can still perfect a part 2 of the Fedson connection? You mean continuity as the PDP slogan. Yah man that is our gold mine. It is simple the security has not improved instead it has diminished. All we do is to have a combine force with our rejoinder who has busted our Jackboot war. Remember we have to package them as they came from far away north.

On the 29th of March being Easter Monday the convoy left for a cruse driving through the town. "Can it be real" Nicky said don't tell me it's possible. Drive master stopped in front of the premises he tapped his horn and the security opened the gate wide. As the man was about to close the gate a Honda car followed preceded by a spots car. Get down one man kill shouted as he fired the Jackboot man trying to raise his gun. Serves you right when ever don't delay in using your fire arm. The group rushed into the banking hall, no body moves if you try playing hard you will be dead on the hour.

Outside the bank a man shoulders high suspended his berretta rifle he kept on firing on the quite street kill all the Jackboot no one must leave this place alive. Jude my Brother oh! Jackboot I can't wait to revenge, he fired at the Jackboots position inside the bank premises. Where is the bank manager? Or is he in the toilet again. Get the man out in the open or we will kill any man we see. The Manager remained in the toilet. 'If you like kill everybody, I can't fall for that treat. Safer and lonely I had remain in here rather than face cruelty he opened the vault electronically. The vault is open so the manager can go to blazes. But if I luck these people inside oh they will have back up. He thought. The people regroup rush, use your to the SARS men at Mandela hotel. The man screeched almost hitting his car he drove straight to Mandela hotel. Calm down no be robbers who want to die I can hear the sound of the gunshot from this point forget that one if they are through they will leave the town and no body will get hurt. The SARS man advised. As for me I like my family too well or you don't like your family; look at how you are looking or should I give you my gun.

Give him na! if that is what he want to take a fellow SARS man said. O boy! you guys are butch of a disgrace to our tax payers. Oh! So that is how you have become? Scared of these robbers, he entered his car and drove off.

At the bank premises the people gathered waiting for the SARS team. The old road was filled with spectators the robber displaced his rifle swinging it left, right and front. "No body" he said onto his telephone mouthpiece. I will get back to you. span o the riffle released smoke as it double fired. The robbers inside the banking hall had so much confidence; they were not in a hurry. Time to go Greg ordered as he saw One man kill dragging the bags from the corridor, did you get enough cash" he asked. Sure yes trust these people they are river never ends. Greg laughed accompanying him outside. "Ready to go he spoke into his radio." Okay we have no enemy the people have cooperated to far all we got is blockages but that is no problem he fired as he kept talking on his hands free. The boot filled bring the Honda fast no time left remember our friend have a long drive to make.The jeep lead the way with it's rear light fully on other cars followed. Oh! No the tyre is down' drive only said. Why didn't you say so earlier. Okay small boy look out for a convenient place we have to change our tyres Nicky said. No problem. Small boy cleared the way as he fired into the air. Deem! Leave the way, he shouted; the youth was so sure of his witch master pulled the drum into the road. Deem small boy released his trigger the bullet cut the boy at the back as he took cover. What was that Nicky barked on the radio sorry I didn't mean to kill but he got on the way. Never I repeat you have succeeded in taking their funds don't add killing to the business we are no killers small boy. Yes boss. Small boy fired as he remove the last blockage. We are there drive into this primary school we can be safe here. The men in the Jeep all came down dangling the riffle on their shoulders. One after the order they fired into the air. "this will checkmate anybody" Greg said Drive only parked the Honda and came down he took his time went to the booth brought his spare tyres and the jack. As he jacked the car Alone known as lonely man help in loosening the tyre. The tyre was replaced and alone tightened the nuts. We are ready to go drive only informed the crew. The people watched from a distance no body's nerve carried him near the school entrance as the crew embarked the car small boy kept firing he pulsed to drink his star beer. As the last car got to his position he threw the bottle of star away and entered through the open door.

Pals, is of no use rushing off, better you hang on so that we can finish with this matter before you can go back to your base; our men will always act as back up team. Nicky said. Drive slowed down on approaching the low bed as the driver of the low bed turned off his work man a sound from his walking talking 'ready to go' he watched the cars as it neared his position the skippers were let down and the three vehicles drove in, the driver pressed a button and the low bed was covered revealing nothing apart from the trucks metals, the men disembarked and entered the second low bed. The low bed containing the money bags moved towards the Sapele bridge while the other low bed heading to warri reduced his speed on getting to a lonely road, ensuring there was no close observers he pulled over along the narrow road mostly used by farmers, the skippers were lowered. 'operation detachment commence' Nicky ordered. The cars slowly rolled down, no one was on sight maneuver right ahead and the low bed followed behind at it's own safe pace.

Hello, Nicky said on the mouth piece. Please Nicky I need you guys at Ughelli as speedily as you can come over. Why? We are on our way to complete Irraw assignment, remember Tennyson has an unaccomplished deal last night in some elements shop and made it look as if we were some jock crackers, if they see comedians can't they easily distinguish between comedians and we want to clean the area. Put Tennyson on hold this is very important, if we can't float this one right away we will be in deep shit; the field men have finished with the seismic line creation, we can easily access the target from the river side. So why delay, if we afford an extra day you never can tell who will come around the scene. Mind you the villagers are waiting for seismic equipment to arrive and we cannot afford to pay more workers. We have all other preparation almost complete. please do this for us and we shall always remember.

Ok you call the shot, can count on us we will be there swiftly. Nicky said. Nicky forgot his initial consultation, to redeem his traits he spoke through the wireless so that all team mate could hear him. "We have got to kick at Ughelli town, right now, Brown has been worried over nothing but I can envisage his fears. The line has been mapped out by our surveyors and the line cutters have done part of their job waiting for the shooting crew. The team have left the sight, for any reason what so ever and there is slight delay in us moving in, 'maimi' the game will be easily detected. Remember employment for the propose exploration is on, that means we have to disguise absolutely so that our espionage cannot be detected before the job commence.

Do you see why it has to be today? I mean right on the hour. Check your backup armory he added. No cause to worry Jonah said we did not waste much today. okay we shall capitalize on our exit, a fast get away boat is there. What happens to the boat driver? He will be forced to get us over to a safe place where we can join our cars.

Speak out boys, we have 35 minutes to dawn. Greg bit his cigar; he chewed the tip and spat out through the window. Why are we in such a hurry? Jonah asked. I feel we just have to consult with papa Mudi, remember he said blood is not a good custodian of his antidote. I know the old man is always very sensitive to his antidote. That is a wise decision but time is of essence. "that antidote he uses to call someone at all times I trust so much. Pat said . 'You've been off this track for a while I know why I'm concern of this neighborhood.

"Gentlemen do we all agree to protect our finances." Vicky asked. Yes, yes, yes, yes, yes, yes, and yes they all responded. Driver, straight to the river bank Greg said. The jetty being an isolated makeshift plank construction where speed boats can easily belt to drop off it's crew men. Standing on the jetty was a respondent text for all the crew members. Greg counted the team mate ensuring the gang was enough to do the job he said. "we have two assignment on hold. "why don't we split ourselves into two group, as both parties finishes we can then regroup. At least that will save us the trouble of timing. 'Nicky you will have to lead a group, if anything goes wrong take the Agharo uto road out of the scene. Nicky breath in and out. Paul, Collins, Nat ,Ben, Jonah, Andrew, Dave, Steve, join Vicky ,Simon, Mac, peter, Felix, better join Vicky You have to come back this way as we will complete this job at this end.

Vicky please you have to survey the bank first before you go in and call me once you are in. Ok, dash my life I will do just that Vicky assured. My war men time in, is of essence so we better keep moving right away.

At Agbaro Uti the news circulated as the okada rider got to town. The town crier did not wait to be informed he picked his gong beating it he shouted "come together, come together, there is a meeting at the kings palace, punctuality is our watch word remember our town has been at siege. The people responded urgently to the call as the kings palace was over populated. 'where are the volunteers? Please come forward the king announced. Six heavily built men bare chest stepped out. "remember a warrior does not return home unsuccessful, you must come back victorious if not we shall have no choice but to banish you. Our king we have taken this vow to succeed and not to disappoint and bring shame to our fatherland. A traditionalist assembles some concoction he raised the native chock sprinkling it on them. "powers is never sufficient when it comes to the peoples war my people I leave them at your mercy do to them what you feel best for your own true kinsmen. They suddenly separated into two groups one facing the north while the other one faced south. The people followed as they left dangling on their shoulder as they held tight to the outdated gun offered to them by the renounced hunters in the village. Julius remembered the horrifying night as he walked along the Ughelli/Agbaro Uti road. All Agbaro Uti citizens were asleep when the men of the underworld visited gun short paralyzed the town no body could come out of his door. 'Open the door or we break it' they basked, a cracking sound as an iron protection was open. 'you failed in your duty as a husband and you have to pay right now, the robbers barked. How much do you have? Take it all please Samuel shouted. 'how much is in there? One hundred thousand naria, the man replied. What! You think we came to play? While will you say you have only one hundred whereas you are wearing a gold necklace.

Oh! Oh! it is easy to get such money and you go about to rob? The man's wife replied. Woman? you dare us, Samuel pulled out his gun and fired at the man his skull split open. She fainted as she saw her breadwinner dropped to the ground. Oh! My life wire she screamed and dropped by her husband. Row out all I hate blood, Kenneth barked as the group went over to the next house the woman complied on hearing the gently knock at her door. Fine lady why? You mean you have reserved this bottom for whom then? Ha Nat said as she twisted on changing position. Come here let me have a feel. The woman knelt down pleading, stop that Kenneth bark. Don't tempt me four of the robbers held her while Kenneth raped her. Like a sampler in signal encoding, the robbers trusted their weaponry supported by a native concoction tied to their gun mouth capitalizing on the peoples weakness they ravaged the whole village. The following day the people assembled in the kings palace. "Eze! The otota called. 'what do we do? We rely on you to do something. Patient my people the camel is not too happy yet it's load is not reduced, we are all in this 'remember the cock is yet to crow when the egret took over it's home be wise my people for patience is a virtue. The people grumbled as they left the kings palace disappointed. The devils is at it again the woman shouted as she stood face to face with the robbers; being a market day the robbers fell a log along the road blocking the road from one side and any incoming vehicle slows on getting to the location attracting a rush from the nearby bush the robbers dressed in Jackboot uniform. "Thank you madam but we would have preferred to have you instead, the woman wept knowing what they were capable of doing. A close section with you one of the robbers hit her bottom. "Can you preserve this for long?' the whole traders were relieved of their money. Time is of essence, let's go' woman you will go with us, she was pushed into the raving car as all the robbers dashed into the car and zoomed off the car suddenly reversed and faced the village. The Kings did not wait to confirm, he slide through the aluminum window he could not shout, an anonymous car pulled over and the king on noticing the man by the wheel jumped in and the man drove off. 'that is the kings bodyguard.' Oh! Yes I now know why he did not hesitate to enter the car. the people jubilated. My family' the King panted as the driver stopped the vehicle. They will not do anything to your wife, I guess is a threat to convince you to come out. God forbid you did not yield, it would have been a let down on us. How could we have explained nor tell it that our honorable king had face to encounter with these hoodlums. The man shake his head, no way. The subsequent day the elders of the neighborhood met in the Kings palace, while the King presided over the meeting an image in the Kings palace dropped to the ground. No! the King screamed, the native doctor moved forward and picked the object. My king if we continue to wait without acting, just as this lifeless object dropped to the ground, so will you drop out of your throne. The whole palace was swiftly crowded. "Most accepted King, we have endured as much as necessary. Please spare us I mean permit us cause we are tired of this humiliation and intimidation.

Let us venture at least one bit will not kill all the warriors in this town. As much as we do want peace our King, remember that without justice there can't be peace no matter how you try. The people groan. Our King approve and we will never let you down. The spokesman said. All the while the people voiced out their grievances the King rested his head on his kneel. As the last speaker finished speaking, he raised his head. Dry tears rested on his eye lid. A pity the King cannot weep in front of his subjects he fought back with all his might. My people he called shaking his head 'sleep has not spoilt the eyes, I was in a trance I knew it is a semi judgment day. I will not fail you this time, we shall do all that is required, pardon and forgive my relapsed nature all this week. The bullet hit the roof top paralyzing the people as they all went down on the ground each man to his tent the fleeing citizen abandoned their King but the Kings bodyguard whisked him into an inner room. Firing at the fleeing crowd the robbers emptied their magazine on the people. "let's see how you will regroup to fight one of the robbers said. The unlucky ones caught were lead to their homes. "listen carefully, Nicky said. If you grumble that means you are not giving willingly Pat said. "if you like run away that does not count because you will not all escape from your home. Make them to know, Festus said. If you run we will definitely come back for you another day.

Bring that basin here Jonah said. It is good this is computerized robbery. Tell it any were after all politicians are stealing, people are stealing with their pen and thereby looting the nations treasury and no body is checkmating them. 'who be fool' 'abeg' play me that old jam. Nicky said as the driver was about to change the CD. If you like call the Jackboot and they will fail you again, or you don't know that it is only the Jackboot force that dog eats dog. Imagine only the inspector general of Jackboot forces worth 17.4 billion and man can not afford a round square meal or you think we are happy collecting from you. This is the toughest of them all that we do with ease. After all we rig election for the politicians and what do they pay us with neglect. Put that in the basin it is your contribution to bad governance. Time is of essence hasten up Nicky ordered. Fear was the capturer of the wick in spirit; the people complied the second man smiled as he parted with his cash. how much is that? Jonah asked. Shakily the man answered. Twenty thousand the man answered. Thank you my brother you tried after all it is not easy. Next the man did not want to let go he stood by the basin. Drop it and leave or it is difficult to part with? Jonah said laughing.

As a group we must agree to dislodge our enemies, we are sending you to give the devil a run for his money. Courage, is the key to countless fear. If you must succeed don't count on your loss but your gain that way you definitely will over run your enemy. Julius kept imagining the brutal murder of the aged woman who refused to be seduced by the team of the robbers in their last encounter. Nicky rammed into the reversing car. 'get down all, Pat clear the nobility line cut across so that they cannot regroup. Dave get the cars rolling. Greg the operation is aborted; the police has backed down but the people seem very anxious to regroup. He jumped into the moving car. 'Get ready, once you hear my last command, fire he shouted on noticing the large turn out of the people. Move, move, move, the team mate were all inside the car, the car pulled over avoiding a narrow bed. Better be on defensive drive straight into Agbaro Uti road and heard straight to the village. The firing persisted until the cars were safely out of Ughelli town moving into a close circuit. The party halted on hearing the persistent firing of gun short . Don't fire yet , let them draw nearer. Samson said as Joel raised his gun to return the firing . Joel's gun was still suspended Samson could not resist the wage he sprang into a race docked by a huge rubber tree and started firing at the incoming cars, he stopped. 'We are trapped, never mind we, can manage, he spoke into the receiver. Get down and let's waste these sentry position. The bang of the gun short emanating from the robbers side deafened the people as such reduced the followers number. Fear override a whole lot of the people but the determined ones motivated quite a number of the villagers who kept their line of pursuit. The bullet spindled on the bare floor as it failed to hit any target . But sides walked on mounting pressure on the people the robber kept shooting until there was no more noise from the two side . Julius stopped short he tied his gun with dusty particles he fired into air. The people dropped their gun and chased at the robbers . The robbers were mesmerize, they eventually succumbed as fifteen men to a robber. Victory is ours today the people sang as they retuned back to the village with their captives.

When the sun rose today God the Father rose on our Behalf, we have gone into a new day with confidence and are singing victoriously a pastor in the town said. Congregation, bring those element here the king said. No use wasting time on them, we have to administer copra punishment to them. Justice is all we seek. The youth leader said. Positioned that very well the youth leader said. Chick's leg was on a rocky ground. The women closed their eyes as the axe hit Chikes ankle the more you see the less you see Chike. As the axe hit Chikes leg he vanished from the scene to the peoples astonishment leaving in his position sprinkles of water. Disappearing was not common not to talk of when a large crowd was watching. 'Chike was no where; how lucky he walked along the bush part leading to his village. Stripped this braggarts now Bishop barked. Untie that rubbish dangling on his waist, the bone fractured and the piece scattered littering all over the place as the axe torched his leg. Second leg, Bishop called out. No time to waste, the sound echoed into the forest as the whole fourteen robbers ankles fractured. Women and children pulled out their knifes ,first on the lead position near the robbers, "feel free" Julius encouraged her, the woman slit part of the mans flesh, he wailed as other people took their share of his body blood spilled, the fleshy tissue yielded to different knife cut. The people exited lined in a single file one after the order they sliced each man's skin until the men were satisfied lifeless.

THE END

www.ingramcontent.com/pod-product-compliance
Lightning Source LLC
Chambersburg PA
CBHW020602310726
48979CB00008B/1310/J

* 9 7 8 1 4 2 6 9 3 3 8 1 3 *